I0712695

JUSTIN PETTYJOHN

Monster John

*To those who hide their pain behind quiet smiles, may your monsters never win,
and may the light inside you always find its way through the darkest nights.*

In Oakhaven, quiet streets are only paint on
a cracked wall. A man named John wears
routine like a mask, while trauma sharpens
its teeth behind his eyes. When love walks
the river path, the woods answer. Monsters
don't appear - they remember. And the abyss
is patient.

— MONSTER JOHN

Contents

Foreword

Some horrors don't arrive with a scream. They arrive with a whisper—so soft you mistake it for wind in the trees, so ordinary you file it away as "nothing," until "nothing" becomes a pattern and the pattern becomes a pulse. That is the particular dread that lives at the heart of Monster John: the slow corruption of the familiar, the way a quiet town can become a stage without realizing the curtain has risen.

At first glance, the setting feels almost too safe to fail. Oakhaven is painted in warm, recognizable strokes—front porches, routine greetings, children in the square, couples tracing the river path as though the future is guaranteed. Then the murders start. The town's comfort doesn't shatter in one clean break; it fractures in hairline cracks—locked doors, sideways glances, interrupted conversations, a creeping suspicion that safety was only ever an agreement everyone *assumed* was permanent.

What makes this story hit harder than a simple "serial killer" premise is that it refuses the easy distance we try to create between ourselves and the unthinkable. It doesn't let the terror remain "out there," roaming the woods like a campfire legend. Instead, it plants the nightmare in plain sight—in routine, in politeness, in the mask of normalcy that can hide a storm behind calm eyes and careful habits.

The book also understands something grimly modern: when violence enters a community, it doesn't only harm the victims. It changes the town's bloodstream—how people interpret sounds, how they read strangers, how quickly they trade trust for vigilance. And into that wound steps the media machine, eager to name what it can't explain. A label becomes a myth. A myth becomes a shortcut for fear. "Monster John" is not merely a nickname; it becomes a public artifact—something people can point at, whisper about, and blame, even as the real danger stays maddeningly human.

But if the novel were only about fear from the outside, it would be brutal—and forgettable. The deeper engine here is psychological: the way trauma, buried and unattended, can metastasize into identity. The story pushes into that uncomfortable space where the mind becomes a battleground—where memory fragments, guilt bleeds into obsession, and dissociation turns hours into missing time. The result isn't a monster in the supernatural sense; it's something more unsettling: a person whose internal rupture starts making choices in the dark that the daylight self can barely recognize.

And still—this isn't exploitation dressed as horror. The narrative keeps returning to consequences: to the investigators straining against the noise of rumor, to the survivors who carry the near-miss like a second spine, and to a town that can't unsee what it has learned about itself. It asks a quiet but relentless question: once a community's innocence is broken, what does "normal" even mean—and who gets to have it back?

So as you step into these pages, expect suspense and brutality, yes—but also expect a story about *rupture*: the rupture of a town's certainty, the rupture of a mind split by childhood horror, and the rupture between who we appear to be and what we're capable of becoming when pain is left to ferment. By the time the abyss opens in this book, you'll understand why it doesn't feel like a plot device.

It feels like a destination.

Justin Pettyjohn

Preface

Every town has a story it tells itself.

In Monster John, that story begins with comfort: a quiet place tucked between woods and hills, where the loudest sounds are familiar ones—church bells, frogs by the lake, wind in the leaves. But comfort can be deceptive. Sometimes it's not peace—it's **permission**. Permission to ignore the cracks. Permission to assume the worst things only happen elsewhere.

This book was written from that tension: the fragile boundary between "normal" and "unthinkable," and the way that boundary can fail without warning.

At the center of the story is a man who looks like background noise—polite, routine, dependable. But behind the mask is a childhood event so violent it fractures identity itself. The premise is simple and brutal: when trauma is buried instead of confronted, it does not disappear. It mutates. It waits. And eventually, it returns with a hunger that feels less like impulse and more like inevitability.

I wanted to explore a kind of horror that doesn't rely on the supernatural to feel impossible. The killings in this story aren't treated as "shock scenes" meant to be consumed and forgotten. They're treated as **contagion**—something that spreads through a community's bloodstream and changes how people lock their doors, how they look at their neighbors, how they interpret every rustle in the dark. Fear doesn't just make people cautious; it makes them suspicious. It turns togetherness into surveillance.

You'll also see how quickly the world tries to package terror into something digestible. A name becomes a headline. A headline becomes a myth. A myth becomes a substitute for understanding. The town starts chasing a "monster," because a monster is easier to believe in than the more disturbing truth: the threat may be human, close, and quietly ordinary.

While the story moves like a hunt—murders, investigation, escalation—it is also an interior descent. The chapters are structured to show two kinds of pursuit happening at once: law enforcement racing toward a suspect, and a man's mind splitting further under the pressure of memory, guilt, and a secondary self that grows stronger each time it is fed. If the book feels claustrophobic at times, that is intentional. The psychological cage is as important as the physical setting.

Finally, this novel is for people who understand that darkness is not always loud.

It can hide behind routine. It can live under politeness. It can wear the face you wave at in the morning. And it can survive for a long time—until the night gets too quiet and the thing you thought was gone remembers what it was doing.

Thank you for stepping into Oakhaven.

— Justin Pettyjohn

Acknowledgments

The shadows that John Vance cast during his reign of terror may have finally faded away, but many people owe a lot to the light that is needed to see through such darkness. To Detective Brody, for always looking for the truth, even when it took him to the most disturbing places. To the strong people of Oakhaven, whose spirit, though tested, won in the end. I am also very thankful to the criminologists and mental health professionals whose knowledge of how the mind works helped me understand the broken mind at the center of this story. Their commitment to understanding trauma and violence, both in theory and in practice, is a sign of the best in people. Lastly, to my family and friends for being patient with me, encouraging me, and putting up with my trips into the darker parts of my mind.

Introduction

Ravenshade had always been a quiet town. It was the kind of place where everyone knew everyone—or thought they did—because it was hidden between rolling hills and endless woods. The only sounds that broke the silence of its nights were the hum of streetlights, the low croak of frogs by the lake, and the rustle of leaves in the fall. Until the murders started.

A young couple out for a late-night drive found the first bodies near the old mill road. People in the area talked about wolves, drifters, and even cults. But the truth was much worse. A human thing. Something is wrong. Something that looked like a man named John Mercer.

During the day, people who passed by John didn't think much of him. He was just a quiet mechanic with distant eyes and a polite nod. But there was something terrible going on behind that calm front. Memories he couldn't get rid of. A childhood full of blood and screams. That night, John's father painted the walls of their home with the lives of their family, leaving young John to watch the horror unfold. That night, something inside him broke. One part of him was still alive, but it was empty and full of guilt. The other one waited, hungry.

The wait is finally over, decades later.

Every murder that happens in Ravenshade is like a message written in blood, a reminder of the violence that made him. People in the news call him Monster John, but they don't know what they're talking about. Monster John isn't just a name; it's a sign. It's what happens when trauma stays in the dark for too long and pain learns to walk and breathe.

And when a pair of lovers narrowly escapes his grasp, the façade begins to crumble. The police will have to chase the criminals through the thickest fog, over the sharpest cliffs, and into the heart of madness itself. When John falls into the abyss, they will think it is over. But the abyss knows how to keep what it wants.

Monsters like John never die. They stay out of sight.

And sometimes, when the night gets too quiet, they remember what they were doing.

Chapter 1: The Whispers of Oakhaven

A Town Frozen in Fear

The old oaks that surrounded Oakhaven had leaves that were a rusty color and wouldn't let go. Their brittle fingers scratched against a sky that looked like bruised plums. The town was proud of how quiet it was. The loudest sounds were often the church bell ringing in the distance or neighbors saying hello over picket fences. Oakhaven was a sanctuary for most of its residents because it was deep in a valley and surrounded by rolling hills that turned into dense, whispering forests. A place where time moved more slowly and the worries of the outside world rarely broke the peace. Kids played in the town square without a care in the world. Their laughter was a bright, fearless tune against the stoic fronts of Victorian homes. Couples walked hand in hand along the winding river path, their futures as clear and calm as the sky's reflection on the water. This was the Oakhaven that the people who lived there loved.

But under this facade of pastoral perfection, a different kind of chill had begun to creep in, not from the autumn air that was coming in, but from a much more evil source. It started out small, like a whisper or a rumor, or a brief feeling of unease that brushed against the edges of awareness like a spider web. The first event was written off as a tragic accident, a robbery that went horribly wrong. A young couple who were very much in love and still wearing their engagement rings were found dead in their remote cabin on the outskirts of town. The details that came out in the quiet conversations at the general store and the worried looks exchanged over coffee at Mrs. Gable's diner were scary. In fact, it was too disturbing to be a coincidence. There were signs of a fight that was too violent to be just a robbery. A week later, there was another couple. This time, their lives were cut short in a way that was impossible to understand in the quiet woods on the other side of the valley. The distance between the two scenes didn't help; it just made the terrifying realization that this wasn't an isolated event even stronger.

The first wave to hit Oakhaven was disbelief. The town wasn't used to such darkness, and its people weren't ready for the real horror that was about to happen. People were more careful around each other. The easy familiarity of neighbors was replaced by a growing sense of distrust. The calm front started to break. The doors that used to be open were now locked tight. Kids could no longer go out on their own. People in the town square started to laugh less, and they kept looking nervously at the darkening woods. Every car that wasn't familiar and every person who walked down Main Street became something to watch closely. The solitude that used to make them feel safe now felt like a cage. The thick forests, which used to be a symbol of nature's embrace, now seemed to press in on me, their shadows getting darker and hiding unseen dangers. The winding river, which used to be a sign of life and flow, now seemed to reflect the mood getting darker, with its waters reflecting a sky full of unspoken fear.

The first news reports were scattered and full of guesswork. They were picked up by local TV and radio stations and online news sites. They talked about a "growing sense of panic" and a "series of brutal murders" in the "picturesque town of Oakhaven." The residents' worries only grew because there was no real information. Every new piece of information, no matter how small, made the picture more frightening than the last. People talked about a careful killer who left little behind, like a ghost moving through the night. The police, who were used to dealing with small crimes like theft and bar fights, were overwhelmed. Their first attempts didn't get them very far, which only made the town's fear grow stronger. The closest city's detectives were called in, and their presence was a grim sign that Oakhaven's peaceful life had been forever ruined.

It was very clear how weak Oakhaven was. It was a small town where everyone knew each other and privacy was often given up for the sake of the community. Now, that very connection made people very afraid. Who among them had such darkness in their hearts? Could the friendly wave from the mechanic or the smiling face at the post office hide something terrible? The fear wasn't just because of the murders; it was also because trust was slowly being destroyed and the nagging feeling that the monster could be anyone, living among them and breathing the same air. The town's isolation, which used to be a nice thing about it, now felt like a huge problem. There were no quick ways to get away or get help. In a way, their fear kept them trapped.

The sounds of Oakhaven, which used to be familiar, started to sound creepy. The wind made the leaves rustle, which sounded like footsteps. The sound of a twig breaking in the woods made people shiver. The hoot of an owl at night, which used to be a soothing natural sound, now sounded like a sad cry, a sign of darkness. The shadows themselves looked like they were getting longer and moving around with threats that weren't visible. The air in Oakhaven felt heavy, full of fear and dread that couldn't be put into words. The town was holding its breath, waiting for the next horrible sound. Its once-peaceful heart was now beating a frantic, scared rhythm against the darkness that was closing in. The front of Oakhaven had fallen apart, showing a raw, exposed nerve of fear. The community was frozen in the grip of a nightmare it could no longer deny. The whispers had turned into a roar, and Oakhaven was no longer a safe place; it was a stage for unimaginable horror. The perfect surface had cracked, and the darkness below was starting to seep through, leaving everything it touched with its cold, all-encompassing gloom. The silence that followed the initial shock was not peaceful; it was full of anticipation, like the calm before a storm that had already begun to break.

The Medias Monster John

The horrible things happening in Oakhaven, which were once just a local tragedy, quickly became known across the country, thanks to the media's never-ending need for news. As the investigation stalled because there were no solid leads or real suspects, sensationalism rushed in to fill the gap. Regional news vans with whirring cameras and eager reporters came to the quiet town, turning its calm streets into a morbid curiosity show. Without any official information, people started to guess what was going on, and the media, always eager to give the public what they wanted, started to make up their own stories.

It began with vague descriptions of a "phantom killer" or "shadowy figure" that was stalking couples without them knowing it. Then, as the details, even though they were few and not confirmed, started to come together, a name was born. First, people in the newsroom said it in low voices. Then, people in broadcast studios shouted it from the rooftops. "Monster John." The name was a stroke of journalistic genius, a chillingly effective piece of branding that instantly caught the public's attention and added to the fear that was already growing in Oakhaven. It was simple, powerful, and scary, bringing to mind a primal, mindless force of destruction. Both local and national newspapers jumped on it with both feet. "Monster John Strikes Again!" and "Oakhaven Terrorized by Monster John!" were some of the headlines. The phrase became a public face for the killer, who was still unknown.

The way the media talked about "Monster John" was a masterclass in how to scare people. He was described as a monster of pure evil, a psychopath with no empathy for others, and a bloodthirsty person who couldn't be satisfied. Reporters put together bits and pieces of reports and eyewitness accounts, which were often unreliable and based on panic, into a coherent but scary picture of the person. They did this with little more than a police scanner and a lot of imagination. He was shown to be a master manipulator, a ghost who could vanish into the Oakhaven woods like mist, and a predator who stalked his prey with terrifying planning. The crimes were very carefully planned, there were no clear motives, and the victims were chosen at random, which made it seem like the criminals had an almost supernatural intelligence and cunning that was beyond human comprehension.

The public's view, shaped by these constant reports, started to differ greatly from the investigators' grim reality. "Monster John" was a real person to the people of the country. He was a huge, scary figure that represented all of their deepest fears about the darkness that lies beneath the surface of civilized society. He was the real-life boogeyman, a scary story that parents told their kids and that people talked about for hours at the dinner table. His image, though never seen, became imprinted on the collective consciousness: a hulking silhouette against a moonlit sky, a glint of madness in unseen eyes, a chillingly detached presence that could strike anywhere, at any time. This over-the-top persona was good for getting headlines and boosting ratings, but it only made the fear in Oakhaven worse. The media's graphic descriptions made the residents' fears even worse, which were already bad. People now blamed "Monster John" for every sound and rustle in the leaves that they couldn't explain. The town, which used to be a peaceful place, was now part of a national horror story, and its residents were unwittingly taking part in a drama they wanted to end.

The local government was already stretched thin and under a lot of pressure to find the killer. Now they were fighting a war on two fronts. On the one hand, they were fighting the killer himself, a ghost who didn't leave them with many clues. On the other hand, they were up against the media, which was a constant force that often twisted the truth, spread false information, and made people panic, all of which made their work harder. Detective Harding, whose rough exterior hid a deep-seated tiredness, was getting more and more angry with the media circus. He knew that people needed information, but the constant stream of speculative news was not only unhelpful, it was also harmful.

He complained to Officer Miller one night while looking at a particularly bad headline in a national tabloid, "They're not reporting facts; they're writing fiction." "This 'Monster John'… It's a cartoon. It's making a complicated and very scary crime into a cheap ghost story. And that isn't helping us catch him. "It's just terrifying everyone and making their jobs harder."

The media's constant focus on the "monster" side of things also made the killer less human by making him a one-dimensional embodiment of evil. This made it harder for the investigators to look at the case with the analytical and nuanced mind needed to understand a criminal's mind. They were being pushed to see a force of nature instead of a person, no matter how disturbed they were. Detective Harding knew this was dangerous because figuring out the killer's motives, patterns, and weaknesses was the key to catching him. But how could they get into the mind of a "monster" when the media had already made everyone think he was something that couldn't be understood?

People's views of "Monster John" were not based on the truth of the crimes, but on the media's need for a story. The killer, whoever he was, was turning into a character in a sensationalized drama instead of a suspect. People could more easily separate the horror from their own lives and see it as something that happened outside of their peaceful town because of this story of the horrible, inhuman killer. But the truth, as the investigators knew all too well, was much more disturbing. The "monster" wasn't a creature from hell; it was a real person, probably living among them, whose actions were based on human, though twisted, reasons. The scary truth that the monster could have been walking among them was what really scared Oakhaven. Ironically, the media's exaggerated "Monster John" story made the monster seem less personally threatening by making it easier to define.

The people in the town, who were in the middle of all the media attention, started to take on the "Monster John" persona. Their fear, which was already strong, grew even stronger. It wasn't just the fear of an unknown attacker anymore; it was the fear of a force so evil that it didn't make sense. Children, whose imaginations were sparked by scary stories and quiet conversations, whispered stories about "Monster John" hiding in the dark, his presence marked by an unholy chill. Adults, even though they knew better, found themselves looking at people's faces for signs of darkness, for the hint of a monster in their neighbors, friends, and even their own family members. The media had made a scary figure, and Oakhaven was now living in its shadow.

This false information, along with a steady stream of sensationalized speculation, made people feel like they couldn't trust anyone and were always on edge. The investigators had to deal with not only the killer but also the flood of false theories and wild accusations that spread through the town because the media kept making guesses. Every anonymous tip and whispered rumor, no matter how crazy, had to be looked into, which took valuable time and resources away from the real investigation. Sheriff Brody and his team were under a lot of stress. They had to keep the peace, calm down a scared public, and catch a killer, all while dealing with the dangerous currents of public opinion, which were often manipulated by the very media that said they were informing them. The name "Monster John" was, in a way, a strong anesthetic for the public. It made the real world less sharp by making a fictional villain that was easier to handle, even though it was scary. It let the rest of the country enjoy the Oakhaven tragedy as entertainment, a scary but ultimately far-off show, while the town itself was stuck in the painful, scary truth of the situation. In its quest for the sensational, the media had accidentally built a wall of myth around the crimes. Investigators would have to work hard to tear down this wall in order to find the truth.

John The Mask of Normalcy

Hey John. The name was as boring as the man himself. Like the soft rustle of leaves in the many oak trees that gave the town its name, it blended into the background noise of Oakhaven. John was the most normal person anyone who knew him or even just knew of him could think of. He was the kind of guy you wouldn't notice at the store or on the road, the kind whose car you would pass a dozen times a day without a second thought. His life was like a tapestry made up of threads of routine, a boring but comforting pattern that made Oakhaven feel safe.

Every morning, he followed the same exact routine. The simple digital alarm clock would beep softly at 6:15 AM. There would be no sudden jarring or fumbling with bleary eyes. Instead, John would wake up and swing his legs out of bed as if someone were nudging him with a hand. He moved in a way that was efficient and didn't waste energy. The mirror in the bathroom showed a face that was, for all intents and purposes, forgettable. Brown hair that is about mid-length and neatly parted. There were some faint lines around the eyes that were a dull shade of hazel. He wasn't ugly or plain; he was just there. He would shave quickly and efficiently, and the sound of the razor scraping against his skin was a quiet counterpoint to the gurgling of the coffee maker below.

Every morning, he had the same thing: two slices of whole wheat toast with a little butter and a cup of black coffee. He would sit at his small kitchen table, and the worn linoleum under his feet showed that he had been doing the same thing every morning for years. He didn't read the newspaper; the national headlines, even those concerning the escalating terror in Oakhaven, held no particular sway over his placid demeanor. As he sipped his coffee, his eyes were unfocused, as if he were thinking about something very ordinary, like the exact angle of the sunlight hitting the chipped Formica countertop.

His job as a bookkeeper at the local lumber mill made people think of him as a quiet, capable man. He got there on time at 7:30 AM, and his old briefcase was a familiar sight. His desk was spotless, and the ledger books were stacked in a way that made sense. He would spend his days in a world far away from the quiet, panicked conversations that filled the town's public spaces. The smell of pine and sawdust would comfort him. His coworkers thought he was hard-working, dependable, and completely boring.

"John? Frank, a big man whose overalls are always covered in sawdust, says, "Yeah, he's a good worker." "Not much of a talker, though. Stays to himself. Does his job and clocks out on time. "Never a problem."

Martha, the office manager, said, "He's… steady," as she adjusted her glasses. "You can always trust John to get the numbers right. Not one for small talk, though. But that's not a bad thing in a place like this, is it? "Simple."

Easy. That was the word that went with John's name the most. He lived in a small, two-bedroom bungalow on the outskirts of town. The house was just as plain as he was. The hedges were always trimmed and the lawn was always neatly mowed. There were no fancy flowerbeds or funny garden gnomes; just a clean, useful space that showed how careful and boring he was. His neighbors thought he was a good neighbor, even though they didn't see him very often. He would nod politely and wave when they passed, but he never stopped to talk.

Mrs. Gable, who lived across the street and watered her prize-winning roses, would say, "He's polite, John is." "Always makes sure his property looks nice. I've seen him out there late at night, just puttering around. I never heard a sound from his house. He is as quiet as a mouse.

At first, this outward show of normalcy was not a deliberate attempt to trick anyone. It was just the easiest way to go, a natural desire for order and predictability. John felt better when things were the same every day. He watched the chaos that was starting to take over Oakhaven and the fear that hung in the air like a damp fog from a distance, like someone might watch a strange weather pattern. The whispers of "Monster John," the frantic news reports, and the obvious worry were all things that happened outside of his orderly world of ledger books and neatly trimmed hedges.

He would sometimes see the news vans parked near the town square, with their satellite dishes looking like metal sunflowers. He would notice them, maybe with a hint of mild curiosity, and then go on his way. When he saw the sensationalized headlines at the corner store, he thought they were just more noise from the outside world intruding on Oakhaven's quiet life. He could see the fear in the eyes of the people in his town. They held their keys tighter as they walked, and conversations stopped suddenly when he came near. He thought it was because everyone was on edge and anxious. He didn't think he was a part of that equation at all.

His evenings were just as planned as his mornings. After a simple dinner, which was usually something he had made ahead of time or could easily put together, he would spend his time quietly. He might read, not the thrillers that were suddenly popular at the local bookstore, but boring, scholarly books on history or bugs. He could also do what Mrs. Gable called "puttering." This usually meant taking apart and putting back together small mechanical things with great care. He spent his free time fixing things like a broken toaster, a squeaky door hinge, and a complicated clockwork mechanism he found at a yard sale. His small garage, which was usually used for lawnmowers and gardening tools, had a perfectly organized workbench with a wide range of specialized tools, all of which were shiny and in the right place.

There were no signs of stress on the outside, like quick movements or nervous tics. He looked like a picture of calm happiness, a man who didn't seem to be bothered by the worries that bothered his neighbors. The rising fear in Oakhaven, the growing paranoia, and the very real terror that lurked in the shadows of its streets didn't seem to bother John at all. He walked through town like a ghost of normalcy, a living example of the life Oakhaven was trying so hard to hold on to but was quickly losing. His lack of interest in anything was his shield, his daily routine was his fortress, and his calm demeanor was a masterful, unconscious trick. He was the perfect disguise, blending in with everyday life so well that no one in Oakhaven would ever suspect the darkness that was lurking just below the surface, waiting for its chance to strike. His mask of normalcy was so well made and so convincing that even he might have thought it was the face of his true self at times. He carefully built the everyday world around him and played the part of the ordinary man with an unsettling level of dedication that would soon be put to a much more evil purpose. The whispers of Oakhaven were getting louder, but they were aimed at a ghost. The real source of the fear, on the other hand, was moving around in plain sight as John.

Echoes of a Shattered Past

John's life was starting to fall apart. He had a calm surface that he kept up with routines and an almost pathological fear of change. It wasn't a violent break yet, but a slow, sneaky erosion, like water seeping into stone. These cracks showed up in the middle of the night, when the carefully built walls of his mind fell apart and the shadows of Oakhaven's growing fear were covered by even older, deeper shadows. Sleep, which used to be a safe place to forget everything, had turned into a war zone.

He would wake up with a gasp, his heart pounding against his ribs, and the taste of fear like metal on his tongue. The dreams were not coherent stories; they were more like a patchwork of broken sounds, images, and feelings. It sounded like a woman's terrified scream was coming from the walls of his bedroom. Even though his home was always clean and crisp, the smell of coppery blood, thick and cloying, would fill his nose. And then there were the flashes of light: the harsh, blinding glare of a bare bulb in a room he couldn't quite place, followed by the darkness that seemed to swallow everything. These weren't the usual worries of a man living in a town with a predator; they were deep, primal echoes of a trauma that had been buried so deep it had changed the way his mind worked.

He would lie there, stiff in the suffocating silence, trying to remember the details and put the confusing pieces together. But like fog on a cold morning, the memories would disappear as soon as he tried to grab them, leaving behind only a lingering chill and a deep sense of unease that lasted long after the dream had faded. He would look at the ceiling, where the familiar patterns of the plaster changed into blurry shapes in the dim moonlight. Then, at 6:15 AM, the first soft beep of his alarm clock brought him back to the comforting, if increasingly fragile, reality of his everyday life. The sound of the razor scraping against his skin was familiar to him and helped him feel grounded for a moment. He would do his morning ablutions with practiced, almost automatic, efficiency. But under the calm surface, his hands trembled slightly, a barely perceptible vibration that showed how uneasy he was inside.

The routine worked as a strong sedative during the day, dulling the sharp edges of his broken-up nighttime experiences. The ledger books at the lumber mill had exact columns of numbers, the machines made a steady hum, and the smell of pine and sawdust were all things that kept the chaos at bay. But even in the middle of this orderly world, the whispers would sometimes come out. A certain color of light coming through the dusty windows might make you feel strange for a second. The sudden clang of metal, which was too sharp and too sudden, made him flinch, which made a passing coworker look at him for a moment, as if to ask what was wrong. He would blame these times on stress or the general unease that was going around Oakhaven, which was an easy way to explain the tremors inside.

He started to look at the other women in town with a new, unsettling focus. Not with desire or even open curiosity, but with a strange, detached interest. The way they moved, the sound of their laughter, and the small changes in their faces were all like characters in a play he had seen a long time ago. Their actions and reactions were strangely familiar, but he couldn't remember them. He'd see a woman walking alone at dusk, her silhouette standing out against the fading light, and a knot of fear that he couldn't explain would tighten in his stomach. It felt like a phantom limb that had been cut off long ago was suddenly hurting with a phantom pain, a sign that something terrible was about to happen.

He found a faded picture in a drawer that he had forgotten about while going through old bills one afternoon. It was a picture of his mother from school, with a bright, hopeful smile and wide eyes that looked like they were from a long time ago. He looked at it, and a strange emptiness opened up inside him. He remembered her laugh, which used to fill their small home with a beautiful sound. Now, though, the sound was lost in the maze of his mind. But the memory was like a ghost: it was there but not there, and he couldn't touch it. He tried to picture her face, her voice, and the warmth of her touch, but the picture stayed stubbornly incomplete, like a puzzle with important pieces missing.

Along with the broken memories came a strong sense of guilt, a feeling that he had failed in a deep, unexplainable way. He would think about twisted and nightmarish situations from his childhood when he was small and helpless and saw something terrible that he couldn't stop. The people in these visions were hard to see because they were always in a kind of twilight, but you could feel how scared they were. He saw the glint of metal, heard the wet thud of impact, and felt the presence of a darkness that was older and more evil than anything Oakhaven had ever released. And there was always the picture of a woman with a twisted face and eyes that begged for help that never came.

He started to carefully write down these brief thoughts and memories that were hard to understand. He would write down broken sentences, random phrases, and rough drawings in small notebooks. A doll that is broken. A mark on a wooden floor. A flame that flickers. He didn't want anyone else to read these notes; they were his own desperate attempts to make sense of the storm raging inside him and bring some order to the chaos that was threatening to take over. He would read these notes over and over in the privacy of his garage, where the smell of oil and metal was strangely comforting, as if the realness of his tools could somehow ground him and keep him in the present.

The perfect picture of Oakhaven, the town he had worked so hard to build for himself and others, was starting to fade. The happy face of normalcy was cracking, showing the open, festering wound underneath. He could see it in the way his neighbors looked away from him, in the quiet conversations that stopped when he got close, and in the fear that hung in the air like the smell of wet earth after a storm. He knew on a deep level that the discomfort wasn't all outside of him. It was a dark mirror that showed him something that was growing inside of him. People in town used to think the whispers of "Monster John" were just the scared town's superstitious talk, but now they were starting to sound like a chilling, undeniable truth. The desolate nature of these memories and the overwhelming sense of loss and fear they brought on were a grim sign of what was to come. The path he was on, a path paved with routine and cloaked in normalcy, was leading him not towards peace, but towards a precipice, a descent into the very darkness he was so desperately trying to outrun, a darkness that was intricately, irrevocably, intertwined with his own shattered past. The dam he had built to hold back the floodwaters of his trauma was starting to give way, and the first signs of the destructive tide were already starting to get through.

The First Glimpse of the Predator

John's carefully planned stillness, which had once been a fortress against the chaos that was coming, was no longer a safe place. It was a prison. The phantom feelings and broken visions that had started as strange whispers in the back of his mind were now coming together to form a clearer, more terrifying picture. Sleep didn't help; it just made things worse by making the broken pictures of his past more clear and frightening. He would wake up with a shock, not from the cold sweat of a bad dream, but from a heat that seemed to come from deep inside him. It was a feeling that was strange for him, like a burning ember that wouldn't go out.

He kept going back to memories from his childhood, not with the calm sadness of remembering grief, but with a strong sense of agitation. The teasing on the playground, the mean things other kids did, and the way his mother's eyes would flash with fear that she tried to hide—these were no longer memories from long ago. They felt fresh and painful, like each perceived wrong was a new wound. The carefully planned logic of his adult life started to fall apart at the edges, unable to hold back the strong wave of emotion that was about to take over. He would look at his hands, which were rough and steady like those of a working man, and a tremor would run through them, as if there was some kind of primal energy buzzing beneath the skin. It was like a spring that was coiled up and waiting to be let go.

The "Monster John" persona didn't come out of nowhere; it grew slowly, like ink spreading through paper. It came from the pain that he didn't want to admit, the shame that he kept hidden, and the small hurts and insults that had built up in the dark corners of his mind for years. The victim from childhood, who would never be able to do anything about it, was starting to wake up and demand justice. This wasn't a logical response; it was a primal outburst fueled by the dark magic of his trauma. The anger wasn't his own, not completely, but it ran through him like something he had known for a long time, a terrifying echo of something old and deeply ingrained. He felt more and more disconnected from what he was doing, as if an invisible hand were directing his actions and pushing him toward a limit he had never thought about before.

It was getting harder and harder to keep up the appearance of normalcy during the day. The accuracy of his work at the mill, which used to bring him comfort, now felt like a pointless attempt to bring order to the chaos inside him. The rhythmic thud of the saws and the smell of sawdust had always calmed him down, but now they seemed to make the growing unease worse. He would stare into the middle distance, his mind lost in the swirling vortex of anger that wasn't going away. A misplaced tool, a careless word from a coworker, or even the constant chirping of a bird outside could make him feel more angry than he should have. He would quickly hide the dangerous look in his eyes. It was hard to keep control; it was a constant, draining fight against an enemy that was getting stronger inside of me.

He began to notice the small changes in how he looked. His walk became more purposeful, and his shoulders were a little straighter, as if he were carrying an invisible weight of power. His gaze, which used to be soft and unassuming, was now sharper and more penetrating, which could make people feel uneasy. It was like the sleeping predator inside was waking up, sharpening its senses and honing its instincts. He started to look at the other men at the mill in a new, almost predatory way, as if he could see their interactions and perceived weaknesses with an unsettling clarity. The whispers of "Monster John" no longer felt like an accusation from the outside; instead, they felt like a growing truth inside him, a name he was slowly and surely starting to embody.

The dreams that kept coming back got worse. The distorted screams and the sickly sweet smell of blood were no longer just sounds and smells. They started to come together around a scary image: a woman's face twisted in fear, her eyes wide with a plea that tore at something deep inside him. He couldn't see her features clearly, but he could see the raw, primal fear on her face. But he couldn't shake the feeling of being deeply responsible for her pain, which made him feel bad. The guilt was like a corrosive acid that ate away at the last bits of his ordered self, making him more vulnerable to the dark forces that were pulling him down.

He felt drawn to the edges of Oakhaven, to the dark parts of the woods that surrounded the town. The paths he used to walk as a child now seemed full of hidden energy and a sense of waiting. He would stand at the edge of the trees, where the dappled sunlight came through the leaves, and feel like he finally belonged and was seen. The forest, with its quiet, ancient presence, seemed to know what was going on inside him and offered a stark, wild comfort that the civilized world couldn't. He'd look at himself in a calm pool of water, and for a brief, scary moment, the face looking back wasn't his own. The eyes had a glimmer of something wild and hungry, a sign of the darkness that was closing in on him that he could no longer ignore.

The primal urge started to show itself in small but important ways. He was becoming more and more interested in violent thoughts, even though they weren't physical yet. The little injustices he saw, like people being rude to him or people he thought deserved protection, would make him very angry. He would think about different situations over and over again, imagining harsh punishments and his mind making clear pictures of quick, decisive action. This inner conversation, this practice of violence, was a scary sign of how strong the secondary personality was getting. It was as if his mind was carefully getting him ready for the eventual descent into open violence.

He began to have moments of complete dissociation, when he would lose all sense of his surroundings and be left with a disorienting blankness. These gaps in his awareness were like little black holes that sucked up parts of his day, making him feel lost and confused. He would be in a different part of the mill or looking at a task he had already finished but didn't remember doing. His coworkers would notice how he acted strangely, how he looked far away, and how he mumbled his answers. But there was an undercurrent of fear in their concern, a sense that something was changing in the quiet, dependable

John.

The trauma, which had been a buried ghost, was now a real thing that controlled how he felt and how he saw things. The world started to look different, and every interaction was looked at closely for possible threats or insults. The politeness that had always been a part of his personality felt like a thin layer that could be easily broken. He got angry when he thought someone was being condescending, and he responded with cold, cutting sarcasm that even shocked him. The anger was a familiar but unwelcome visitor who was becoming a permanent resident. The careful balance he had kept for so long was starting to tip, and the forces of darkness were getting stronger and stronger. He was no longer just a victim of his past; he was becoming its tool, the way that its old rage would be let loose on Oakhaven. The whispers were getting louder. They weren't just in the shadows of his dreams anymore; they were echoing in the waking hours, getting ready for the storm that was about to break. His carefully planned daily routine, which used to be a comfort, now felt like a frantic attempt to hold back the tide, a desperate, pointless effort to keep control of a self that was quickly slipping away. He was seeing himself fall apart, and a scary part of him that had been quiet for a long time wasn't completely against the change.

Chapter 2: The Shadow's Embrace

Rituals of the Night

The moon, which looked like a bruised, swollen eye in the velvet sky, cast long, bony fingers over the sleeping town of Oakhaven. During these stolen hours, when the world held its breath and the line between the normal and the horrible got thinner, "Monster John" came to life. His coming out wasn't a sudden change; it was a slow, planned process, like a poisonous flower opening its petals in the dark. The John that the people of the town knew—the quiet, unassuming mill worker who kept to himself and whose days were set by the rhythmic sound of machinery and the comforting smell of sawdust—was gone. In his place came a creature of instinct, a predator that had been held back by rage for a long time and was now free.

His preparation was not a frantic rush of impulse, but a methodical ritual that sent shivers down his spine. It started days or even weeks before the act itself. John would carefully scout the area he had chosen. Not the busy center of Oakhaven, but its forgotten edges, where the asphalt turned to gravel and the streetlights flickered and went out, leaving dark spots that couldn't be seen. These were the liminal spaces, the empty places where weakness thrived and a life could be snuffed out with almost no sound. He knew these places well: the old logging roads that were now overgrown with trees, the empty farmhouses that had been taken over by the wild, and the quiet coves along the river that made no noise. His mind, which used to be full of the practicalities of his job, was now a blank canvas for his dark plans, mapping out routes, figuring out escape routes, and noting the lack of watchful eyes.

He carefully chose his victims as well, which was a sickening extension of his new predatory focus. He wasn't interested in random chance; he was interested in a specific, scary type. Someone on the edge, whose disappearance would be a minor problem for society rather than a major disaster. The drifters who came through town, their faces showing signs of tiredness and anonymity; the people who lived on the outskirts, their lives full of quiet desperation; and the people whose cries for help, if they ever made them, were lost on the world. He saw in them a reflection of how he used to feel invisible and a twisted sense of family that drove him to do terrible things. He watched them from a distance, his gaze unnervingly steady, keeping track of their daily activities, habits, and times of unguarded solitude. There was no passion in these observations, no sign of human connection; only the cold, analytical look at prey.

The night of the hunt was a symphony of planned actions. He would drop the persona of John like a snake sheds its skin and take up a position of silent, coiled alertness. His movements became smooth, efficient, and free of any extra motion. The rough fabric of his work clothes, which used to be a sign of his normal life, now seemed to soak up the shadows, making him a part of the dark that was coming. He didn't have a weapon that could be easily found, like a shiny sword or a rough club. Instead, his tools were more sneaky and personal. A strong piece of rope that has been used a lot and has knots tied with the skill of a craftsman. A small, tarnished silver locket that he had both rejected and brought back to life. The cold metal was a contrast to the growing heat inside him. And sometimes he would give a single, perfect rose with deep, dark red petals as a creepy gift to the powers he thought were guiding him.

He moved through the night with an eerie silence, and his senses were almost superhumanly sharp. The sound of leaves crunching underfoot was meant to hide the sound of the snapping twig, which was meant to draw attention away from it. He could hear the distant hum of traffic, the lonely howl of a dog, the wind sighing through the eaves, and he could put them all together into a soundscape that guided his every move. He was a ghost, a shadow that had come to life, a silent hunter moving through the town while everyone else was asleep. It was very important that his chosen hunting grounds were isolated. A deserted stretch of highway where the only witnesses were the stars, which didn't care; a secluded clearing deep in the whispering pines, far from the prying eyes of civilization; and a decaying boathouse by the river, its timbers groaning under the weight of time and neglect. These weren't just places; they were parts of his own inner emptiness, places where the normal rules of life didn't work anymore.

He always approached his victim the same way, with careful planning and patience. He would wait like a statue made of shadow for the right time. A door left open, a window unlocked, a moment of being vulnerable. Then, without warning, he would hit with a speed that was unusual for him. There was no doubt or inner conflict. The primal urge took over after being carefully nurtured and expertly directed. At first, the victim was shocked and let out a short, startled cry. But his quick, practiced actions quickly silenced it. He didn't enjoy the fight; he just put up with it because he saw it as a necessary step in carrying out his dark plan. The act itself wasn't a violent explosion; it was a controlled, almost surgical end. It showed how well he had honed his chilling skills, which were a dark form of art that came from trauma and twisted logic. The silence that followed was deep. The only sounds were the frantic beating of his own heart, a drumbeat of grim satisfaction, and the distant, uncaring sigh of the night. He was the shadow, and at those times, Oakhaven was its unwilling, unaware embrace.

The Innocent Targets

Tonight, he wasn't looking at the lonely people on the edges of town or the people who were just passing through. Tonight, his predatory gaze changed, drawn to a different kind of weakness and a different kind of light that the darkness wanted to put out. It was the innocent, pure, and bright flames of new love that he could see now. The young couples, who were the living examples of Oakhaven's fragile hopes and growing futures, became the new, terrifying focus of his sick desires. They were the opposite of his lonely life, bright flowers in a garden he thought he would never be able to enter.

As they walked along the riverbank, Sarah and Mark's hands were always linked. Their laughter was a song carried by the evening breeze. Sarah's hair and eyes were sun-kissed, and they had the hopeful shimmer of a summer dawn. She dreamed of opening a small bakery that would fill Oakhaven with the sweet smell of cinnamon and sugar. Mark, steady and kind, already had a plan for his future as a carpenter. He saw their life together as a sturdy, well-built home filled with warmth and the sound of tiny feet. They talked about their wedding, which would be a small event at the old chapel by the lake. Their dreams were painted in soft pastels, and they didn't notice the shadows that were creeping up on them just outside of their happy vision. Their love was strong and quiet, based on shared looks, comforting silences, and the deep, simple joy of finding your anchor in someone else. John watched them from the thick brush, a ghost in the dusk. Their carefree happiness was a painful, stark contrast to the emptiness he felt inside. He didn't see two people; he saw one perfect being that stood for everything he had never known and probably never would.

Chloe and David were the rebels in their graduating class. Their love was a fierce, defiant flame against the predictable currents of small-town life. Chloe, who was rebellious and had a mind that raced ahead of Oakhaven's quiet pace, wanted adventure and a world beyond the familiar cobblestones. David, who wanted to be a musician, found inspiration in Chloe's fiery spirit. He played guitar with a raw, wild passion. They spent their evenings in the quiet, messy garage of David's house, where the air was thick with the smell of oil and dreams that were just starting to form. Their conversations were a quick exchange of ideas, hopes, and stolen kisses. They were going to leave Oakhaven to chase the bright lights of faraway cities and make a place where their unusual hearts could beat freely. Their future was a thrilling, unknown horizon, like a canvas with bright, clashing colors. John watched them with a heart that was as cold and hard as a stone. Their youthful energy and bold plans were an insult to how stuck he felt in his own life. Their love was a strong, almost violent force that challenged the way things were, which he felt stuck in. He saw their shared defiance as a reckless disregard for the natural order and a show of freedom that he thought was unfairly denied to him.

Emily and Thomas lived in a small, vine-covered cottage at the edge of the woods, a little farther away. They were a quiet couple. Emily was a talented artist who saw beauty in everyday things. Her paintings were full of the soft, muted colors of Oakhaven's landscapes and the subtle expressions of its people. Thomas, a kind man who worked at the library, found comfort in the quiet stories that were hidden in the worn pages of books. Their love was like a rare, fragile flower that grew in their shared solitude and deep, unspoken understanding. They were happy with the simple things in life, like morning walks, cups of tea by the fire, and evenings spent working on their own crafts. Just being with each other made them feel better. Their future was not a big announcement, but a quiet promise to keep building on the peaceful sanctuary they had made together. John thought of them as weak butterflies whose wings were too easily broken by the harsh realities of life. He wasn't inspired by their quiet happiness; instead, it reminded him of how alone he felt and how peaceful he couldn't be, which he thought meant he shouldn't exist.

These couples, who were like beacons of hope and new happiness, were everything that John thought had been systematically taken away from him. Their shared futures, their intertwined destinies, and their naive belief that love and friendship are good things—these are the things that made his pain worse and turned it into a weapon. He didn't see their happiness as proof of how beautiful life is; instead, he saw it as a cruel joke about how empty his own life was. Every stolen look, every whispered sweet word, and every shared dream only made the gap between his inner darkness and their bright light bigger.

He looked at them not with lust, but with a cold, detached interest, like a scientist cutting up a specimen. He kept track of their schedules, where they met, and the little things that showed how much they cared about each other. He remembered how Sarah leaned into Mark, how Chloe's hand rested possessively on David's arm, and how Emily's eyes softened when Thomas spoke. These observations, which had no real emotion, became data points in his creepy equation. He didn't want to copy their happiness; he wanted to destroy it, to take away the very things that made them alive and full of life. He thought their love was a flaw in reality, like a wrong note in the quiet symphony of his own pain. He felt like he was doing the right thing by going after them, and he was happy that their bright futures would never happen.

What drew him to these young lives was their innocence. They weren't jaded or tired like he was; they were fresh and new. Their dreams were pure, and their love wasn't weighed down by the problems and compromises that often ruin romantic ideals. Because they were so pure, they were the perfect canvas for him to show how deeply he felt about losing and being betrayed. He didn't want to share their happiness; he wanted to take it away, to suck out its color and light until all that was left was the stark, empty landscape of his own sadness. He didn't feel bad about their impending doom; it was a grim necessity, a last-ditch effort to make the universe he saw as fundamentally unfair more fair. Their growing love, a sign of life's lasting power, became, in his twisted mind, a sign of defiance, a challenge to the bleak order he felt he had to impose. The difference between their sweet, budding love and his deep, entrenched obsession was so great, so deep, that it threatened to swallow Oakhaven whole. He was the shadow, and these bright, innocent lights were now right in its way.

A Fragmented Consciousness

The air in the rundown boathouse was thick and heavy with the smell of damp wood, stagnant water, and something else… something metallic and definitely scary. John stood in the heavy darkness, and his own breathing made a rough sound in the deep silence. The deed was done. The young couple's once-strong energy was gone, leaving behind a cold emptiness that echoed his own. But in this emptiness, a storm raged.

A sliver of moonlight, like a ghost, came through a hole in the rotting boards and lit up a dirty spot on the floor. There were signs of their shared hope on it: a broken picnic basket, a crumpled map of hiking trails, and the faintest red stain that John couldn't ignore even in the dark. In these quiet moments after the war, the real war within him began.

A phantom limb of his old self twitched, bringing back memories of the sun on his face, the simple pleasure of doing a good job at the mill, and the taste of a home-cooked meal. John, the man who was worried about his rising utility bills and whether Mrs. Henderson would notice his overgrown lawn, flickered at the edges of his mind. He saw the life he was supposed to be living: a quiet, unremarkable life. A wave of something like regret, a weak version of real remorse, washed over him. It was a short-lived feeling, as weak as a soap bubble, that popped easily under the heavy weight of what he had just become.

Then, the dark would rise. It wasn't a conscious choice or a planned embrace; it was an involuntary submersion, like being pulled under by an unseen undertow. The predatory persona, the being that planned these nighttime hunts, showed that it was in charge. This wasn't "John." This was something else, something old and hungry, a physical form of all the anger, resentment, and deep loneliness that had been a part of his life for so long.

He could feel it as a separate being, living in his own head. It whispered reasons and twisted logic that made his actions seem like a way to bring the universe back into balance, a necessary cleansing of the world's too much happiness. It hissed that they were too bright, and the voice wasn't quite his own; it was a deeper, guttural sound that shook his bones. Their happiness was an insult. A falsehood.

John's mind turned into a battlefield. The mill worker's rational, organized thoughts would come to the surface as a last-ditch effort to stay grounded in reality. He would carefully go over the events again and again, breaking them down with a detached, almost academic accuracy, looking for a way out, a hole in the horrible story that was unfolding. He would remember the faint smell of pine needles crushed underfoot, the almost imperceptible tremor in the victim's voice, and the way their eyes widened in a primal, animal fear. These were sensory details, the raw data of his actions, and he would try to make sense of them by looking for a logical order, a cause and effect that didn't involve the terrifying lack of his own will.

But the predatory mind was always one step ahead. It would add its own scary meaning to these observations. The shaking in the voice wasn't fear; it was a song of giving up. The eyes that were getting bigger weren't scared; they were a last, desperate plea for oblivion, which it had so kindly granted. The smell of pine needles was not a natural smell; it was the smell of incense used in a holy ceremony to clean the world's impurities.

There were times, though they were very short, when the two minds fought with such force that it almost broke him. He'd feel sick and dizzy, as if the ground beneath his feet had disappeared. He'd see the innocent faces of his victims, their youth and weakness made worse, and a deep cry would rise in his throat, begging for freedom. He would scratch at the edges of this inner pain, trying to find an identity that felt like it was slipping through his fingers like sand.

He might see how terrible his actions were and how completely wrong they were in those broken seconds. In the dark, unblinking eyes of his prey, he would see a twisted version of himself. A ghostly hand would reach out, not to hurt them, but to pull them back from the edge and offer a silent apology for the darkness that was about to take them. These were the times when "John" fought back, a spark of humanity against the dark.

But the fight was never fair. The predatory persona was a skilled warrior who had been neglected for years and was driven by an insatiable hunger. It knew John's weaknesses and deep-seated fears, and it used them to its advantage with ruthless efficiency. It would turn his loneliness into a weapon and use his desire for connection as a reason to destroy. It would bring back memories of every time he felt left out, every time he felt like he was invisible, and every time he felt like he was being treated unfairly. It would use these memories to support the idea that the world was a cruel, unfair place and that he was just doing its harsh justice in his own way.

The fall never happened all at once. It was a slow drowning, a slow giving in to the pull of the abyss that couldn't be stopped. Every act chipped away at the structure of his identity, leaving behind a shell that was more empty. The times when things made sense got fewer and shorter, like dying embers in a storm. The "normal" John was slowly being eaten away, his essence being replaced by the predator's never-ending hunger.

He would stand there, his body moving on its own after the event. He would carefully clean the scene, which was a scary reminder of how methodical he was at the mill, but for a different reason. It wasn't about being efficient or orderly; it was about erasing things, making the world forget, just like he was forgetting himself. He would carefully get rid of any evidence, moving slowly, precisely, and almost peacefully. His carefulness and calmness on the outside were a horrible joke about the chaos inside him.

Sometimes, a random thought would come to him, like the faded picture of his mother on his bedside table. Her gentle smile was a stark contrast to the grim reality he was living in now. He'd feel a pang, a distant echo of love and family ties, and for a split second, he wanted to go home, curl up in his own bed, and pretend none of it had ever happened. But the predatory mind would quickly put out that light. It would say, "Home is a cage." This is being free. This is strength.

The strength. That was the hook. John had never felt so powerful in his life as he did when he was in charge of life and death. He wasn't the invisible man in the background or the mill worker who was never noticed. He was the architect of terror, the quiet power that demanded complete obedience, even if it was the last, unyielding obedience. This intoxicating rush of power, no matter how short-lived and harmful, was like a drug that kept him going back to the dark, even though the parts of him that were still human screamed in protest.

The feeling of having a mind at war was always there, gnawing at me. It made the world outside the fog of his hunts seem strange and not real. During the day, he would walk the streets of Oakhaven. The cheerful greetings of neighbors, the laughter of children playing, and the normal rhythm of daily life all seemed like a show he was no longer a part of. He was a fake, a ghost that haunted his own life, always separated from the living by the horrible things he did at night.

He would look at his hands, the ones that had held the rope and stopped the screams, and they would seem strange and out of touch with his will. He'd make fists with his hands to try to feel the familiar feeling of his own flesh and bone, but the world around him felt muted and far away, as if he were seeing it through thick glass.

The broken mind didn't get worse over time; it broke apart in a series of violent events. One moment, he was John, the man who carefully sorted wood and politely greeted people he knew. The next moment, he would be a primal force, driven by instincts he barely understood, with a warped sense of reality. There was no smooth change or gradual slide. It was like walking through a ripped curtain, going from one reality to another without being able to control the moment of passage.

The memories of the victims became a haunting kaleidoscope. Their faces, voices, and last moments of terror would flash behind his eyes at random times, without him wanting or asking for them to. He'd see Sarah's hopeful look, Mark's protective stance, Chloe's defiant spark, David's passionate intensity, Emily's quiet grace, and Thomas's gentle smile. For a brief moment, the predatory consciousness would fade away, leaving John open to the raw, unfiltered horror of what he had done. These were the times when the carefully crafted mask he wore was about to come off, when the monstrous facade cracked under the weight of his broken mind. He was a man stuck between two worlds, not really belonging to either one. He was a prisoner in his own skin, haunted by the memories of the lives he had so brutally taken. The battle went on, a silent, internal war that kept Oakhaven blissfully unaware of the real monster that lived among them. The monster's worst enemy was himself.

The Silence After the Storm

The boathouse's oppressive silence, which had once been a real thing, faded away and was replaced by a soft hum, a vibration that felt more familiar. The sound of Oakhaven waking up, the distant rumble of the first delivery trucks, and the chirping of birds that didn't know what was going on at night. John took a shaky breath. The metallic smell in the air seemed to fade, or maybe his senses were resetting, blocking out the strong, primal smell of death. He became very aware of his own body, the pain in his shoulders from standing in an awkward way and the stiffness in his knees. These were normal physical feelings that made a person feel stable, and John clung to them with a desperate, almost sad hunger.

He looked down at his hands, which had done terrible things that night, and felt sick. He had used these same hands to carefully fix a broken engine at the mill and to hold a chipped teacup while listening to his mother talk about her day. But now… now they were dirty. The bright and disgusting picture of their last event flashed in front of his eyes. He squeezed them shut, and a silent plea slipped from his lips, a whisper against the huge space of his own conscience. No. Not me.

The thought was like a fragile seedling trying to grow through the burnt ground of his recent actions. That man was coming back: the one who paid his taxes on time, helped Mrs. Gable carry her groceries now and then, and felt bad when he stepped on an ant by accident. He felt like he had to scrub his skin raw to get rid of the lingering touch of his victims and the phantom weight of their lives that seemed to cling to him. He staggered toward the murky water that was lapping at the floor of the boathouse. His movements were awkward and uncoordinated, like a puppet whose strings had suddenly gone slack.

He knelt down by the edge and looked into the dark, oily water. It didn't show any signs of the person who looked into its depths. Instead, it looked like it was soaking up the little light and keeping its secrets. John's mind was like a battlefield where opposing forces were always fighting. It started to frantically try to put together the pieces of his broken reality. The act itself was a blur, a bunch of disconnected images and feelings that wouldn't come together to make a story. He remembered the thrill and the intoxicating rush of power that had gone through him, but it was like remembering a dream: clear at times, but ultimately hard to pin down and not to be trusted.

He tried to make sense of it. They were glad. Way too happy. Their happiness was a joke. The words rang in his head, like a distorted echo of the voice that whispered in the dark. But this time, the voice sounded strange and outside, like an unwelcome guest who had stayed too long. He fought against it, trying hard to take back control. Being happy is not a crime. There is no sin in love. The thoughts were stiff and unconvincing, like a lie that hadn't been practiced enough. He knew, with a cold certainty, that his excuses were just that: flimsy excuses meant to protect him from the harsh truth.

When the guilt finally started to set in, it wasn't a raging fire; it was a slow, poisonous poison. It was the cold fear that settled in his stomach, the shaking of his hands that he couldn't quite control, and the sudden, strong need to run away and hide. He thought about the faces of the people he had killed, how young they were, how much they could have done, and how they had not lived yet. He saw how Sarah looked at Mark, with pure love in her eyes, and the picture made his stomach hurt like a knife. He remembered Chloe's angry look, the fire in her eyes, and he felt a flash of shame, a desperate wish that he had never seen that spark and never been able to put it out.

This was the weak victory of the hidden self, the ghost of John fighting his way back to the top. He held on to these feelings, these pieces of regret, like a man who was drowning held on to driftwood. He would carefully go over his steps again, not in a detached, analytical way, but with a desperate need for understanding. How did I end up here? What did I do? He looked for the turning point, the point of no return, but the answer was still frustratingly out of reach. He felt like he had been sleepwalking through his own life and then waking up in a nightmare.

He thought about the questions that would come up if anyone ever found out what had happened. The questioning, the accusing looks, and the public shaming. The thought made him feel panicked again. This was not for him. He wasn't really a monster. He was a man who had done terrible things and had been taken over by something dark and unknown. This was the story he desperately tried to tell himself, the comforting lie that would let him sleep at night, if he could ever sleep again.

He felt a strong need to confess and let go of his guilt. He imagined walking into the police station and saying a lot of things that made him feel guilty and hate himself. But then the shadows would move. A cold certainty would creep in, a whisper of realism that felt eerily logical. They won't get it. They'll put you in jail. They'll cut you up. Even when it was weak, the predatory consciousness was a master manipulator. It used his deepest fears and feelings of being alone to paint a picture of his future that was much scarier than the pain he was in right now.

He got up, but his legs weren't steady. The terrible things that happened that night were still there, a real stain on the air, his clothes, and his soul. But the strong, instinctive urge to act, to kill, had faded, leaving behind a hollow ache and a gnawing emptiness. He had to go back to acting like the normal person he was supposed to be. He had to go back to the world outside this old boathouse, where people were waking up. He was a ghost in the machine, a wolf in sheep's clothing.

He slowly started to wash himself with a rag that was wet with the still water. He tried to scrub away the evidence of the act itself and the darkness that had taken over his life with each wipe of his skin. He scrubbed his hands until they were raw. The sting was a welcome distraction from the deeper pain. He tried to push the pictures of his victims to the back of his mind, where they would be buried under everyday thoughts like the cost of milk, the weather forecast, and the latest woodworking project he had been thinking about.

He left the boathouse, and the bright light of early morning was too much for him. The air, which was cool and crisp, felt strange on his skin. He looked at the familiar Oakhaven landscape, with its sleepy houses and quiet streets. It felt like he had come back from a place where there was violence and darkness. He was John again, or at least he looked like John. The memories were still there, like a dark current under the calm surface of his mind, but for now, they were kept inside. The fight was far from over. It was only a break, a short break before the storm, which would inevitably come back. He knew with a sickening certainty that this fragile peace was an illusion and that the darkness that was always with him would soon take over again. He was a man torn apart, a prisoner of his own broken mind, stuck in the horrible silence that came after the storm.

Whispers and Rumors

The quiet whispers started slowly, like the first sound of leaves moving in the wind before a storm. At first, they could only talk quietly in the aisles of Miller's Grocery, behind cupped hands at the post office, and in the worried whispers of parents waiting to pick up their kids from school. The sudden disappearance of Sarah Jenkins, a bright and cheerful sixteen-year-old whose smile could light up the whole town square, was a shock and a break in the otherwise calm flow of life in Oakhaven. People talked about teens who ran away, bad choices made in the heat of rebellion, and accidents that happened near the old quarry. Sheriff Brody, who was very serious, told the people of the town that they were doing everything they could to find Sarah. But weeks turned into months, and the hope that had once been a flickering candle faded, leaving behind a gnawing, unsettling fear.

Then there was the second disappearance: Chloe Davison, a quiet art student known for her dreamy watercolors and shyness. Chloe disappeared without a trace from her small cottage on the edge of Blackwood Forest. She left behind an easel with a half-finished landscape on it and the smell of turpentine still in the air. The fear in Oakhaven grew stronger, changing from a general feeling of unease to something more specific and real. Two young women died within a few months of each other. The whispers got louder and had a darker tone. This wasn't just a fluke. People started to whisper the word "monster," and just saying it made people shiver.

The town, which used to be a safe and quiet place, started to feel like a trap. Every shadow seemed to get longer, and every face that wasn't familiar made you suspicious. Parents, whose faces showed how worried they were, kept their kids close. Their kids' free spirits were now stuck in their homes, which they thought were safe. Curfew became a rule that everyone knew about but didn't talk about, thanks to the tension in the air. People at the Oakhaven Diner stopped joking around and started talking quietly about what might have happened. They shared theories over cold coffee and stale donuts. Was it someone from outside? A drifter who is just passing through? Or, the most terrifying thought of all, was the monster one of their own?

Sheriff Brody, a man whose weathered face usually showed an unflappable calm, now had the town's fear on his broad shoulders. His office was flooded with calls from worried citizens reporting strange behavior, parents who were worried about their children's vague fears, and lonely people who thought they had seen something. He and his small team worked around the clock, following leads that often led to dead ends and chasing shadows that disappeared into thin air. At first, the press was only a trickle, but soon it became a steady stream. Their sensational headlines only made people more scared. One particularly bad tabloid screamed, "OAKHAVEN MONSTER STRIKES AGAIN?" This headline sent a new wave of fear through the already scared community.

When a group of hikers found the first body, Sarah Jenkins, near Miller's Creek, it shattered any remaining hopes of safety. When the details came out, they were horrible and suggested a level of violence that Oakhaven had never thought possible. The fact that Chloe Davison's body was found in an old hunting cabin deep in the woods only made the town's worst fears come true. This wasn't a case of someone running away or an accident. Someone who was sick and enjoyed causing pain and fear did this. The police were no longer just looking for people who were missing; they were also looking for a serial killer.

Fear in Oakhaven became a living thing, a heavy blanket that smothered happiness and normalcy. The sound of children's laughter, which used to fill the summer afternoons, now seemed quiet and full of fear. Adults who used to greet each other with big smiles and easy conversation now looked at each other nervously and talked about the latest bad news or the newest crazy theory. The annual summer fair, which everyone loved, was called off because the thought of large crowds was too scary. The town's only movie theater closed because not many people went to see movies there. This felt like another nail in the coffin of Oakhaven's former peace.

Paranoia started to set in, ruining relationships and trust. People were now suspicious of a neighbor who had always been friendly. Did they see something? Were they keeping something from you? A passing car, a stranger walking down the street, or a loud noise in the night could all be signs of danger. The police were under a lot of stress and were the target of public anger. The Sheriff's office got a lot of angry letters, some of which called for immediate action and others that said Brody and his team were incompetent. There were small but loud protests outside the police station, which showed how sad and hopeless the people in the town were.

Sheriff Brody knew he didn't have much time left. There was a lot of pressure, both from the people who were scared and from within himself. He could see the fear in his children's eyes and how his wife jumped at every little noise.

He knew how big of a responsibility he had: the lives of people depended on his ability to bring the light back to Oakhaven. He went through the case files, forensic reports, and witness statements over and over again, looking for a pattern, a clue, anything that would help him find the killer. He could feel the weight of Oakhaven's collective gaze and their silent cries for help.

The media, a hungry beast, fed on the town's fear. Reporters set up tents outside the Sheriff's office and kept asking officers for any information they could get, often with a morbid curiosity. The killer, whoever they were, had become a kind of celebrity, a boogeyman whose fame spread far beyond the borders of Oakhaven. The local newspaper used to be a place to get news and ads about the community. Now, though, its front pages are full of articles and interviews with scared residents about the tragedy that is happening. The name "Monster John," which came from the whispers, started to show up in print. This made the image of a savage, unfeeling predator stalking their peaceful town even stronger.

It had a big effect on the community. The feeling of shared history and comfort that had been a part of Oakhaven for generations was broken. People who had known each other for a long time suddenly didn't trust each other anymore. The perfect image of small-town life had been torn away, showing a weakness that scared everyone. A killer who worked in the shadows and fed on their deepest fears was tearing apart the very fabric of their community. Every day that went by, every missing person case that wasn't solved, and every horrible discovery made them less able to handle what was happening. They felt exposed, helpless, and completely alone. The whispers in Oakhaven were no longer just rumors; they were the desperate prayers of a town that was trapped in terror's tight grip and begging for the light to come back and drive away the darkness.

Chapter 3: The Hunt Begins

Detectives on the Trail

The fear that Oakhaven had caused had settled not only on Sheriff Brody, but also on the two men who were now in charge of figuring out the nightmare. Detective Miles Corbin, who had moved to the city and had an unsettling stillness about him, had been brought in from the regional task force. He was known for getting to the bottom of the darkest parts of the human mind. His eyes, which were the color of a winter sky, always had a quiet intensity, as if they were constantly sifting through data that wasn't visible. He didn't say much, preferring to watch. His silences were often more scary than any questioning. His drive came from a cold, analytical search for truth, a need to make sense of chaos, and a need to understand the "why" behind the "what" with an almost detached interest. Thorne couldn't resist the puzzle that was Oakhaven, with its growing horror. It was a morbid intellectual challenge. He didn't see the town's clear fear as a reason to stay away; instead, he saw it as a key, a reflection of the killer's own mind.

Detective Lena Hanson stood next to him, and they were very different in how they acted. Her family had lived in Oakhaven for generations, so her roots there were strong. She was the epitome of local toughness and determination, and her anger at the tragedy that was happening was clear and real. Her dark, expressive eyes often flashed with anger, which was very different from Corbin's calm gaze. Hanson had a personal reason for doing it: she had known Sarah Jenkins and had seen Chloe Davison's soft drawings at the town's annual art show. This wasn't just a case; it was an attack on her community and an attack on the innocence she had promised to protect. Her methods were more straightforward, and her interrogations were full of a simmering anger that could push suspects to the edge at times. She was Corbin's hammer and scalpel.

At first, their time in Oakhaven was a lesson in how to deal with frustration. The crime scenes, which Brody's already overworked local police had to carefully process, only gave them painful echoes of the violence. The forensic teams had searched the creek bed where Sarah's body was found, carefully sifting through mud and other debris. They had gathered every fiber and every trace, but the killer had been so careful that they left behind a perfect void. The air at the abandoned hunting cabin where Chloe was found was still thick with the smell of old blood and decay. The scene was also very clean. It was as if the person who did it had disappeared with the dust motes, leaving no fingerprints, stray hairs, or DNA that didn't belong to the victims.

"It's like he's a ghost," Hanson said quietly, running a hand through her already messy hair as they went over the first reports in a small, temporary office set up in the back of the Sheriff's department. The air was thick with the smell of old coffee and the tension that hung over the whole building. "There was no forced entry at Chloe's, no signs of a fight, and nothing to suggest a break-in." And Sarah… they found her miles from anywhere, with no witnesses and no idea how she got there.

Corbin sat on the edge of a worn desk, staring at a picture of a crime scene. He gave a quiet, almost imperceptible nod. "Not a ghost, Detective." A ghost. Someone who knows how to get rid of patterns and knows how to do it. This isn't violence for no reason. The lack of evidence is a work of art on purpose. He pointed with a long, thin finger at a small mark on the floor of the cabin that was hard to see. "This mark. It's too exact and clean for a fight. It implies a certain intentionality in movement, a planned distribution of weight, perhaps. Or a well-kept area.

Hanson leaned in closer, her brow furrowing. "On purpose? Do you think he's cleaning up after himself? That's very careful. Most murderers leave something behind. "A signature, a mistake."

"Or they are so sure of their power that they think they haven't left anything," Corbin said in a low, measured voice. "The psychological profile is evolving. We are looking at a person who is very smart, very organized, and very troubled. Someone capable of extreme patience and meticulous planning. The lack of a signature, in itself, becomes a signature. It's a taunt. He says he can't be touched.

But the pressure was very real. Sheriff Brody, who was usually as steady as the old oaks around Oakhaven, was not himself anymore. His phone rang all the time, and each call was full of worried questions, desperate pleas, and sometimes even direct accusations. The town council, with serious looks on their faces and the weight of their constituents' fear on their shoulders, had asked for daily updates. The media, like a pack of hyenas around a hurt animal, had come to Oakhaven, making the town even more anxious and giving rise to the sensationalist nickname "Monster John." Corbin and Hanson were stuck in a never-ending loop of reporting to their bosses, answering questions from reporters whose questions often turned into morbid speculation, and trying to calm down the people who were getting more and more scared.

Hanson slammed a file down on the desk and said, "They want answers, Corbin." "Not ideas. They want to catch "Monster John." A lot of people are giving Brody a hard time. The governor's office is calling. The papers are almost asking for Brody's head on a platter. She pointed to the window, where a single reporter was still outside the Sheriff's office, ready with a camera and tripod. "Every minute we spend looking at scuff marks, he's out there, feeding the frenzy and making us look like we're not doing enough."

Finally, Corbin stood up, moving smoothly and slowly. He walked over to a wall that had maps, pictures, and timelines on it. Detective, you need to understand to do enough. To understand this killer, we need to look beyond what is clear. The mark on the surface is more than just a scuff mark. It's a small thing. And that's where the truth is. He tapped a pin on the map to show where Sarah found it, then another pin to show where Chloe's cottage was. "The geography is disparate, yet connected by the dense Blackwood Forest. He is taking advantage of the natural landscape by moving around without being seen. This isn't a killer who works in the dark on a well-lit street in the city. He does well in the wild, dark places.

Their early attempts to investigate were a never-ending grind. They went back to the crime scenes many times, and Corbin's quiet observations often caught things that had been missed in the initial panic. He spent hours in the Blackwood Forest, not looking for clues in the usual way, but taking in the sights and sounds and trying to picture how the killer moved and where he was. He looked at the plants, the ground, and the possible ways in and out, putting together a mental picture of the killer's hunting ground. Hanson, on the other hand, looked into the lives of the victims and carefully put together the last days, hours, and minutes of their lives. She talked to friends, family, and coworkers to look for anything strange, any strange encounter, or any hint of a threat that might have been ignored at the time.

"Sarah was…" "She was a good kid," Mrs. Jenkins told Hanson, her voice hoarse with grief. "She wouldn't have gone anywhere with someone she didn't know. Not unless they knew her or somehow tricked her. She was looking forward to prom and applying to college. "She had her whole life ahead of her."

Chloe's parents, who were quiet and artistic and lived in a nearby town, talked about how she was a loner, how much she loved her art, and how connected she felt to nature. Her father had said, "She found peace in the woods," and his eyes were far away. "She would spend hours drawing and just being. We never had to worry. It was her safe place.

There was a big difference between the two victims, but their fates were the same. One was outgoing and lively, while the other was shy and creative. What could possibly connect them in such a terrible way? Corbin thought about how the predator needed a variety of prey, which is a psychological sign of power and control. Hanson, however, felt the insidious reach of the killer into the very heart of Oakhaven, suggesting that perhaps the killer was someone who knew the town, who understood its rhythms and its inhabitants.

They talked to people in the area who had been in trouble with the law before and had a history of violence, but every lead led to a frustrating dead end. The profiles didn't match, the alibis, no matter how weak, held up under scrutiny, or the fact that there was no real link to Oakhaven made them unlikely. The clock was ticking, and every day that went by was another wound on the town's mind. There was a lot of pressure to make an arrest, a real force that could have clouded their judgment and pushed them toward a quick, possibly wrong, conclusion. But Corbin's unnerving calm and Hanson's fierce determination kept them steady, keeping them tied to the slow, often soul-crushing process of real investigation. They were trying to catch a ghost, a phantom, or a monster who loved being hard to find. They knew that using brute force or making quick guesses would only help him. The hunt had begun, but it was going on in the woods as well as in people's heads.

A Flaw in the Predatory Design

The lack of evidence, which was deafeningly silent in the forensic reports, had first seemed like an impossible problem. But as Corbin and Hanson carefully and almost obsessively went over the few details again, they began to see a symphony of small omissions, a deliberate gap that said a lot. It wasn't just what the killer left behind; it was also what he didn't leave behind. This wasn't the crazy mess of a crime of passion that happened without planning, nor was it the bragging signature of a murderer with a big ego. This was the work of a predator who knew what would happen, weighed the risks, and had an almost scary level of self-control.

The embankment of the Willow Creek at Sarah Jenkins' discovery site had been thoroughly searched, but the churned mud didn't give up much except for the grim fact that she was dead. But what caught Corbin's attention wasn't the fact that there weren't any footprints leading away; it was how exact the few that were found were. They were faint, almost erased by the shifting earth and recent rain, yet their placement suggested a careful, deliberate tread, not a panicked flight. He thought about how the killer got there and left, picturing a hunter who knew the area well and used the natural features of the land to hide his tracks. He might have even carried Sarah in a way that left as little of a mark on the ground as possible. He didn't picture the killer as a clumsy brute; instead, he saw him as a skilled tracker who knew how to disturb the ground as little as possible. The fact that it was so far from any road or inhabited area made it seem like a planned meeting, a staged scene meant to throw people off and move the discovery far away from where the abduction happened. The river itself, which is a natural channel, could have been used to move the victim, making the trail even harder to follow. Corbin's mind, which was always working to figure things out, started to come up with scenarios in which the killer carefully planned his movements, maybe even using a boat or some other hidden way to get away from the area without leaving a traceable path on land. It was especially telling that there were no signs of a struggle near Sarah's body. There would have been problems, a mess, or maybe a dropped item if she had been attacked and killed there. The clean, if muddy, state of the area around her suggested that she had been put there after the main act had taken place somewhere else.

Chloe Davison's old hunting cabin, which had once brought her peace, had turned into a charnel house. The first search didn't find anything useful. There were no hairs, fibers, or blood that wasn't Chloe's. But Corbin, who had an almost supernatural ability to see things that weren't there, saw a faint, almost invisible sheen on the doorframe inside, close to the lock. It was too smooth and even to be normal wear and tear. He carefully took a sample, and later tests showed that it contained traces of a high-quality, specialized lubricant, the kind used in precision mechanics or, even more frighteningly, to keep specialized tools in good shape. This wasn't something a casual trespasser would use, and it wasn't something that most people would have around the house. It made me think of someone who took care of his tools like a professional, someone who valued efficiency and quiet in his work. When Corbin compared the lubricant to his growing mental database of criminal modus operandi, it pointed to people who used careful, controlled violence instead of acting on impulse. He thought about the possibility that the killer had carefully cleaned the lock mechanism itself, maybe to make sure that no one could hear them come in or out. This small detail said a lot about how well he planned and how much he hated leaving anything to chance. He also pointed out how strange it was that a small, chipped ceramic bird figurine was on the mantlepiece. It didn't fit with Chloe's usual artistic style or the rustic look of the room. Corbin thought that the killer might have brought something with him, like a subtle, almost subconscious marker, or maybe even a twisted gift to his victim. Its displacement, a mere inch from its original position, suggested a moment of interaction, a fleeting, chilling acknowledgment of the scene beyond the purely functional.

Hanson, on the other hand, looked at the victims' online activities and social interactions, which was just as frustrating. Sarah Jenkins' social media was a colorful picture of teenage life, with parties, friends, and school events. But when we looked closely at her direct messages and online activity, we saw that she suddenly stopped talking to people in the days before she died. Her usual long, enthusiastic posts became shorter and more guarded. One conversation, with a username that wasn't real, was especially worrisome. The messages were short and almost cryptic, suggesting a secret meeting or something they both knew about. The username didn't make any sense; it was just a bunch of random letters and numbers that looked like they were meant to be impossible to find. Corbin thought it was a planned effort to make a digital ghost, a ghost in the machine, to match the killer's physical ability to hide. He thought that the killer might have been watching Sarah online to learn about her habits and weaknesses before getting in touch. The fact that the communication was anonymous was a planned way to control the story and keep Sarah alone without raising immediate alarm.

Chloe Davison, on the other hand, didn't have much of an online presence; most of her life was lived offline. But her sketchbooks told a different kind of story. Most of the recent sketches were of local plants and animals, but some showed strange, abstract shapes and dark, swirling patterns that suggested the artist was becoming more and more troubled. There were also a few disturbing, almost disturbing, pictures of shadowy figures hiding in thick woods. Their shapes were hard to make out, but they looked threatening. Corbin didn't think of these as just works of art; he thought of them as Chloe's subconscious way of showing her growing fear and awareness of an unseen presence. He thought the killer might have been subtly affecting Chloe, maybe through meetings in the woods, which made her feel uneasy and affected her art. Corbin said that the recurring image of the shadowed figure was Chloe's mind's way of trying to deal with an outside threat and give shape to the terror that was creeping into her life. It made it sound like Chloe had at some point felt like someone in the woods was watching her or even threatening her, and she had put that feeling into her art.

Their investigation started to show that the predator was not only smart and careful, but also very patient. The times when he wasn't doing anything were not just breaks; they were times when he was carefully watching and planning. He wasn't just hitting things at random; he was picking them out. Corbin looked closely at a map of Oakhaven and the nearby Blackwood Forest and started to see a pattern in the land that was not very obvious but still there. There were a lot of logging roads and game trails that weren't used very often that connected the places where Sarah and Chloe were found, even though they were miles apart. It seemed that the killer had set up a territory, a hunting ground in the thick forest where he felt safest and most hidden. He lived in the woods, and its rhythms controlled how he moved. He knew all of its secret paths better than anyone else. Corbin saw him as a ghostly hunter who blended in perfectly with his surroundings. His presence was as natural and unnoticed as the sound of leaves rustling. The logger's roads, which were often overgrown and not used very much, would have let him get to remote areas where he could move his victims and get rid of evidence without being seen by people who weren't paying attention.

"He's using the forest," Corbin said in a low voice as he ran his finger along a faint, dotted line on the map. "Not just as a background, but as a friend." He is familiar with these paths. He knows where the camera can't see him, where the canopy is thickest, and where the ground is softest so he can hide his tracks. "It's his domain."

At first, Hanson was only interested in the people, but he soon realized how important the land was. She remembered Sheriff Brody talking about an old logging camp deep in the Blackwood that had been abandoned and mostly forgotten. It was the perfect place to set up shop, where someone could do whatever they wanted without being seen by the townspeople. The camp's isolation and distance from other places made it a good place for the killer to work. She imagined the killer using this forgotten outpost as a base of operations, where he could plan his hunts, get his tools ready, and maybe even keep his victims there before their horrible deaths. The camp's remoteness, which had caused it to be abandoned, now gave a predator a dangerous edge.

Hanson thought about "the old logging camp" as she looked at the map. "My grandpa used to tell me stories about it. He said it was rough land where it was easy to get lost. "Nobody goes there anymore."

"Exactly," Corbin said, his eyes flashing with something that looked like grim satisfaction. "And that's exactly why he would pick it. It is off the grid in both a physical and mental sense. A place where the rules of Oakhaven don't work anymore.

The investigation was moving from a broad look at things to a more detailed look. They weren't just looking for a killer anymore; they were also looking for a ghost who had left the faintest of trails. The lubricant, the precise footprints, the digital ghost, the creepy drawings, and the geographical advantage were all parts of a puzzle that was slowly, painfully, coming together. Every piece, no matter how small, was a thread in the killer's complicated mind, and Corbin and Hanson were carefully pulling on each one, determined to find the monster that was hiding in the shadows of Oakhaven. The killer's attention to detail, which had once been his best quality, was now his worst enemy. He had unknowingly left a trail of small clues that showed he was there, each one a breadcrumb that led them deeper into his darkness. The hunt had really started, and the hunter was starting to show himself, even though he didn't want to.

The NearVictims Testimony

At 03:17, a frantic, jumbled burst of fear broke the quiet of the Oakhaven Sheriff's Department before dawn. Dispatcher Henderson, a man whose jaded composure had been forged over decades of domestic disputes and drunk-and-disorderly calls, felt a prickle of unease that transcended the usual noise. This was different. The voice on the other end, a young woman named Emily Carter, was a raw, ragged thing, her words tumbling out in a desperate cascade, punctuated by gasps and choked sobs. She was calling from a pay phone miles away, and her cell phone signal had died hours before. She talked about being chased, a dark car, and a man. She had only seen the man once, but his presence had left a mark on her soul.

Before the first official report could even be typed, Corbin and Hanson were already at the precinct. Emily Carter was huddled in a small interview room, a blanket clutched tightly around her, her eyes wide and vacant, darting at every shadow. She was young, no older than twenty, her face a pale mask of shock, streaked with dirt and tears. Her clothes were torn, her left arm bearing the angry red marks of what looked like deep scratches, as if she'd been clawed by a wild animal. The payphone booth, miles from where she had finally gotten away, was a stark reminder of her ordeal, a lonely light of hope in the growing darkness.

"He… he almost had me," she stammered, her voice barely a whisper, her gaze fixed on some unseen horror. "I was walking home from my friend's house. It was late. The streetlights are terrible on Elm Street, you know? "Always flickering." Her words were broken up, and the memories that came back to her mind made it easy for her to lose her train of thought. Corbin saw that her hands were shaking as she tried to drink the water Hanson had given her. The plastic cup rattled against her teeth.

"Take your time, Emily," Hanson said, her voice a soothing balm. "Just tell us what happened. Anything you remember."

Emily nodded, a small, jerky movement. I heard a car. Slowing down. I thought… I thought maybe someone I knew. But it was dark, the windows were tinted. Then it stopped. Next to me. She swallowed, and her throat worked. "He opened the door. Just… a crack at first. And he said something. I couldn't make out what it was. It was muffled. Like he was… holding something over his mouth?" She frowned, and for a moment, the fear was replaced by confusion. "Then he made it even bigger. He had this strange smile. Not happy. Twisted. Like he was enjoying my fear."

Corbin leaned forward, his gaze unwavering. "What did he look like, Emily?"

Her eyes, a startling shade of blue even in their current state of distress, widened further. "He was… tall. Very tall. And broad. He was wearing a dark jacket. Could it be leather? And a baseball cap. Pulled down low. I couldn't see his face clearly. The shadows, and the cap… but his eyes. They were… cold. Like ice. And his hands. They were… big. Strong. Also, his fingernails were dirty. Like he had been digging in the ground. She shivered and pulled the blanket around her more tightly. "He reached out. I… I panicked. I just ran. I didn't even think. I just ran."

"Which way did you run, Emily?" Hanson prompted gently.

"Towards the old mill. I know it's not safe, but it's the only way I knew how to get to the main road without going further down Elm. I heard him… I heard the door of the car slam. Then, he was gone. He was chasing me. He was really quick. Faster than he looked." A fresh wave of sobs wracked her body. "I could hear him breathing. A lot. It seemed like he was really enjoying the chase. He kept calling out to me. His voice… it was rough. Deep. Not like any man I've ever heard."

"Did you even see his face, Emily?" Corbin pushed, his voice calm and low. "Just a peek?"

She shook her head, tears streaming anew. "No. That smile, though. And his eyes. And… and one more thing. Something on his face. A… a mark? On his cheek. Like a scar? Or… a birthmark? It was dark. Irregular. I only saw it for a second when he turned his head. It was… unsettling." She stopped for a moment, trying to find the right words to describe how she felt. "It made him look… not human."

Corbin exchanged a meaningful glance with Hanson. A scar. A mark. It was the first potentially concrete piece of identifying information they had received since the beginning of this nightmare. It was a small ray of light in the thick darkness that had taken over Oakhaven.

"And what about the car, Emily?" Hanson asked, holding her pen over her notepad. "Can you describe the car?"

"It was dark. Black, maybe? Or a very dark blue. A sedan. Nothing fancy. But it was dirty. Mud splatters on the sides. And the windows… they were really dark. Colored. So dark I couldn't see inside at all. And the headlights… they were off when he stopped. He only turned them on after I started running. Like he didn't want me to see him coming."

The details, though fragmented, were beginning to form a picture. A tall, broad man, likely wearing dark clothing and a baseball cap, with cold eyes, dirty fingernails, a distinctive mark on his cheek, and driving a dark, nondescript sedan that was visibly dirty. The precision of his movements, the almost playful cruelty of the chase, the deliberate concealment of his face and vehicle – it all painted a chilling portrait of a predator who was not only methodical but also deeply manipulative. This wasn't the frantic, impulsive act of a stranger; this felt calculated, deliberate, and terrifyingly familiar in its cold efficiency.

"And the voice, Emily," Corbin said, his mind already sifting through the scant evidence. "You said it was rough. Deep."

"Yes," she confirmed, her voice still trembling. "And... there was something else. Something I can't quite place. A... a slight slur? Or an accent? Not like anyone from around here. It was almost... guttural. And when he breathed, it was loud. Like he was... wheezing? Or something in his throat."

Corbin's brow furrowed. A slight speech impediment. A wheezing breath. These were subtle nuances, easily overlooked, but in the context of their investigation, they were invaluable. They added another layer of specificity to the ephemeral image of their suspect. He recalled the almost imperceptible sheen of lubricant on Chloe Davison's doorframe, the meticulously placed footprints near Sarah Jenkins' body, the chillingly precise nature of the attacks. This man was a creature of habit, of detail, and these small inconsistencies, these seemingly minor physical traits, were the cracks in his carefully constructed facade.

"He seemed to know the area," Emily added, as if reading Corbin's thoughts. "He didn't seem surprised when I turned towards the old mill. He just... kept coming."

"Did you hear any music from the car?" Hanson asked, ever the pragmatist. "Anything distinctive?"

Emily shook her head. "No. It was quiet. Just the engine. And... and his breathing. And his voice." She paused, her eyes unfocusing again. "He was... I think he was wearing gloves. Even though he reached out. They were dark. Like the jacket."

Gloves. Another detail that spoke of premeditation. He was covering his tracks, both literally and figuratively. The lack of discernible fingerprints, the absence of any DNA evidence at the previous crime scenes – it was all starting to coalesce around a singular, chilling pattern. This wasn't an amateur. This was someone who had clearly thought through the implications of his actions, someone who understood the importance of leaving no trace.

"Emily, did you happen to notice anything about the car's tires?" Corbin asked, his voice deliberately calm, as if discussing the weather. "Any particular tread pattern? Or perhaps the condition of the tires?"

She hesitated, her brow furrowed in concentration. "I… I don't think so. It was dark, and I was running. But… I remember seeing mud on the wheels. Lots of it. And… and maybe something else? Like… like gravel caught in the spokes? If it had spokes. I'm not sure. It was just… dirty. Very dirty."

Mud and gravel. Oakhaven, especially the outskirts near Blackwood Forest, was rife with dirt roads and logging trails. This detail, while seemingly minor, could be crucial in narrowing down the search area, particularly if they could cross-reference it with recent rainfall patterns and known off-road routes used by individuals with access to the more remote parts of the county.

"And when you finally got away," Hanson continued, her tone encouraging, "where did you go?"

"I ran and ran. I don't know how I got to the payphone. My legs were burning. My lungs felt like they were going to explode. I just… I saw it and I ran for it. I fumbled with the coins. My hands were shaking so badly. I almost dropped them. Then I dialed 911. I just kept thinking… he's going to come back. He's going to find me." She buried her face in her hands, her shoulders heaving with silent sobs.

Corbin and Hanson let her weep for a moment. This raw, visceral fear was a potent antidote to the detached, analytical nature of their investigation. It reminded them of the stakes, of the human cost of the monster they were hunting. Emily Carter's terror was the first tangible evidence of his presence, the first breath of life he had inadvertently blown onto the cold embers of their investigation. Her survival was not just a lucky break; it was a lifeline.

"Emily," Corbin said, his voice softening, "you've been incredibly brave. What you've told us is… it's going to help us. A lot. We're going to find him."

She looked up, her blue eyes red-rimmed and brimming with a fragile hope. "You will?"

"We will," Hanson assured her, offering a small, reassuring smile. "We're going to catch him. But we need you to try and remember anything else, no matter how small. Think about the car again. Any logos? Bumper stickers? Anything that stood out?"

Emily closed her eyes, her lips moving silently as she replayed the terrifying encounter. The silence in the room stretched, thick with anticipation. Then, she spoke, her voice barely audible. "There was… a small dent. On the rear passenger door. Like someone had bumped into it. And… and a sticker on the back windshield. Faded. I think it was a… a fish? A religious fish symbol. But it was old. Peeling."

A dent. A faded fish sticker. Small details, yes, but in the grand, terrifying puzzle they were assembling, each piece was a revelation. The dent suggested a past mishap, perhaps an indication of carelessness in an otherwise meticulous individual, or simply an overlooked imperfection. The fish sticker, though faded, offered a potential clue to the owner's affiliations or beliefs, however tenuous. It was another thread, however fine, to tug on.

Corbin felt a surge of something akin to adrenaline, a raw, primal excitement that had been absent for too long. This was it. This was the break. The near-victim's testimony, the raw, unfiltered terror of Emily Carter, had given them more than just a description; it had given them a direction. It had transformed the phantom hunter, the shadowy enigma, into a tangible, albeit terrifying, possibility. The hunt had truly begun, and for the first time, they felt they were no longer chasing shadows, but a man. A man with cold eyes, a twisted smile, and a distinctive mark on his cheek, driving a dirty, dark sedan, a predator who had almost claimed his next victim but had instead, inadvertently, signed his own indictment. Emily Carter's ordeal, a nightmare for her, was the dawn of hope for Oakhaven. The silent predator had finally made a mistake, a near-fatal one, and in doing so, had put himself squarely in their sights. The woods of Blackwood might offer him sanctuary, but the terror of a survivor had finally breached his carefully constructed defenses.

Piecing Together the Puzzle

The sterile air of the Oakhaven Sheriff's Department buzzed with a new kind of energy. It was a clear change from the stagnant fear that had settled over the precinct after Sarah Jenkins' murder. Emily Carter's frantic call, which came in broken pieces, had been a lifeline, a light cutting through the thick fog of doubt. Now, in the harsh glare of fluorescent lights, her testimony was being dissected, reassembled, and cross-referenced with an almost obsessive focus. Detective Corbin, his usual weary stoicism etched with a newfound urgency, hunched over a corkboard, pinning up the scant details gleaned from the near-victim. There was a picture of Sarah Jenkins next to a quick sketch of the "dark, nondescript sedan," with Emily's description of its muddy wheels and the faint impression of gravel stuck in what could have been spokes on top of it.

"Tall, broad build, dark jacket, baseball cap pulled low," Corbin murmured, tracing the outline of the sketch with a calloused finger. "Eyes that are cold." Fingernails that are dirty. And the mark on his cheek – irregular, dark. Scar or birthmark." He then added a note, scrawled in red ink: "Unsettling. Inhuman." He also pinned a small, torn piece of paper next to it with Emily's description of the voice: "Rough, deep, slight slur, guttural, wheezing breath." They treated the faded fish sticker on the back windshield and the dent on the passenger door with the same respect, seeing each as a possible breadcrumb that could lead them out of the woods.

Detective Hanson, her brow furrowed in concentration, sat opposite him, a laptop screen casting a cool blue glow on her face. She was meticulously sifting through Oakhaven's database, her fingers flying across the keyboard. "Nothing on the vehicle description yet, Corbin," she reported, her voice a low drone. "Dark sedan, generic… It's like trying to find a certain raindrop in a storm. The mud and gravel are common enough out here, especially with the recent rain. But that fish sticker…" She stopped and held her fingers over the keys. "That's something." A faded, peeling fish sticker. "Not quite a billboard."

Corbin grunted, running a hand through his already disheveled hair. "It's something. And the dent. It means he's not perfect. He makes mistakes, or at least, his car has seen better days. This guy is careful, but he isn't perfect. He gestured to the board. "The gloves. The intentional hiding of his face. The way he waited for her to run before he even got out of the car. He wants to be unseen, but he's also… enjoying it. That smile Emily described. " The word 'inhuman' hung in the air, a dark omen.

Hanson nodded, but for a moment her eyes were far away. "He is methodical. He is patient. He plans things out. But he's also starting to show signs of weakness. The wheezing breath, the slur… these aren't things easily masked. They're physical characteristics. And the cut. "It's important if she can see it while being chased." She tapped a key, bringing up a list of registered vehicles within a fifty-mile radius. "I've put out a BOLO, but with this vague description, it's a long shot." We need something more solid.

Corbin got a new marker. "What about things that have happened before? Anything that matches the MO? The pattern?" He tapped the photograph of Sarah Jenkins. "No forced entry, no signs of struggle inside the house. Clean. Very clean, like a surgery. And the way she was positioned…" He shuddered inside and pushed the horrible images out of his mind. "It's like he's… putting them in a pose. Or presenting them."

Hanson looked through a lot of reports. "On the other side of the county, there were a few disappearances a few years ago. Not solved. All of the victims were young women, about the same age as Sarah and Emily. But the circumstances were different. No bodies found, no definitive evidence of foul play. Just… gone." She zoomed in on a blurry picture from one of the cold case files. A young woman with bright, hopeful eyes. "This was Clara Bellweather. Vanished five years ago. Last seen walking home from the library."

Corbin leaned in and squinted his eyes. "Any vehicle descriptions from those cases?"

"Nothing concrete," Hanson said. "Witnesses saw cars, but again, generic. Dark sedans, nothing remarkable. The families were distraught, grasping at straws. It was all speculation." She leaned back in her chair and sighed. "We're chasing ghosts, Corbin." This guy is good. Too good."

"He's not a ghost, he's a man," Corbin countered, his voice firm. "And men leave traces. Even the most meticulous ones." He tapped the sketch of the car again. "That fish sticker." It's a common symbol. But combined with everything else… it's a thread. Let's start there. Let's see if we can find anyone in our recent databases who owns a car that fits that description, even if it's not exactly right, and who has a history of assault, stalking, or anything else that suggests this kind of predatory behavior.

Hanson began a new search, her fingers dancing across the keys. The ticking of the clock on the wall seemed amplified, each second a beat in the escalating tension. Corbin watched her, and his stomach knotted up. They had a near-victim, a terrifying glimpse of their predator, but no name, no face. The woods around Oakhaven, which used to be a peaceful place, now felt like a huge, suffocating space where a monster could hide.

Suddenly, Hanson gasped, her eyes widening. "Wait a minute. This is strange.

Corbin turned, his attention instantly captivated. "What is it?"

"I'm running a cross-reference on individuals with registered vehicles matching 'dark sedan' and 'minor damage' within a fifty-mile radius, with a history of any kind of reported suspicious activity, even minor infractions," she explained, her voice barely above a whisper. "And I'm getting a hit. A hit, but not a strong one. She pointed to the screen. "Robert Vance." Lives out near Miller's Creek, about twenty miles from here. He has a dark blue 2018 Ford Fusion. It's registered as having sustained recent damage to the rear passenger door. Minor collision report filed six months ago."

Corbin's breath hitched. "Robert Vance. Anything else?"

"He had a brief encounter with law enforcement about two years ago," Hanson continued, her voice gaining a note of excitement. "A noise complaint that escalated. He was aggressive, agitated. Neighbors reported he had a... a peculiar way of speaking. Slurred words when he was upset. And he had a visible... dark, irregular mark on his left cheek. They described it as a birthmark, but it was quite prominent."

Corbin felt a chill snake down his spine, a potent cocktail of dread and exhilaration. The pieces were clicking into place with a horrifying finality. "What about the fish sticker, Hanson? Did anything come up about religious affiliations or symbols associated with him?"

Hanson typed furiously, her eyes scanning the limited public records. "He's a recluse, not much out there. But his estranged sister mentioned in a past interview... she said he used to have a morbid fascination with... ichthys symbols. The Christian fish. Said he'd even had a faded one on his old car, years ago. She described it as 'worn out and almost gone.'"

The 'aha!' moment struck with the force of a physical blow. It wasn't a shout, but a profound, internal resonance. The tall, broad man, the dark clothing, the baseball cap, the cold eyes, the dirty fingernails, the distinctive mark on his cheek, the rough, slurred, wheezing voice, the dark, dirty sedan with a dent on the rear passenger door and a faded fish sticker on the back windshield. Every detail Emily Carter had provided, every terrifying fragment of her ordeal, pointed with chilling accuracy to this one man: Robert Vance.

"Miller's Creek," Corbin said, his voice low and steady, though his heart hammered against his ribs. "That's deep in the woods. Lots of unpaved roads. Perfect for a man who wants to stay hidden." He looked at the sketch of the car, then at the photograph of Clara Bellweather. "He's been out there. He's been waiting. And now he's escalated."

Hanson closed the laptop, a grim determination settling on her face. "He's not going to get another chance, Corbin. Not with Emily, and certainly not with Sarah. We have a name. We have a car. We have a direction."

The abstract profiling, the hours spent poring over databases and cold cases, had suddenly coalesced into a single, terrifyingly tangible target. The hunt had shifted. It was no longer a blind pursuit of a phantom in the dark. They were hunting a man, a man named Robert Vance, a man whose carefully constructed anonymity had just been shattered by the desperate courage of a survivor and the meticulous work of two determined detectives. The silence of Oakhaven had been broken, and the echo of that scream was now leading them directly to their predator. The puzzle was far from complete, but the key piece, the one that unlocked the door to confrontation, had just been found. The woods would soon feel less like a sanctuary and more like a trap.

Escalating Stakes

The air in the Oakhaven Sheriff's Department crackled with an electric charge, a potent blend of adrenaline and grim determination that had replaced the earlier, gnawing anxiety. Finding Robert Vance was like a huge earthquake that changed the direction of their whole investigation. Detective Corbin, his usual exhaustion momentarily banished, felt a surge of primal urgency. They weren't just chasing a shadow anymore; they were hunting a man, a man whose address in Miller's Creek now served as a focal point, a dark star around which their efforts would orbit. The clock was no longer a passive observer of their painstaking work; it was an active adversary, ticking down the precious seconds until Vance might strike again.

Corbin said, "We can't afford to be careful right now," and his voice became more intense. He stood in front of the expanded corkboard, which was now a messy collage of Vance's few personal details, his car, and the chilling echoes of Sarah Jenkins' murder. "Emily's testimony was a gift, but it also means he knows we're onto him. He could be scared or getting ready. Either way, we need to move. Now."

Detective Hanson, already immersed in the operational logistics, looked up from her laptop, her eyes sharp with resolve. "I've asked the patrol cars to quietly set up a perimeter around Miller's Creek. No immediate approach, just eyes on. We don't want to tip him off unless we're sure he's in his residence or we have eyes on the Fusion." She stopped, her fingers hovering over the keys. "We're also pulling surveillance footage from the routes leading to and from Miller's Creek. Vance's car could have been at gas stations, convenience stores, or anywhere else in the last 48 hours. It's a long shot, but we need to know if he's moving.

The stakes, which had once been vague, were now brutally and terrifyingly real. Vance was no longer an unknown person; he was a name, a face in a blurry picture, and a known person with a disturbing history of becoming more violent. The memory of Clara Bellweather's hopeful smile, now juxtaposed with the stark reality of Sarah Jenkins' fate, fueled their resolve. Each unsolved disappearance, each unpunished act of intimidation, had been a building block in the foundation of this monster's reign. They couldn't allow him to add another brick.

Corbin went on, "We need to lean on the resources we have," looking over the officers who were there. A small, hand-picked task force had been quietly mobilized, a testament to the seriousness with which his superiors were now treating the case. "Sergeant Miller, I want your team to start canvassing the area around Miller's Creek. Not overly aggressive, but hard-working. Talk to your neighbors and anyone else who might have seen something strange. Look for anyone who fits Vance's general description or who might have seen his car. Ask about strange sounds, people coming and going at odd times, or anything else that seems "off."

Miller, an old pro with a strange talent for dealing with people, nodded sadly. "Got it, Detective. We'll be careful, but we'll get the job done. We know what's at stake."

"And for God's sake," Corbin said, his voice getting harder, "make sure everyone knows how important this is. It's not just about catching a suspect; it's also about stopping another murder. This man is a predator, and he is probably getting worse. The longer we wait, the higher the probability of him finding another victim."

Hanson chimed in, her fingers flying across the keyboard as she accessed warrant requests. "I'm drafting a search warrant for Vance's residence and property. We have enough evidence to believe that Emily is telling the truth and that the evidence points to her. We'll need SWAT on standby, just in case he's armed or decides to resist. I'm also coordinating with the state police for a wider BOLO on the Fusion, flagging it as a vehicle of interest in a potential homicide investigation."

The sterile office, which used to be a quiet place to think and analyze data, had become a center of action. Maps were unfurled, communication channels were established, and contingency plans were rapidly being drawn up. The hunt had moved from the realm of deduction to the visceral reality of pursuit. There was no room for mistakes or second thoughts. Vance was a cornered animal, and cornered animals could be dangerously unpredictable.

Corbin's mind kept going back to what Emily Carter had said, how her voice shook, and the vivid details of her close call with death. The attacker's cold, calculating nature and the way he calmly watched her fear said a lot. This was not an impulsive act of violence; it was the culmination of a carefully cultivated obsession. He saw Vance not as a man driven by sudden rage, but as a patient, methodical hunter, one who had honed his craft over years of lurking in the shadows.

"We need to consider his habits," Corbin mused aloud, pacing the small space. "He lives alone in Miller's Creek. He's clearly comfortable with solitude, perhaps even thrives on it. This means he knows how to take care of himself and work alone. He might have a backup place to go or a planned escape route. We can't just assume he'll be in his living room waiting for us.

Hanson nodded, pulling up satellite imagery of the Miller's Creek area. "The ground out there is thick. There are a lot of wooded areas and old logging roads. If he wants to disappear, he has the perfect environment to do so. Once we see the vehicle or him for sure, we'll need to work with air support to get a better picture and keep an eye on any movement.

Everyone was starting to realize how big the operation was. This wasn't a simple arrest; it was a manhunt, potentially a dangerous confrontation. Sarah Jenkins' murder made it clear how dangerous the killer was, so every move had to be planned. They couldn't afford to make a mistake that would let Vance get away or, even worse, take another life.

"I want a full background check on Vance, everything we can dig up," Corbin commanded. "Financial records, any social media presence, no matter how old or obscure. Any connections, past or present, that might explain his isolation or his motivations. We need to know both the "why" and the "how."

"His sister said he had a 'morbid fascination' with symbols," Hanson remembered, tapping a note on her screen. "While the fish sticker seems to be a key element, there might be other, more subtle indicators of his psychological state. We need to look for any signs of obsession or fixation on certain themes that could have brought him to this point.

People had whispered the word "monster" because they were scared and couldn't understand what Vance was doing. Corbin, on the other hand, wouldn't let it stop them. He focused on the tangible: the vehicle, the address, the known physical characteristics. He saw a man, a flawed and dangerous man, and their mission was to bring him to justice.

"The urgency is paramount," Corbin reiterated, his gaze meeting each officer's in turn. "We're not just trying to catch a criminal; we're also trying to stop one." Every minute we delay, Vance could be planning his next move, choosing his next victim. We are under a lot of pressure, and we need to face it. No one can go home until Vance is in jail. Understood?"

A chorus of strong affirmations filled the room. The hum of activity grew louder, and the calm determination of the early hours turned into a strong sense of purpose. The hunt had officially begun, and the woods of Miller's Creek, once a sanctuary for a predator, were about to become his cage. The stakes had never been higher, and the Oakhaven Sheriff's Department had never been more determined. The chase was on, and the fate of potential future victims hung precariously in the balance.

Chapter 4: The Desolate Ravine

A Labyrinth of Shadows

Detective Corbin's unmarked sedan crawled along the bumpy road that led deeper into the area around Miller's Creek. The air was thick with the smell of wet earth and rotting leaves. The paved road had long since given way to a messy mix of mud, gravel, and branches that hung down. Every bump and lurch of the car was a clear sign of how alone they were becoming. The late afternoon sun, once a benign presence, now struggled to penetrate the dense canopy, casting long, distorted shadows that danced like specters in their peripheral vision. The place was so quiet that it felt like a suffocating blanket that absorbed all sound, leaving only the thrum of their own worries and the distant, sad cry of a hawk.

This was Vance's territory, where the lines between man and nature were blurry and the basic instincts of survival would soon clash with the cold, calculated logic of the police. Corbin's mind, however, was less focused on the immediate surroundings and more on the unfolding psychological landscape. He didn't see Robert Vance as a man who had accidentally gotten into a life of violence. Instead, he saw him as a creature who had carefully planned it out, finding comfort and strength in the world's most desolate places, like this one. The ravine, according to the preliminary aerial sweeps and the hushed whispers of local legends Corbin had managed to unearth, was not merely a geographical feature; it was a scar upon the land, a place whispered about with a mixture of fear and reluctant respect. People said that the earth itself seemed to hold its breath there, that shadows clung to things in an unnatural way, and that the air felt charged with an old, dark energy.

The ravine wasn't just a remote place; it was a carefully chosen stage, a natural fortress that gave the killer an edge and scared and confused his pursuers. Its sheer walls, shaped by water and erosion over millions of years, looked like huge, jagged teeth. The surfaces were always wet and covered in moss. They were impassable for most, a natural deterrent that funneled any approach into a limited number of treacherous routes. The floor of the ravine below was a mess of fallen trees, boulders the size of small cars, and thick undergrowth that made it impossible to see any clear path. The plants were a dark, tangled mass of thorny bushes, gnarled roots, and ferns that thrived in the constant twilight. They made a maze where you could only see a few feet ahead. Even the best tracker would get lost in the thick plants, which made them feel like they were in a small space.

The ravine was so empty that it felt like it was in my bones. It was a place that seemed to push life away. The usual symphony of forest sounds was muted, and the only sounds were the rustling of unseen creatures or the wind whispering through the skeletal branches. This silence wasn't peaceful; it was the tense quiet of a predator holding its breath and waiting. It was a quiet that told of secrets hidden deep in the ground, of histories that only the elements could tell, and of a darkness that looked like the broken mind of the man they were looking for. Corbin imagined Vance moving through this terrain with a predatory grace, his steps silent, his senses honed to the slightest disturbance, a ghost made manifest in the shadows. The ravine was a reflection of Vance's own internal landscape – a place of deep fissures, overgrown with the weeds of his obsessions, and shrouded in a perpetual gloom.

The chosen spot, which was a very deep and narrow part of the ravine, was even scarier. The cliffs came closer together here, and their stone faces looked like old, scarred faces that had been through a lot. A small, sluggish creek, more of a dark ribbon of water than a flowing stream, meandered through the debris-strewn floor, its sluggish movement adding to the oppressive atmosphere. The air was cooler here, always damp, and smelled like minerals that were hidden from view. This was where the shadows truly began to take hold, even in the mid-afternoon, clinging to the crevices and pooling in the dips and hollows like spilled ink. The place was so tall that it felt like I was stuck there, like I was at the bottom of a well where getting out felt like a far-off, almost impossible dream. For Vance, it was probably a safe place where he felt most in charge and in tune with the rhythms of his troubled mind. For the Oakhaven Sheriff's Department, it was a crucible.

Corbin remembered what he had learned from Emily Carter's scared retelling. Vance's careful planning, unnerving calm, and ability to blend in with normal life and then come back with a chilling purpose all showed that he knew how powerful the environment could be. He wouldn't be in a place where he could be easily seen and caught. He would pick a place that made his strengths stronger: hiding, scaring people, and surprising them. The ravine was a perfect match for this. It was a place that could eat a man whole, and the natural world itself worked against him to hide him.

Corbin said in a low voice that barely broke the silence of the car, "We have to be ready for anything." "This isn't just a chase; it's a hunt in his element. He'll know every hidden path, every treacherous drop. He is the top predator, and we are the intruders. He thought of Vance watching them from a place they couldn't see, with a hint of dark amusement on his lips as they tried to figure out how to get around the land he knew so well. The steep hills would wear them out, the thick underbrush would tear at their clothes and skin, and the shadows would always be there, making every rustle of leaves seem like a threat.

Hanson, her gaze fixed on the unfolding landscape, nodded. "The thermal imaging will be very important when we get closer. It will help us see through the mess and find any heat signatures that don't belong. But even then, the sheer density of the vegetation… it's going to be a challenge to track him effectively on foot." She pointed to a part of the woods that was especially thick and seemed to be swallowing the light. "We might not see him until he wants us to, even if he's only a few yards away."

The place's psychological weight was also a factor. The oppressive atmosphere of the ravine was designed to disorient, to amplify fear, and to foster a sense of hopelessness. It was a physical representation of the darkness that had taken over Vance, a place that echoed the chaos inside him. The cliffs were so big, the narrow passages made people feel trapped, and the constant darkness all made for an unsettling place that was meant to break down the will of anyone who dared to enter it. Corbin knew that Vance would get stronger from this very oppression, and the fear of his pursuers would make him feel more powerful.

"He's been operating in the shadows for a long time," Corbin said, the words tasting like ash in his mouth. "He feels at home here." He feels like he can't be hurt here. We want to break that illusion, free him from this place, and free him from his own twisted reality. But we can't let this place get to us. "We need to stay focused and sharp." He saw Vance moving through the ravine not as a man running away, but as a creature showing its power. His movements were precise, and his intent was terrifyingly clear. The ravine was more than just a place to hide; it was a sign of his strength.

The ravine was a natural amphitheater of despair, with walls that trapped sound and made every snap of a twig and every shouted command louder, making them easy for Vance to hear. It was a place where the very earth seemed to conspire against them, where the terrain itself was a weapon. The steep hills would take all of their strength, the loose scree underfoot would make them fall, and the thick undergrowth would always be in the way. Vance knew every little detail of this dangerous terrain, so he could move with a speed and grace that his pursuers could only dream of. He could disappear into the bushes, climb rock faces that looked impossible to climb, or blend in with the shadows cast by the tall cliffs.

Corbin's knuckles turned white as he tightened his grip on the steering wheel. He could feel the tension building in his stomach, a familiar knot of fear and grim determination. This was it. The hunt had taken them to the center of the beast's lair. The ravine wasn't just a place; it was a character in this story, a silent witness to the coming battle between order and chaos, between hunter and hunted. Its dark, dangerous beauty made it even more so. And in its empty depths, the shadows were not just a physical thing; they were a symbol of the darkness that lay at the heart of Robert Vance's soul, a darkness they were about to face head-on. The air itself seemed to press in, heavy with the weight of anticipation, a chilling prelude to the storm that was about to break.

The Predator Cornered

The sound of sirens in the distance, which had once been a faint tremor on the edge of perception, grew into a real vibration in the ground. John, or Vance, as everyone else insisted on calling him, could feel it in his teeth: a low thrum that spoke of order coming, of cages being built around his wild heart. He didn't turn around. To look back was to acknowledge the pursuers, to give them weight, to grant them a victory before the final act had even begun. He owned the ravine. It had always been his, even before he knew the word for it, before the suffocating normalcy of the town had begun to press in. The air here tasted different, raw and wild, and it smelled like wet earth, old stone, and something primal that made him feel something deep inside.

His breath hitched, a ragged sound in the suddenly charged air. He felt desperate, like an animal, and he fought hard to keep it down. Not completely, but it wasn't fear of being caught. He was afraid of being trapped, of being made smaller, and of being forced back into the pale imitation of the life he had worked so hard to get rid of. Rage, hot and bitter, bubbled up from below, fighting the nagging worry. They thought they were after a man. They didn't get it. They were chasing a force, a spirit that had finally found its real home in the harsh grip of this empty gorge. This wasn't just a retreat; it was an ascent, a shedding of the last bits of the obedient, meek boy. This is where they would really give birth to the monster, or maybe finally admit that he existed.

Every step was a planned act of defiance. The loose scree under his worn boots offered little purchase, but he moved with a preternatural grace, a predator instinctively navigating its territory. He climbed over rocks that were slick with moss, using his hands to find places to hold on that would have sent a normal person falling into the dark depths. The ravine was a living entity, a vast, breathing organism that had absorbed him, welcomed him, and promised him sanctuary. Its tall, rough walls looked like old sentinels, their faces marked with stories he understood. They talked in hushed tones about strength, loneliness, and a beauty that was harsh and unforgiving.

He dove deeper, and with each step down, the light got dimmer. The thick canopy above acted like a natural roof, turning the last bit of daylight into a soft twilight. This was his element. The claustrophobia that would have unnerved others was, for him, a comforting embrace. It made the world smaller, sharpening his senses and instincts. The tangled underbrush, which looked like a thorny, oppressive mess to someone who wasn't used to it, was a familiar maze. He knew where the hidden paths lay, where the roots snaked like tripwires, where the shadows were deepest, offering an impenetrable cloak. He could feel the eyes of the forest upon him, not judging, but simply observing, a silent witness to his reclamation.

His mind, which was usually full of conflicting thoughts and violent urges, started to calm down. The encroaching police presence, the flashing lights he'd seen on the distant ridge, the distant wail of sirens – they were becoming muffled, their urgency muted by the immense stone walls and the dense foliage. They were outside, in the world that tried to define him, to mold him, to break him. But down here, in the heart of the ravine, he was unbound. The fractured pieces of his psyche began to knit together, not into a cohesive whole, but into a unified force, driven by a singular, primal instinct: to survive, and to reclaim his power. This ravine was more than just a place to hide; it was a crucible, where the bad parts of his old life would be burned away, leaving only the pure, unadulterated essence of who he really was.

He got to a narrow ledge that looked out over a deep hole. The air here was cooler, carrying the metallic tang of stagnant water and something else, something wild and untamed. The smell brought back memories of a time before fear, before compromise, and before the heavy burden of what society expected of him. He could feel the raw power of the earth flowing into him, a force that calmed his racing heart. He was not escaping; he was returning. This was not a defeat; it was a homecoming.

He thought about how carefully he had planned and built his defenses. Not only the physical walls of the ravine, but also the mental walls he had built over years of anger and feeling wronged. The world had tried to tame him, to fit him into its neat, sterile boxes. It didn't work. And now, in this desolate sanctuary, he would finally unleash the fury it had so cruelly cultivated. He thought about the faces of the people who were chasing him, how determined they looked, and how wrong they were to think they could catch him. They were blinded by their own righteousness, their own rigid adherence to rules that meant nothing in the face of true primal instinct.

The ravine not only hid them, but it also gave them a deep sense of belonging. The gnarled trees, which had been twisted and bent by the weather, looked like his own soul. The oppressive darkness was not a threat, but a comforting shroud, a familiar blanket that had always offered solace. In this place, the silence wasn't empty; it was full of potential and the promise of unrestricted action. He could move without being seen or heard, like a ghost from the shadows, a force that the orderly world couldn't understand, much less control.

He found a shallow cave, a natural alcove carved into the sheer rock face, hidden behind a curtain of thick ivy. It was dry, safe, and gave him a good view of anyone coming near. He sat down on the cold stone floor, his senses on high alert. The sounds of the ravine, which used to be a symphony of nature, now seemed to get sharper. Every rustle of leaves and every distant bird call could mean movement or an intrusion. He belonged to this wild place, and he would protect it with the rage of a trapped animal and the smartness of a hunter.

There was still desperation, a low hum beneath the surface, but it was now covered by a strong, defiant will. This was his last stand, his last act of defiance against a world that had kicked him out, judged him, and not understood the wild, untamed spirit that burned inside him. He wasn't a victim; he was a force of nature. This ravine was the place where his true self would finally come out. The sirens that were coming were no longer a threat; they were a call to arms, a call to his most basic instincts. He wouldn't be trapped; he would be let loose. The ravine was his home, his fortress, and his battlefield. And here, in the middle of all this emptiness, he would finally fight for the right to be who he was, wild and unyielding. The world had turned him into a monster, and in this empty ravine, he would show them they were right, not as a broken man, but as a creature reborn.

The Manhunt Intensifies

The cold, biting wind whipped through the ravine, carrying with it the amplified sounds of human endeavor. It was a stark contrast to the primal silence that had previously enveloped John, or Vance, as the relentless pursuit had rebranded him. Now, the ravine, his sanctuary, was being invaded. The methodical, almost unnerving rhythm of the manhunt began to press in, a tangible force against the natural cacophony of the wilderness. Officers, clad in tactical gear that seemed to absorb the dim light, fanned out across the lower reaches of the gorge. Their movements were slow, deliberate, each step a carefully calculated risk. The terrain, which Vance knew well and felt at home in, was giving his pursuers a lot of trouble. Loose scree shifted treacherously underfoot, sending small avalanches of gravel skittering down the steep slopes. Gnarled roots, like the grasping fingers of some ancient earth spirit, lay hidden beneath a thin veneer of decaying leaves, ready to trip the unwary. The sheer, damp walls of the ravine, which had offered Vance such intimate protection, now presented an impassable barrier to those trying to encircle him.

The crackle of radios, a constant, intrusive static, punctuated the hushed commands and the labored breathing of the officers. "Sector B, clear. No sign of movement." "Alpha team, give a report. Do you have anything on thermal? The voices, tinny and distorted, seemed to echo and bounce off the rock faces, amplifying the sense of unease. Each transmission was a stark reminder that his carefully constructed solitude was being systematically dismantled. He could see them in his mind's eye, painting a clear picture of their coordinated but ultimately useless sweep. They were playing by the rules, by the book, expecting a man to react in a predictable fashion. They failed to grasp that the ravine had transformed him, that he was no longer merely a man being hunted, but an extension of the very landscape that sheltered him.

He moved further into the shadows of the alcove he had chosen, and the rough fabric of his clothes brushed against the cold, hard stone. His senses were heightened, finely tuned to the subtlest anomaly. The metallic tang of sweat from the approaching officers mingled with the earthy scent of the ravine, creating a new, unwelcome olfactory signature. He could discern the heavier tread of boots on more solid ground, the lighter, more cautious shuffle on loose shale. The beam of a tactical flashlight, a brief, searching arc of artificial light, played across the opposite wall, momentarily illuminating the dark, glistening moss. It was a dance of shadows and light, and he was the master choreographer, a ghost moving just beyond their reach.

The systematic nature of their search was both infuriating and oddly exhilarating. They were leaving no stone unturned, no crevice unexplored. But their very thoroughness was also their undoing. They were looking for a conventional fugitive, a man trying to hide. They weren't looking for a creature of the ravine, a spirit that could meld with the shadows, that could use the very contours of the earth as a shield. He heard the distinct thump of a K9 unit being deployed, the excited bark of the dog a sharp, piercing sound that momentarily sent a tremor through the usual fauna of the ravine. But the dog's confusion was also palpable. The scent, so strong in the open air, became a tangled, misleading web once it hit the damp, convoluted paths of the gorge. The dog would pick up a trace, follow it with feverish intensity, only to lose it on a gust of wind or a trick of the terrain, its barks of pursuit turning to frustrated whimpers.

He watched, unseen, as a team carefully rappelled down a section of the cliff face, their headlamps cutting narrow paths through the gloom. They moved with practiced efficiency, their gear clanking softly, a metallic symphony of invasion. He knew this section. He had scaled it countless times, finding handholds and footholds that would be invisible to the untrained eye. Their descent was slow, painstaking. One wrong step or a moment of not paying attention, and the ravine would take one of them. He felt no pity, only a detached observation, a scientist studying a foreign specimen. They were breaking the rules and ruining the sacred balance of his safe place.

The pursuit was not just physical; it was a battle of wits, a clash of opposing philosophies. They operated on logic, on deduction, on the assumption of rational behavior. He operated on instinct, on an intimate understanding of the ravine's hidden language, on the raw, untamed power that surged within him. He could hear the frustration in their voices, which were strained and showed that they were losing their patience. They were accustomed to quicker resolutions, to cornering their prey. This never-ending, twisting maze of stone and shadow was an oddity, a problem in their well-oiled machine.

He mentally mapped their progress, anticipating their next moves. They were tightening the noose from the outside in. But the ravine was vast, its depths far greater than they could comprehend from the limited vantage point of the surface. He had been getting ready for this for years, maybe even his whole life. Not on purpose, but in the simmering anger, the quiet rage, and the deep-seated feeling of being different that had always set him apart. This ravine was not a sudden discovery; it was a homecoming. And he would defend it with every fiber of his being.

He froze when he heard the crackle of a radio that was closer this time. A voice, sharp with urgency, broke through the wind. "Command, we might have seen something. In the south sector, close to the old waterfall. Moving to confirm." The old waterfall. A natural bottleneck with dangerous drops and slippery rocks. They were good, he grudgingly admitted. They were learning. But still, they were looking for him, a distinct entity to be apprehended. They weren't looking with the ravine, as he did. He was a whisper in the wind, a shadow in the darkest corner, and a ripple in the still water. He could be in a lot of places at once and not be in any of them.

He began to move, not in a panicked flight, but with a calculated fluidity. He used the natural acoustics of the ravine to his advantage, his footsteps deliberately placed to mimic the sound of falling debris. He slithered through narrow crevices, his body contorting to fit where they could not. He climbed, not with the brute force they might expect, but with a spider-like tenacity, finding impossibly small holds, his muscles coiling and uncoiling with practiced ease. The ravine was his ally, a living, breathing entity that aided his escape. The loose rocks he dislodged weren't accidents; they were distractions, carefully orchestrated diversions designed to draw their attention elsewhere.

He heard people yelling, and the sudden urgency in their voices told him that his trick had worked. They were converging on the area he had just left, their hopes momentarily rekindled. This was the ebb and flow of the hunt, the feints and parries of a deadly game. He pressed on, deeper into the heart of the gorge, towards the places where even the most determined search party would eventually falter. The air grew colder, heavier, thick with the scent of decay and the unseen. This was not a place for the faint of heart, or for those bound by the comforts of the civilized world. This was his world now.

He paused, catching his breath, the raggedness of his respiration barely audible above the rush of unseen water. He could feel the vibrations of their search, a slight shake in the ground that showed how hard they were working to find him. They were thorough, undeniably so. But they were also easy to guess. They relied on technology, on brute force, on the assumption that sheer numbers and organized effort could overcome any obstacle. They didn't know how powerful being wild could be or how it could give them a strategic edge.

He knew that the ravine held secrets, places where people could be alone for a long time, and natural defenses. He had explored them in his previous life, seeking solace from a world that never truly accepted him. Now, those memories, those hidden pathways, were his weapons. He wasn't just running; he was moving strategically, using the ravine's maze-like shape to get away and make things more confusing. The systematic search, while a threat, was also a guide. It showed him where they expected him to be, and therefore, where he absolutely would not be.

The sound of crunching gravel under heavy boots was growing more distinct, closer than he liked. He could hear the muffled commands, the sharp, clipped orders that betrayed the growing tension. They were a pack, moving with a shared purpose, but lacking the individual cunning, the primal awareness, that he possessed. He could feel the eyes of the ravine upon them, the ancient trees, the weathered stones, all observing this intrusion with a silent, indifferent gaze. They were not from around here, and their presence was a problem.

He made his way towards a narrow fissure in the rock face, a place so tight that it would require him to contort his body almost impossibly. Years ago, he found a secret passage that led to a hidden grotto, a place of deep darkness and silence. It was a gamble, a desperate move, but his instinct screamed at him to take it. He squeezed through, the rough rock scraping against his skin and the darkness wrapping around him like a shroud. The sounds of the search immediately muted, the world outside receding into a muffled hum. He was in the belly of the beast, the heart of the ravine, a place where even the most determined pursuer would struggle to follow. He could feel the cool, damp air seeping into his bones, the absolute silence a balm to his frayed nerves. He had bought himself time, precious time. But he knew this was only a temporary reprieve. The hunt had gotten more intense, and they wouldn't stop until they caught him. The ravine protected him, but the war was just getting started.

Confrontation at the Precipice

The wind, a relentless sculptor of the ravine, clawed at John's ragged clothes, whipping tendrils of damp hair across his face. Every gust brought with it the metallic taste of fear—his own—and the strong, sharp smell of the men getting closer. He could hear them now, not the far-off crackle of radios or the muffled thuds of boots on shale. Instead, he could hear their sharp, short breaths of effort and the strained grunts that showed how desperate they were. They had found him. After days of being a phantom, a rumour whispered on the wind through the echoing chasm, he was finally trapped. The ravine, his sanctuary, his intricate labyrinth of escape, had finally offered up its most elusive prize to the relentless machinery of law enforcement.

He stood at the precipice, a narrow ledge barely wide enough for a single man, overlooking a sheer drop that plummeted into the bruised, twilight depths of the gorge. The world had shrunk to this precarious perch, the sheer rock face behind him, the abyss before him, and the hunters fanning out from the edges of his limited sanctuary. He could see them clearly against the fading light. Their tactical gear had a dull shine that spoke of purpose and finality. Three of them stood with their arms crossed and ready. Detectives, not uniformed officers. These were the ones who had pieced together the puzzle, who had tracked the fragments of his fractured existence to this desolate, unforgiving place.

Detective Miller, the one with the perpetually furrowed brow and the eyes that seemed to bore into the very soul of whomever he faced, was the closest. He held his firearm steady, not pointed directly at John, but held low, a promise of immediate, devastating action. Beside him stood Detective Harding, younger, her face a mask of grim determination, her hand resting on the butt of her own weapon. Completing their triumvirate was Sergeant Davies, a hulking man whose presence radiated a coiled, controlled aggression, his gaze fixed on John with an intensity that was almost palpable. They were the vanguard, the ones chosen to make the final move, to bring the hunt to its brutal, inevitable conclusion.

John's breath hitched, not in fear, but in a strange, primal surge of adrenaline. His eyes, wild and unfocused from days of deprivation and the raw, unfiltered essence of the ravine, darted from one pursuer to the next. He could feel his own blood beating, like a frantic drumbeat against the silence that had fallen between them for a moment. The wind seemed to stop and wait. The ravine itself felt like a silent witness, its ancient stones absorbing the tension, the raw, unvarnished confrontation playing out on its stony stage.

"John. Vance. "Whatever you call yourself now," Miller's voice, which was rough and strained, broke the silence. It was a voice that had lost its usual authority, replaced by a weary, desperate edge. "It's over. There's nowhere else to go."

Nowhere else to go. The words echoed in the vastness of the ravine, a hollow pronouncement that felt both true and utterly false. He looked down at the chasm, at the swirling mist that hinted at the unknown depths. He looked back at the detectives' determined faces, which were like hard shells. They saw a trapped animal and a broken man who had finally given in to the stress of being chased. They saw the result of all their hard work, the prize they had worked so hard to get.

But they didn't see the truth. They didn't see that this was not an ending, but a transformation. The ravine had stripped him bare, not of his identity, but of the superficial layers that had burdened him in the world outside. It had exposed the raw, elemental core of his being, a core that resonated with the wildness, the ferocity, the untamed spirit of this place. He was not just John, the hunted fugitive; he was Vance, a creature forged in the crucible of isolation, a product of the very wilderness they now sought to reclaim.

A flicker of something – amusement? Defiance? – crossed John's face. His lips, cracked and dry, pulled back in a semblance of a smile that held no warmth, only a chilling, predatory glint. His eyes, sunken and shadowed, held a frantic luminescence, the kind that speaks of a mind teetering on the edge, or perhaps, a mind that had finally found its true north in the wilderness. He was a reflection of the ravine itself – jagged, unpredictable, and infinitely dangerous.

"Over?" he rasped, his voice a dry rustle of leaves. It was a sound that seemed to come from the rock face behind him, an echo that made the detectives uneasy. "You think this is over?"

Harding stepped forward, her voice sharp and clear in the wind. "Yes, John. We have you. Don't make this harder than it needs to be. Drop the weapon."

Weapon. The word hung in the air, absurd. He had no weapon, not in the conventional sense. His weapons were the skills he had learned from years of hiding, his knowledge of this dangerous land, and his strong desire to live. His weapon was the terrifying, unpredictable madness that seemed to be bubbling just below the surface. They had only seen it in his victims, but they had not yet seen it in all its wild glory.

He took a step back, his heel brushing against the crumbling edge of the precipice. A shower of loose stones fell into the void, and the sound of them hitting the ground was lost in the deep silence. It was a deliberate move, a provocation. He wanted them to feel the precariousness of his position, to understand that he was not merely trapped, but poised on the brink.

Miller's voice got tighter, a warning mixed with anger. "Vance, I swear to God, if you jump—"

"Jump?" John's laugh was a harsh, broken sound. "Do you think I'm scared of falling?" He spread his arms wide, the tattered sleeves of his jacket flapping like broken wings. "This is not a fall, Detective. This is flight."

His eyes fixed on Miller's, a silent challenge passing between them. He saw the flicker of doubt, the grudging acknowledgement of something beyond their understanding. They had hunted the man, the monster, the perpetrator. They had not anticipated the embodiment of the wild, the spirit of the ravine itself. He was not a defendant; he was a force of nature, momentarily contained, but never truly captured.

The wind swirled around him, a vortex of sound and fury, and for a fleeting moment, John felt a profound sense of belonging, of homecoming. The chasm below was not a terrifying void, but an invitation. The sheer rock walls were not a prison, but a canvas upon which his will could be etched. He was the predator now, not the prey, and his territory was vast and unforgiving.

Davies moved his weight, and his huge body tensed up. "Don't do anything stupid, Vance."

"Stupid?" John's gaze swept over them, a slow, deliberate assessment. He could see the tiredness on their faces and the stress of the long chase. They were good, he conceded that. They were persistent. But they were also human. They were bound by the rules of their world, by their fear of consequences, by their need for order. He was unbound.

He leaned forward, the wind snatching at his clothes, making him sway precariously. He could feel the vibrations of every move they made, even the tiny tremors of their nerves. They thought they would see a breakdown, a request, or a giving up. They expected the predictable collapse of a cornered man. But John was beyond predictable. He was the anomaly, the ghost in their meticulously constructed machine.

"You've come a long way," he said, his voice a low growl that barely carried over the wind. "You've followed my scent, my trail, my mistakes. You've done so well." He paused, letting the praise hang in the air, laced with a dark irony. "But you still don't get it."

He stepped back again, getting closer to the edge. The detectives tensed, their hands tightening on their weapons. There was a lot of tension in the air, and the balance was so fragile that it could break at any moment. John could feel the weight of their collective gaze, the desperate hope that he would simply fall, that fate would deliver the justice they craved.

But John's fall would not be an accident. It would be a choice, a statement, a final, defiant act of rebellion against a world that had never truly accepted him. He had embraced the darkness of the ravine, and in doing so, had found a freedom that the light of their civilization could never offer. He wasn't a monster to be caught; he was a force to be reckoned with, proof of the wild heart that beat beneath the surface of human society. And as he stood on the edge, with only the wind at his back and the abyss below him, he knew he was finally free. His wild eyes, reflecting the dying embers of the sun, held a spark of something ancient and untamed, a flicker of defiance against the encroaching darkness of their world. This wasn't giving up; it was going beyond. This was not the end of the hunt; it was the beginning of something much deeper and scarier.

The Fall into the Abyss

The wind, which had been a mere whisper of menace, now shrieked like a banshee, tearing at John's tattered clothes and whipping grit into the eyes of his pursuers. He had felt the shift, the subtle change in the air, the collective intake of breath from Miller, Harding, and Davies. They saw his defiance, his unsettling calm, and the primal instinct to reassert control, to end the game on their terms, surged through them. It was a mistake, born of protocol and a desperate need for a clean resolution. They mistook his stillness for a prelude to surrender, his quietude for exhaustion.

Miller, who was always practical, made the first move. Not a shot, not yet, but a calculated advance. He lunged, not right at John, but to block his imagined escape route a few feet to his left. His movements were surprisingly quick for a man his age. It was a tactical feint, designed to provoke a reaction, to force John's hand. Harding, anticipating this, mirrored his movement, a fraction of a second behind, her firearm now leveled, her finger tightening on the trigger. Davies, the immovable object, began to flank from the right, his heavy boots crunching on the loose scree, his eyes never leaving John.

But John was not tethered to their logic. He saw the shift, the tightening of their formation, the predictable, almost theatrical approach of men closing in on their quarry. He didn't see a way out in the way they moved; he saw a noose getting tighter. The ravine had taught him to read more than just the terrain; it had taught him to read the intent in the tension of a shoulder, the subtle tremor in a hand. And he saw it now: a desperate, clumsy attempt to herd him, to corral him.

He didn't retreat. Instead, he took a step forward. Not towards the abyss, not yet, but towards Miller. It was a calculated risk, a gamble played with the raw, untamed forces of the ravine as his unwitting accomplice. As he moved, his left foot landed on a patch of damp moss clinging precariously to the rock face. The treacherous footing, a deceptive trap laid by nature, gave way. It wasn't a dramatic slip, not at first. It was a subtle loss of purchase, a terrifying moment of near-balance.

Miller instinctively moved to stop John's sudden, aggressive lunge. He was only thinking about John, the man himself, and not the dangerous ground he was walking on. As John's foot skidded, his body lurched forward, an uncontrolled momentum carrying him towards Miller. The detective, caught off guard by the unexpected trajectory, reacted with a shout, his hand reaching out to grab John, to steady him, to pull him back from the brink he was so clearly tempting.

It was a fatal mistake.

Miller's hand brushing against John's arm was enough to throw the scales off balance. John's already compromised footing gave out completely. He didn't leap. He didn't leap. He fell down. It was a clumsy, ungraceful descent, a tangle of limbs and ragged cloth. But as he fell, his flailing right hand, which was trying to grab anything solid like an animal, found something to hold on to. It caught the edge of Miller's tactical vest.

The effect was immediate and terrible. Miller, his own stance already precarious, was yanked off balance by the sudden, immense weight of John's falling body. His shout turned into a strangled cry as he too lost his footing. His gun went off with a deafening roar that echoed through the ravine, marking the end of the chaos. He scrabbled for purchase, his fingers digging into the crumbling rock, his eyes wide with disbelief and terror.

Harding, with her finger on the trigger, froze for a moment as she watched the disaster unfold. Her training told her to shoot to get rid of the threat. But the threat was no longer a singular entity; it was a maelstrom of falling bodies and loose rock. She saw Miller's desperate fight, John's uncontrolled fall, and Davies, who was on the edge of the scene, momentarily hidden by the dust and spray from the first fall.

John, caught in the violent choreography of his own undoing, slammed against Miller. It wasn't a clean impact. It was a brutal, messy collision. His shoulder struck Miller's chest, knocking the wind out of him. Then, as they both tumbled, John's knee impacted Miller's jaw with a sickening crack. The detective's eyes rolled back in his head, and he lost his grip on the rock face as he fell asleep.

For a terrifying and confusing moment, they were one desperate thing, a human avalanche sliding dangerously close to the edge. John felt Miller's dead weight dragging him down, his own hands scrabbling uselessly at the slick rock. He saw a flash of Harding's horrified face, her weapon now lowering slightly as she grappled with the new, terrifying reality.

Davies, shouting John's name, lunged forward, his massive hands reaching out, desperately trying to grab either man. He was too late. The speed was too fast. Miller, who was now a dead weight, slipped out of John's hands. He let out a guttural groan as he fell over the edge. His fall was not the controlled descent John had imagined, but a wild, uncontrolled drop. He disappeared into the swirling mists below, his final moments lost to the abyss.

John, freed from Miller's weight, was still sliding. The rock face offered no purchase, only a relentless, downward pull. He saw Harding's face, a mask of shock and horror, peering over the edge, her hand outstretched as if she could somehow defy gravity and pull him back. He saw Davies, his face a portrait of grim determination, scrambling along the ledge, trying to keep pace, trying to find a way to reach him.

His own descent was no longer a deliberate act of defiance. It was a brutal, visceral struggle against the inevitable. His ragged clothes snagged on outcrops of rock, tearing further, leaving strips of fabric clinging like desperate prayers. His skin scraped against the unforgiving stone, tearing flesh, drawing blood that mixed with the grit and the sweat. Each impact was a shockwave, rattling his bones, stealing his breath.

He saw, in fragmented flashes, the receding sky, the sheer, indifferent rock face rushing past, the dizzying blur of the ravine's depths growing closer. He heard the wind, no longer a shriek, but a deafening roar, a symphony of his own destruction. He heard Davies's shouts, increasingly distant, increasingly desperate, a fading lifeline in a sea of chaos. He heard Harding's choked sobs, a sad song for a man they had hunted down, caught, and then watched disappear.

His body moved like a rag doll thrown by an invisible hand. He struck a jutting rock face with his ribs, a searing pain that made him gasp, a gasp that was immediately stolen by the wind. He felt a sharp blow to his head, a dizzying, disorienting impact that sent stars exploding behind his eyes. His hands were raw and bleeding, and they clawed at the air, but all they found was the howling void.

For a short, scary moment, he thought he might actually live, hanging on to an unseen ledge by a thread. But the ravine didn't care. It offered no quarter. It demanded a sacrifice. His left leg, which had gotten stuck in a cruel twist, slammed into a rock that was sticking out. Even above the sound of the wind, there was a sharp, sickening snap. A wave of agony, white-hot and blinding, washed over him, robbing him of the last vestiges of his strength, his will.

He saw a fleeting image of the sky, now a bruised, purplish hue, as the last of the daylight faded. He saw the mist below, no longer swirling, but a solid, impenetrable curtain of grey, a shroud for the unknown. He felt himself speeding up as he fell, and the scraping and tearing were replaced by a terrifying, exciting rush of speed.

He didn't feel pain or fear before he died. Instead, he felt a deep, almost divine emptiness. The world, with its hunters and its rules, its judgments and its betrayals, had finally faded away. He was being consumed by the ravine, by the raw, primal power of the earth. He was becoming one with the stone, the wind, and the dark that never lets up.

There was no thought of surrender, no final plea. The only thing I felt was a huge sense of freedom, like I was melting into the vast, uncaring mouth of the abyss. He was no longer John Vance, the fugitive, the killer, the hunted. He was simply motion, a falling object, a temporary disruption in the ancient silence of the desolate ravine. The darkness below swallowed him whole, a hungry void that gave him no answers, no judgment, and only a deep, final silence. Whether he was alive or dead, broken or somehow transformed, remained a question lost to the hungry depths, a secret held by the desolate ravine.

Chapter 5: The Absence of Proof

Searching the Depths

The wind, no longer a frenzied shriek but a mournful, lingering sigh, swept through the ravine, carrying with it the acrid scent of damp earth and something metallic – fear, perhaps, or the ghost of Miller's spilled blood. Harding and Davies stood at the edge, their faces showing a fear that went beyond professional detachment. The sheer, violent spectacle they had just witnessed, the impossible vanishing act of John Vance, had shattered the illusion of control, of a neatly concluded investigation. Miller was gone, not as a casualty of a shootout, but as a victim of the very terrain they were meant to subdue, a victim of the man they had hunted with such relentless, brutal certainty. The ravine, a gaping wound in the earth, had swallowed him, and with him, their quarry.

Davies, his face a mask of grim disbelief, knelt at the edge, his heavy frame hunched as if the weight of the world had suddenly settled upon his shoulders. He peered into the swirling mist that obscured the ravine's floor, his breath misting in the cool air. "Miller!" he called out, his voice a raw rasp, swallowed by the immense silence that had descended after the chaos. There was no response, only the distant, hollow echo of his own voice, a lonely sound in the vastness. Harding lowered her gun, her hand still shaking. The cold metal felt very different from the warmth of her fear. Her gaze was fixed on the same churning grey, a desperate, futile search for any sign, any ripple on the surface of the abyss that might indicate Miller's fate. The protocols, the carefully rehearsed procedures, all seemed utterly inadequate in the face of this primal, untamed power. They had expected a struggle, a capture, perhaps even a final, tragic confrontation. They had not expected the earth itself to rise up and claim one of their own, to erase their quarry from existence as if he had never been.

The subsequent hours were a blur of frantic, disorganized activity. The initial shock gave way to a desperate, almost primal need to find something, anything. Davies, galvanized by the loss of Miller, his friend and mentor, took charge, his grief channeled into a furious energy. He barked orders, his voice rough but steady, attempting to impose order on the burgeoning panic. There were radio calls, and a lot of crackling voices shared the shocking news. Backup units, initially anticipating a routine arrest, now descended on the ravine's edge with a grim, almost somber urgency. The objective had shifted, from apprehending a killer to recovering a fallen comrade and, if possible, confirming the demise of their elusive, terrifying quarry. The code name, 'Monster John,' whispered in hushed tones by the force, now seemed chillingly apt. He didn't just get away; he disappeared, leaving behind only a hole and the smell of something that couldn't be explained.

The search began in earnest, a Herculean task against the unforgiving landscape. Teams of officers, equipped with ropes, harnesses, and powerful floodlights that cut feeble swathes through the deepening twilight, were deployed along the ravine's rim. Davies insisted on leading the initial descent, a risky maneuver for which he possessed the most experience and the deepest personal stake. He moved with a grim determination, his eyes scanning every crevice, every overhang, every patch of treacherous scree. Harding, her face pale and drawn, remained on the upper ledge, coordinating the broader search efforts, her mind replaying the horrific scene over and over, searching for a detail, a missed clue, a flicker of logic in the utter madness.

But the ravine fought back. It was a place of perpetual shadows, where the sun's rays struggled to penetrate the dense canopy of ancient trees clinging precariously to its steep walls. The terrain was a labyrinth of sheer drops, unstable rock faces, and narrow, winding paths that seemed designed to disorient and deceive. Water, fed by an unseen subterranean source, trickled down the moss-covered rocks, creating slick, deceptive surfaces. In the ravine's depths, the air grew heavy, humid, and suffocating, filled with the incessant roar of unseen water – a powerful river or a series of hidden waterfalls, no one could be sure. The vegetation was a tangled, impenetrable mass of thorny bushes, gnarled roots, and colossal ferns, each step a battle, each movement a calculated risk.

The search teams, experienced in wilderness recovery, found themselves outmatched. The size of the ravine was just too much. It was a place that swallowed sound, that devoured light, that seemed to actively resist intrusion. Hours turned into a day, then two. The initial frantic energy of the search began to ebb, replaced by a gnawing sense of futility, a creeping dread that settled deep in the pit of their stomachs. Every shadow seemed to morph into a human form, every rustle of leaves a sign of movement. But these were just the tricks of a tired mind, acting out in the heavy air. They found no sign of Miller – no torn uniform, no dropped equipment, not even a scuff mark that spoke of a prolonged struggle. It was as if he had simply dissolved into the very fabric of the ravine.

And of John Vance, the 'Monster John,' there was even less evidence. No body, no bloodstains that weren't from the plants, and no weapon that had been thrown away. He had, quite literally, vanished. The absence of proof, which had been the insidious foundation of Vance's elusiveness, now stood as an insurmountable wall against their investigation. He had not been caught, killed, or even definitely found. He had simply ceased to exist in the tangible world, leaving behind only the terrifying legend of his disappearance. The ravine, with its shadowed depths and echoing silences, had become Vance's ultimate sanctuary, a place where the rules of the world, and the laws of physics, no longer seemed to apply. The investigators, seasoned men and women who had stared into the abyss of human depravity countless times, found themselves adrift in a sea of the inexplicable, their certainty eroded, their resolve tested by the sheer, unnerving emptiness where their quarry should have been. The quiet of the ravine was no longer just a lack of noise; it was a powerful presence, a sign of the ultimate disappearing act, and a chilling reminder that some monsters might be too wild and basic to be contained or understood.

The sheer difficulty of the terrain was a constant, demoralizing adversary. Rappelling down sheer rock faces, only to find that the ropes barely reached the next precarious ledge, became a maddeningly repetitive exercise. The rushing water made it almost impossible to talk and made the ground so slippery that it was hard to believe. Officers slipped, fell, and were narrowly saved from serious injury by their colleagues, the constant threat of a similar fate to Miller's hanging heavy in the air. Every shadow seemed to hold a hidden pitfall, every patch of seemingly solid ground threatened to give way beneath their boots. The dense undergrowth, thick and clawing, tore at their gear and their skin, leaving them scratched, bruised, and utterly exhausted. It was a hostile environment, one that seemed to actively reject their presence, to conspire with Vance's escape.

Davies, despite his own raw grief, was a force of nature. He pushed his teams relentlessly, his eyes burning with a fierce, desperate hope. He refused to believe that Miller was simply gone, swallowed by the earth without a trace. He carefully searched every inch of the ravine's walls that he could reach, using his fingers to feel for any cracks and his eyes to look for anything unusual. He directed spotlight beams into every dark corner, every shadowed overhang, his voice, hoarse from shouting over the din of the water, a constant presence, urging them on. "He has to be here," he would mutter, more to himself than anyone else, and the wind would take his words away. "Miller wouldn't just… vanish." But the evidence, or rather the profound lack of it, whispered a different, more terrifying narrative.

As the second day of the search drew to a close, the atmosphere among the investigators grew palpably heavy. The initial surge of adrenaline had long since dissipated, replaced by a bone-deep weariness and a growing sense of unease. They were starting to get tired of how pointless their efforts were. They had searched miles of the ravine, but their progress was painfully slow, and there was still nothing. There was no sign of Miller. No sign of Vance. It was as if the ravine had a will of its own, a primal force that had decided to protect its secrets. The idea that Vance had somehow survived the fall, battered and broken, and managed to escape into the labyrinthine depths of the ravine, was becoming increasingly plausible, and terrifying. How could a man, injured and alone, navigate such a treacherous environment and disappear so completely? It defied logic, defied everything they understood about survival.

Harding, back at the makeshift command post established on the rim, was poring over maps and drone footage, her brow furrowed in concentration. She went over the last few seconds of the chase again and again, looking for a way out, a detail that had been missed in the heat of the moment. But the footage, grainy and distorted by the ravine's inherent challenges, offered little. Vance had simply… gone. The drone was supposed to take pictures of the ground from above, but the thick canopy and the changing air currents in the ravine made it hard for it to do its job. It had shown the fall, the chaotic tumble, and then… nothing. A void. An abrupt end to the visual narrative, leaving only the chilling implications.

The media, alerted to the ongoing operation, began to descend on the area, their presence a further unwelcome intrusion. Rumors, born of desperation and speculation, began to circulate like wildfire. Vance had somehow used the ravine's natural features to his advantage, a phantom moving through unseen tunnels. He had been consumed by a hidden chasm, his body lost forever. Or, most scary of all, he had just walked away, disappearing back into the shadows from which he had come, leaving the police to chase ghosts. The narrative of the 'Monster John,' the seemingly unkillable, untraceable phantom, was solidifying, taking on a life of its own. The absence of proof was not just a procedural hurdle; it was becoming an almost supernatural element in the case, a testament to Vance's terrifying ability to elude capture, to defy the very boundaries of reality. The ravine, with its huge, quiet indifference, had become the perfect partner in crime, a place where the rules of pursuit and capture no longer applied and a man could, quite literally, disappear into thin air. The officers were not just searching for a fugitive; they were searching for a ghost, in a place that seemed designed to make ghosts.

No Body No Closure

The ravine offered no solace, no definitive end. Days bled into a week, then another, and still, the search yielded nothing. There was no fabric, no bones, and not even a glint of metal from Miller's gun. The unforgiving earth, a voracious entity, had consumed him whole, leaving behind only an aching void where a life had been and a gaping hole in the fabric of their understanding. This absolute absence was more insidious than any gruesome discovery could have been. A body, no matter how badly damaged, would have given a clear end, even if it was brutal. It would have allowed for a funeral, for grief to be processed, for the finality of death to settle. But this… this was an open wound that hurt all the time with unanswered questions.

For Harding, the psychological fallout was a creeping, insidious poison. Each dawn brought with it a fresh wave of dread, a gnawing certainty that the search was, and always would be, futile. She found herself replaying the incident in endless, agonizing loops in her mind, scrutinizing every millisecond of the drone footage, every inflection in the radio chatter, searching for a detail, any detail, that might explain the impossible. Had Miller slipped? Had Vance pushed him? Had he simply… vanished? The lack of evidence, the sheer void, was a canvas onto which her imagination painted the most horrific scenarios, each one more debilitating than the last. Sleep offered no respite, haunted by the echoes of Miller's cries, or perhaps just the roar of the ravine's unseen water, and the phantom shape of Vance, dissolving into the mist like a specter. The protocols she relied on, the logical steps that had always guided her through the darkest corners of crime, were useless here. They were made for a world where there was real proof, where actions had consequences that could be seen, and where death left a mark that couldn't be denied. Vance, and the ravine, had broken those rules.

Davies, too, was a shadow of his former self. He used to be full of life and energy, but now he was quiet and serious, with a deep sadness that seemed to make his already weathered face look even worse. He pushed himself and his teams with a relentless, almost self-punishing zeal, holding on to the hope that they would find Miller as a lifeline. But with each fruitless hour, that hope dwindled, leaving behind a raw, exposed vulnerability. The camaraderie that had once bound the precinct felt strained, fractured by the unspoken anxieties. They were a team that had lost a soldier, but also a team that had been outmaneuvered by something that defied their understanding, something that made their skills, their training, their very purpose, seem laughably inadequate. Every officer who had been at the ravine's edge carried a piece of that helplessness, a silent testament to the power of the inexplicable.

This deep uncertainty also had an effect on the town. John Vance, 'Monster John,' had been more than just a criminal; he had become a local bogeyman, a dark legend woven into the fabric of their everyday lives. His capture, or even his demise, would have been a moment of collective exhale, a chance to finally exorcise the fear that had been a constant, low-level hum in their community. Instead, his disappearance, coupled with the tragic loss of Officer Miller, had amplified the dread to an unbearable pitch. The ravine, once a natural wonder, a place for hikers and nature lovers, had been transformed into a symbol of their deepest fears. Whispers turned into panicked speculation. Had Vance survived? Was he lurking in the shadows, biding his time? Was he watching them, his absence a chilling promise of his eventual return? Children who had once played near the ravine's edge were now kept indoors, their imaginations fueled by the hushed, fearful conversations of their parents. The fear wasn't just about a missing body; it was about the absence of closure, the terrifying possibility that the monster had not been slain, but had merely retreated, a predator waiting for the opportune moment to strike again.

This pervasive fear was a breeding ground for paranoia. Every strange sound and every shadow that moved quickly became a possible sign that Vance was there. People in the area began to lock their doors more carefully, and they nervously looked at the trees that lined the edge of the ravine. The absence of proof was not just an investigative stalemate; it was a psychological siege. Vance had become an idea, a specter of pure terror, more potent in his absence than he had ever been in his physical manifestation. The law enforcement officers, themselves grappling with the trauma and the inexplicable, found themselves unable to offer the reassurance their community desperately craved. How could they promise safety when the threat had literally dissolved into the landscape? Their badge, their authority, their carefully constructed system of justice, all seemed to crumble in the face of an enemy who could seemingly defy the very laws of nature. The story of "Monster John" was no longer just about his past crimes. It was also about how he couldn't escape, how he disappeared in a supernatural way, and how some evils might be too strong to be contained and too hard to defeat. The ravine had become his last, impenetrable fortress, a monument to the terrifying unknown, and a stark reminder that without proof, the imagination would always come up with the most horrible possibilities. Because there was no body, many people thought Vance was still alive. They thought he was a ghostly threat just beyond the veil of their perceived reality, and his continued existence was a chilling reminder of the power of the unknown. The uncertainty gnawed at the edges of their lives, a constant reminder that the monster might still be walking among them, unseen, unheard, a chilling echo of the terror that had once gripped their town. This psychological torment, the fear of the unknown and the unresolved, was a burden far heavier than any concrete evidence could have been. It allowed the terror to fester, to mutate, to become something far more insidious and enduring. The ravine's silence, which had once been a sign of nature's peace, was now the loud roar of their shared fear, a constant, unsettling reminder of what they had lost and what they still feared. The absence of closure was, in itself, a form of violence, a prolonged torment that left the town perpetually on edge, forever looking over their shoulders, forever haunted by the ghost of a man who had ceased to exist, and yet, refused to disappear. The lack of definitive proof, the crucial missing piece, had allowed the legend of 'Monster John' to transcend his physical form, transforming him into a pervasive, intangible force of fear that permeated every aspect of their lives. It was a testament to the power of suggestion, the human mind's desperate need for answers, and its terrifying capacity to fill the void with its darkest imaginings. The ravine, in its silent, enduring majesty, had become the keeper of their deepest anxieties, a constant reminder that some mysteries, once unleashed, could never truly be solved, their shadows forever stretching across the landscape of their lives. The doubt that wouldn't go away was like a poison, eating away at their sense of safety, their faith in order, and their ability to move forward. It was the ultimate victory for Vance, not in his capture or his death, but in his ability to weaponize his own absence, to turn the very lack of evidence into a tool of terror that continued to haunt and torment long after the physical threat had seemingly vanished. Because his fate was still up in the air, the fear was not a memory but a living thing that was always being fed by the worries of the townspeople. Without a body, there was no last chapter, which left the story of "Monster John" open-ended and much scarier. The community was trapped in a state of perpetual anticipation, a chilling limbo where the monster they thought they had vanquished could, at any moment, re-emerge from the shadows, fueled by their own unresolved dread. This psychological void, the emptiness where a definitive answer should have been, was the true legacy of John Vance, a testament to his ability to exert control and instill fear even in his apparent absence. The officers were supposed to bring order and resolution, but they were also caught up in this whirlpool of uncertainty, which made their professional lives unstable because of the terrifying power of the unknown. The lack of tangible evidence had effectively rendered them powerless, their expertise undermined by a quarry that refused to play by the rules of reality, leaving them adrift in a sea of speculation and gnawing doubt, a constant reminder of the limits of their abilities in the face of a truly enigmatic foe. The unresolved nature of Vance's disappearance was a wound that refused to heal, a constant source of unease that gnawed at the psyche of the entire community, perpetuating the reign of terror long after the active pursuit had ended, solidifying his legend as something far more potent than any living, breathing criminal.

Lingering Questions and Doubts

The official pronouncement arrived with the sterile efficiency of bureaucracy, a curt dismissal of the lingering questions that clung to the humid air like a shroud. "Presumed deceased," the report read, the words stark and final, a neatly packaged conclusion to a case that felt anything but. The ravine, in its silent, indifferent grandeur, had performed its grim duty. There was no way to avoid falling from that height into that jagged mouth of rock and rough ground. The forensic teams, armed with their meticulous protocols and the stark reality of physics, had cataloged every plausible scenario. No tracks leading away, no signs of a struggle beyond the precipice, just an almost impossibly clean vanishing act. The official verdict was a surrender to the irrefutable logic of gravity and brute force. For the precinct, it was the end, but it wasn't a very satisfying one. For the town, it was meant to be a catharsis, the final nail in the coffin of 'Monster John,' a definitive severing from the fear he embodied.

But for Detective Harding, the pronouncement felt like a betrayal, a capitulation to the easiest answer rather than the truest. Deep within the core of her being, a dissonant chord vibrated, a persistent hum of unease that no official decree could silence. The absence of proof, the very thing that had stalled the investigation, had now become the foundation of its premature conclusion. And it felt fundamentally wrong. She'd spent years honing her instincts, learning to read the subtle language of crime scenes, to decipher the whispers of guilt and innocence that lingered in the air long after the perpetrators had fled. Her gut, a finely tuned instrument honed by countless nights of chasing shadows, screamed that this was too neat, too convenient. It was the absence of the expected – the absence of struggle, the absence of Vance's body, the absence of any tangible indication of his fate – that was the most damning evidence of all, paradoxically.

She read the investigative reports again, tracing the typed words with her fingers as if they held a secret code. Each page showed how thorough the search was, and it was a well-documented record of how useless it was. Drones had searched the steep, hard-to-reach slopes of the ravine, using thermal imaging to look for any strange heat signature or other sign of life. Ground teams, painstakingly rappelling into the treacherous depths, had combed every ledge, every crevice, their trained eyes searching for the smallest clue – a torn piece of clothing, a discarded weapon, a single, undeniable fragment of John Vance. They had found nothing. Absolutely nothing. It was as if the earth had simply swallowed him whole, a void where a man had once stood. This complete lack of any physical evidence was, in and of itself, the strangest thing. A fall like that, even if fatal, would leave something. Bones, at the very least, would be scattered amongst the rocks. Clothing would snag on jagged edges. The impact would shatter, leaving behind a gruesome tableau that, while horrific, would at least provide a concrete narrative.

It was clear that it was impossible to survive such a fall. Harding understood the science, the brutal physics involved. The terminal velocity, the unforgiving landscape… it defied comprehension that any human being could withstand it. Yet, the absence of Vance's remains gnawed at her. It wasn't just a professional annoyance; it was a deep, almost primal feeling of unease. It made her think of something that her training and experience might not have prepared her for: that Vance hadn't just fallen. That he had somehow cheated death, or, even scarier, that he had planned his own disappearance with almost supernatural accuracy.

She kept going over the moments before the event, looking closely at every frame of the blurry drone footage and analyzing every word of the frantic radio calls. Officer Miller's last moments, the confusion, the sudden loss of sight, and the terrifying silence that followed all played out in her mind like a broken record. Did Miller see something? Did someone push him on purpose? Or had Vance, in a moment of desperate cunning, used the chaotic environment to his advantage, a pre-planned escape route that no one had anticipated? The story had a big hole in it because there was no clear sign of foul play and no clear action. Her imagination, which was already familiar with the darker sides of human nature, was all too eager to fill it.

The official report, with its neat conclusion, felt like a convenient fiction, a narrative constructed to bring closure to an unclosable event. Harding knew that the public needed to think that Vance was dead, like a monster that had been defeated. But she couldn't shake the feeling that the real story was far more complex, and infinitely more unsettling. The lack of evidence didn't mean the end; it was the start. It was the first clue, the most significant hint that this wasn't the end of John Vance, but a new, terrifying chapter in his story. Vance's last, most daring act of defiance was to not provide any proof. He had created a ghost, a phantom born from the emptiness he had so skillfully created, and law enforcement was left chasing it.

The sheer improbability of Vance's vanishing act was what troubled Harding most. The ravine was a natural trap; if you made a mistake, you would die. Yet, there was no body. There were no signs of a fight that would suggest Vance had been pushed over the edge. It was as if he had simply… dematerialized. This kind of ending should only happen in made-up stories, not in the grim world of criminal investigation. Yet, here she was, staring at a case file that offered no tangible evidence of a perpetrator's demise, only the chilling certainty of his absence.

She thought about the sheer psychological toll this uncertainty was taking on everyone involved. Miller's family was lost in a sea of unanswered questions and needed clear answers to start the grieving process. The officers who had been on the scene, haunted by the inexplicable events of that day, by the memory of a colleague lost and a monster who had seemingly evaporated into thin air. And the town, forever looking over their shoulders, their fear amplified by the lack of a definitive resolution. Vance had become scarier than ever in his absence. He was no longer just a man; he was a symbol of the unknown, a specter of pure dread, his potential survival a constant, festering source of anxiety.

Harding's mind, which was always asking questions, wouldn't accept the official story. She saw the holes, the contradictions, and the creepy perfection of Vance's disappearance. It wasn't just a lack of evidence; it was an active, deliberate erasure. It pointed to a level of planning, a calculated precision, that belied the chaotic image of a desperate criminal fleeing capture. Had Vance somehow anticipated the chase, the pursuit into the ravine? Had he prepared an escape route, a contingency plan that involved making his own death appear inevitable?

The thought was like a cold snake wrapping itself around her stomach. If Vance had survived, if he had managed to engineer his own vanishing act, it meant he was still out there. Somewhere. And that was a far more terrifying prospect than a simple, albeit tragic, accident. The monster wasn't dead; he was just hiding, like a predator playing a long game. The fact that there was no body didn't mean the investigation was over; it was a clear sign. It was Vance's way of saying, "You think you've won? You haven't even begun to understand."

She found herself revisiting the known facts, sifting through them with a renewed, almost feverish intensity. Vance's history was one of calculated cruelty, of meticulous planning. He didn't tend to act on impulse, at least not when he was committing crimes. His modus operandi was one of control, of manipulation. Could his disappearance be his ultimate act of control, his final, most devastating manipulation of the system, of the very people who sought to bring him to justice?

The ravine, a place of natural beauty now forever tainted by tragedy, became Harding's obsession. She visualized it, not as the chaotic, unforgiving terrain the reports depicted, but as a meticulously crafted stage. If Vance had known its secrets, its hidden paths, and its dangerous but possibly survivable routes? Did he use the thick trees and echoing canyons to hide his escape? The sheer scale of the place, its vastness and inaccessibility, offered countless opportunities for evasion, for a well-planned retreat.

The drone footage, played and replayed, offered no solace. There was a frantic chase, a sudden loss of sight, and then… nothing. No indication of Vance tumbling, no final struggle against gravity. Nothing but a hole. A black hole in the story that took in all the truth. Harding felt a growing certainty that the official conclusion, while logical on paper, was a dangerous oversimplification. It was a narrative designed to provide closure, but it was a closure built on a foundation of sand, a denial of the profound unsettling questions that lingered in the air like a persistent chill.

The official report was a testament to what they could prove, to the evidence they had meticulously gathered. But Harding was thinking about what they couldn't prove, about the absence of evidence, and what that absence truly signified. It signified the possibility of a meticulously planned deception, a masterful evasion that had left them all grasping at straws. It meant that the monster, the man they had so fervently believed was at the end of his reign of terror, might just be beginning a new, more terrifying chapter. People still had questions, not just about Miller's death, but also about Vance's life, or rather, his continued, unseen existence. And that was a thought that kept Harding awake at night, a chilling whisper in the silence, a testament to the enduring power of the unknown. The ravine had not claimed Vance; it had merely been his accomplice in a grander, more sinister performance. And the world, which thought his fall was the end, had missed the biggest trick of all.

The Town Tries to Heal

The pronouncement of John Vance as "presumed deceased" was meant to be a balm, a definitive closure that would allow Oakhaven to finally exhale the breath it had been holding for years. The official report, crisp and authoritative, was plastered on the town hall bulletin board, a stark pronouncement against the backdrop of cheerful floral arrangements for the upcoming summer festival. Yet, beneath the veneer of returning normalcy, a subtle tremor ran through the community. The fear, once a palpable entity that stalked the shadowed alleys and whispered in hushed tones, had not vanished entirely; it had merely transmuted, becoming a lingering phantom, a shadow in the periphery of their vision.

The shops on Main Street, which had once shuttered their doors at the slightest hint of dusk, now stayed open a little later, the sounds of commerce a determined counterpoint to the silence that had once reigned. Mrs. Gable, at the bakery, still meticulously arranged her famous blueberry scones, her hands moving with practiced precision, but her eyes often drifted to the window, scanning the street with an almost imperceptible flicker of apprehension.

She'd been one of the first to speak out, her trembling voice a catalyst for the fear that had gripped the town. She tried to look strong and unbreakable now, giving each customer a bright, if a little strained, smile. Yet, the memory of Vance's chilling grip on her arm, the predatory gleam in his eyes as he'd demanded her day's earnings, was a phantom limb that ached with a persistent, phantom pain. The aroma of cinnamon and sugar, usually a source of comfort, was now tinged with the faint, metallic scent of fear that clung to her memory.

The library in town used to be a quiet place where people could escape, but now it felt like there was a different kind of quiet there. Children still visited, their laughter a fragile melody against the silence, but their games were less boisterous, their voices softer. They'd grown up under the shadow of Monster John, their innocent minds imprinted with the chilling tales of his atrocities. The absence of Vance's body, the lack of a definitive end, had created a void that their young imaginations were only too eager to fill with even more terrifying scenarios. People told stories in low voices about Vance's escape and how he was always just out of sight, just beyond what they knew. The librarians, accustomed to guiding young minds through worlds of fantasy, now found themselves subtly steering conversations away from the darker corners of Oakhaven's recent past, their own unease a silent undercurrent.

The town square, which is usually a busy place for people, felt different in a small way. People in the town were determined to take back their public spaces, so they held picnics and outdoor concerts. But there was a watchful quality to their gatherings, an almost unconscious scanning of the faces in the crowd, a collective vigilance that had become deeply ingrained. A sudden noise – a car backfiring, a dog barking unexpectedly – could send a ripple of unease through the assembled crowd, a momentary freeze before the collective realization that it was nothing, just the ordinary sounds of life reasserting themselves. The sense of shared vulnerability, born from the knowledge that one of their own had been capable of such unimaginable darkness, had forged a new kind of community, one bound not just by shared history, but by shared trauma.

Sheriff Brody, a man whose gruff exterior had always been a source of reassurance, now carried a heavier burden. The official report said that his department was not at fault because Vance had successfully escaped and the ravine was too difficult to cross. But the questions, the "what ifs," still bothered him at night when it was quiet. He'd been on the scene, had seen the desperate pursuit, the agonizing uncertainty. He had seen firsthand how scared everyone in the town was. The absence of proof, the very thing that had led to Vance's presumption of death, was a nagging anomaly that gnawed at his conscience. He kept going over the events in his head, looking closely at what his officers did and trying to find a detail or moment of oversight that could have changed the outcome. He knew the town needed to move on, but he also knew that a bureaucratic order couldn't really bring that about. It had to be earned, and in Oakhaven's case, it felt like a prize that remained perpetually out of reach.

The kids, being kids, often asked the questions that the adults were too afraid to say. At the playground, little Lily would sometimes yell, "Is Monster John still in the woods?" as she swung higher and higher. Her mother, Sarah, a woman who had once been a vocal advocate for Vance's apprehension, would force a reassuring smile, her heart clenching with a familiar dread. "No, honey," she'd reply, her voice a little too bright, a little too strained. "He's gone. The police said so." But even as she said the words, a part of her wasn't sure. The woods, once a place of childhood adventure, now held a new, darker allure, a forbidden territory whispered about in hushed tones, a place where the monster might still be watching.

The local newspaper, the Oakhaven Chronicle, struggled with how to frame the narrative. Their headlines had been screaming about fear, worry, and the desperate search for months. Now, they attempted to pivot, to focus on the town's resilience, its unwavering spirit. Articles featured stories of community rebuilding, of small businesses recovering, of families finding solace in each other. Yet, even in these optimistic pieces, an undercurrent of unease persisted. The editor, a pragmatic man named Mr. Abernathy, often found himself staring at blank pages, wrestling with the unspoken truth that Oakhaven wasn't truly healed. The scars were too deep, the memories too potent. Vance, in his very absence, had become a permanent resident of their collective consciousness, a specter that cast a long, indelible shadow.

The annual Oakhaven Founder's Day picnic, a long-standing tradition, was met with a mixture of relief and apprehension. It was the first big public event since the official announcement, a test of how willing the town was to come back into the light. Families brought their checkered blankets, their picnic baskets overflowing with homemade treats. At first, there was only a little laughter in the air. Kids ran around the big park, chasing each other. At first, they were shy, but as they got more and more excited about being free, they stopped being shy. Yet, there was a palpable sense of awareness, a constant, almost subliminal scanning of the treeline that bordered the park, a silent acknowledgment that the world was no longer as safe as it once seemed. A sudden rustle in the undergrowth, a distant bird call, could momentarily still the revelry, a collective holding of breath before the normalcy of the day reasserted itself.

Detective Harding, observing the scene from a discreet distance, felt a pang of melancholy. Oakhaven was trying, it was striving to mend. But she knew, with a certainty that chilled her to the bone, that true healing was still a long, arduous journey. The fact that Vance's body was missing was not just a forensic oddity; it was a psychological black hole that had taken away the town's sense of safety. The fear had been replaced by a more insidious, pervasive form of anxiety – the anxiety of the unknown, the fear of what might still be lurking, unseen and unheard. The monster, in his vanishing act, had achieved his most profound victory: he had become a permanent fixture in their nightmares, a testament to the fact that sometimes, the most terrifying monsters are the ones who leave no trace, the ones who manage to disappear into the very fabric of the world, forever haunting the places they once terrorized. The town could rebuild its structures, its businesses, its routines, but the invisible architecture of fear, once erected by John Vance, had been etched too deeply into the soul of Oakhaven to ever be fully dismantled. It was a wound that would continue to fester, a silent testament to the enduring power of a ghost that refused to be laid to rest. The collective denial, while necessary for their sanity, was a fragile shield against the persistent whisper of doubt. Every creak of a floorboard in an empty house, every shadow that danced in the twilight, was a potential echo of Vance's presence, a reminder that the absence of proof was, in itself, the most compelling form of evidence that the story was far from over. The town tried to heal, but it was a healing process complicated by the haunting realization that the wound might never truly close.

A Seed of Suspicion

The official announcement of John Vance's presumed death, which was as final as a coroner's report and made even more clear by the town hall's stark bulletin board, was meant to be Oakhaven's collective sigh of relief. Yet, even as the townsfolk attempted to embrace the fragile dawn of normalcy, a subtle disquiet persisted. The fear that had once been a real ghost had changed into something else, something that wasn't as obvious but still made people uneasy. It was like a ghostly ache in the town's collective mind. Mrs. Gable, meticulously arranging her blueberry scones, found her gaze frequently drawn to the street, a fleeting apprehension in her eyes, a lingering echo of Vance's chilling touch. The children, their laughter now a more subdued melody, whispered stories of Vance's continued existence, their imaginations painting him as a persistent shadow lurking just beyond the familiar. Sheriff Brody, despite the exonerating report, was haunted by the gnawing anomaly of Vance's disappearance, a nagging question mark that refused to be erased. Even the Oakhaven Chronicle, in its attempts to champion the town's resilience, struggled to paper over the cracks of unspoken unease, acknowledging that Oakhaven was a town wounded, its scars far too deep for a simple bureaucratic decree. The Founder's Day picnic was a planned attempt to get back to normal, but there was a sense of awareness in the air, a group scanning the treeline, and a quiet recognition that the world was no longer as safe as it once was. Detective Harding, observing the tentative celebrations, felt the weight of the unspoken truth: Oakhaven was trying to heal, but the absence of proof, the very foundation of Vance's presumed death, was an abyss that had swallowed their sense of security, leaving behind the more insidious fear of the unknown.

It was a Tuesday, precisely three months after the official verdict, when the first, almost imperceptible crack appeared in the carefully constructed edifice of closure. Detective Harding was going through the complicated evidence logs from the Vance investigation when she found herself drawn back to the edges of the case, to the less exciting but more boring details that often get lost in the search for stories that grab headlines. She was carefully comparing witness statements with the forensic data that had been found. This was a boring job that usually only confirmed what was already known. But then, her eyes snagged on a particular entry, a seemingly innocuous detail buried deep within the report from the search party that had scoured the treacherous terrain of Blackwood Ravine. There was a short mention, almost an afterthought, of a small, strange object that was found stuck in the thick underbrush about fifty yards from the edge of the ravine, which is a long way from where Vance was last seen. The report said it was a "fragment of synthetic material, dark green, possibly a piece of torn fabric or netting." It had been logged, bagged, and subsequently dismissed as inconsequential debris, a common enough occurrence in such a wild, untamed landscape.

Harding's brow furrowed. It was a small detail that could have been missed, but the way it was described and the almost apologetic tone of its inclusion in the report made her professional instincts tingle. She brought up the right pictures, which were digital files that had been widely shared and looked at during the first investigation. The images were grainy, taken under challenging conditions, but there it was: a dark, irregular shape nestled amongst the fallen leaves and moss. It wasn't immediately identifiable, but it didn't look like a natural occurrence. The texture looked too smooth and the edges looked too sharp for a piece of rotting plant matter. She asked for the bag of physical evidence that had the piece in it. When it finally arrived at her desk, carefully handled by a uniformed officer, Harding felt a peculiar prickle of anticipation.

She carefully opened the bag, knowing that the sterile latex gloves would keep her safe. Inside, nestled on a bed of cotton wool, was the object in question. It was a shard, no bigger than her thumb, of a dark, almost black-green material. Under the harsh fluorescent lights of the evidence room, it still possessed a faint sheen, a resilience that suggested it wasn't merely dead organic matter. It was stiff, yet with a subtle pliability. Running a gloved fingertip over its surface, she detected a faint, almost imperceptible pattern, a microscopic weave that was clearly man-made. It felt like a piece of some sort of high-tensile netting or possibly a reinforced canvas.

"What do you make of it, Detective?" the officer inquired, his tone laced with the mild curiosity reserved for the mundane sorting of old case files.

Harding turned the piece over in her hands, her mind racing with ideas. It wasn't a piece of clothing, at least not any common garment she recognized. It didn't have the usual drape and weave of denim, cotton, or wool. Is it possible that it's camping gear? A backpack, perhaps? But the search had been extensive, and no such items had been recovered in Vance's vicinity. The ravine itself had yielded nothing conclusive, only the disturbed earth and the chilling absence of its most infamous inhabitant. She remembered the sheer drop, the violent currents of the river below, the unforgiving tangle of the surrounding wilderness. This piece, no matter how strong, should have been swept away, broken, or lost in the wreckage of Vance's fall.

A nagging thought began to form, a whisper of dissent against the official narrative. The search teams had been thorough, yes, but were they looking for this? Were they anticipating the discovery of something that might suggest Vance hadn't simply plummeted to his death? The initial focus had been on finding a body, any trace that would confirm his demise and put an end to the town's torment. Maybe they were too quick to dismiss something less certain, something that suggested a different outcome, in their single-minded pursuit of that goal.

She recalled the testimony of a hiker, a Mr. Abernathy – no relation to the Chronicle's editor – who had been in the general vicinity of Blackwood Ravine on the day Vance disappeared. He said he heard a "sharp, metallic tearing sound" and then a short, muffled cry coming from the direction of the ravine. At the time, his account had been considered anecdotal, easily explained by the natural acoustics of the area, the wind whistling through the trees, or perhaps a falling branch. But now, holding this fragment of robust material, Harding felt a chill that had nothing to do with the evidence room's temperature. A tearing sound. A cry that was hard to hear. And this piece of… what?

Harding meticulously documented her re-examination of the fragment, attaching her own detailed notes and requesting further analysis. She specifically asked for an assessment of the material's tensile strength and potential uses, and whether it could have been part of any specialized equipment. The lab results, when they finally came back a week later, only deepened the intrigue. The material was found to be a strong, rip-resistant composite that is often used in tactical gear, climbing ropes that last a long time, or even parachutes that are made for low-altitude deployment.

A parachute. The word stuck in Harding's mind in a way that made him feel uneasy. Vance, a man who had meticulously planned his crimes, a man who had demonstrated an almost preternatural ability to evade capture, had meticulously planned his disappearance. The ravine, the presumed site of his demise, had always felt too obvious, too theatrical. What if it had been a deliberate misdirection? A staged scene designed to provide a convenient, albeit unconfirmed, end? If he had used some kind of parachute or descent device, the tearing sound Mr. Abernathy heard could have been the material getting caught on something, like a tree branch, while he was making a controlled or semi-controlled descent away from the ravine's most dangerous drop. This fragment, then, wouldn't be evidence of a fatal fall, but of a deliberate, controlled escape.

The implications were staggering. If Vance had survived, if he had orchestrated his own vanishing act, then Oakhaven was not safe. The pronouncement of "presumed deceased" was not closure, but a dangerous illusion. The monster wasn't gone; he was just hiding underground, waiting. This single, overlooked fragment, this tiny piece of dark green composite, was more than just a forensic anomaly; it was a seed of doubt, a chilling intimation that the real story of John Vance had not ended, but had merely begun its most terrifying chapter. Harding felt a cold dread seep into her bones. She looked at the fragment again, this time seeing not just a piece of material, but a tangible link to a predator who had masterfully outmaneuvered not only the law, but the very certainty of death itself. The investigation, she realized with a sinking heart, was far from over. The absence of proof had always been Oakhaven's torment; now, it was becoming Harding's obsession, a terrifying puzzle that threatened to unravel the fragile peace the town so desperately clung to. This small, unassuming piece of composite material was a silent warning, a chilling whisper from the shadows that the monster of Oakhaven had not been defeated, but had only retreated to gather strength for a return that would shatter their hard-won peace. The official report was a lie, a comforting falsehood, and this fragment was the undeniable, albeit silent, proof.

Chapter 6: The Echo of the Past

Johns Childhood Trauma Revisited

The study in the Vance estate was dark and had wood paneling. It smelled like old leather and stale pipe smoke. It held the residue of violence, a spectral stain that clung to the air, invisible yet suffocating. For young John, barely seven years old, it was the epicenter of a universe shattered into a million razor-sharp shards. The night his father, a man whose booming laughter had once filled the grand house with warmth, transformed into a snarling beast, was seared into John's memory with a ferocity that time could neither dull nor erase.

It had begun with a storm. Not just any storm, but one that seemed to claw at the very foundations of their opulent home. The wind howled like a tormented spirit, rattling the leaded glass windows with an insistent, malevolent rhythm. Rain lashed against the panes, blurring the already indistinct shapes of the manicured gardens into a chaotic, watery smear. But inside, a real storm was brewing. His father's whispers, accusations, and a palpable, suffocating rage set off a domestic inferno.

John had been tucked into his bed, the ornate canopy a flimsy shield against the growing unease that permeated the house. He could still hear the quiet, angry voices of his parents arguing as they went up the grand staircase. It was a creepy lullaby that kept him awake and filled him with fear. His mother's voice, usually so melodious, was strained, laced with a desperate fear that clawed at his young heart. Then, the argument escalated, morphing from sharp, angry words into a chilling, guttural roar from his father. The sound was unlike anything John had ever heard; it was the sound of a man unhinged, of a predator finally shedding its disguise.

He crept out of bed, his bare feet silent on the plush carpet. The air in the hallway was thick with tension, heavy with the metallic tang of fear and something else, something acrid and deeply disturbing that he couldn't yet identify. Drawn by an invisible, terrifying current, he edged towards his parents' bedroom door, which stood ajar, a sliver of crimson light bleeding into the dim corridor.

The scene that greeted him was a tableau of unimaginable horror. The room was a chaotic mess. The furniture had been turned over and the velvet upholstery had been ripped. The scent of spilled brandy mingled with the sharp, coppery smell of blood, a scent that would forever be imprinted on his olfactory memory, a primal alarm bell. His father, a hulking silhouette against the flickering lamplight, stood over his mother. Her exquisite silk dressing gown, once a cascade of emerald green, was now a grotesque Rorschach of dark, viscous crimson. Her eyes were wide with fear that would haunt John for years to come. They stared blankly, not seeing.

His father's rage was twisted and not human. It was a mask of pure, unadulterated savagery, a chilling testament to the darkness lurking beneath the veneer of respectability. John stood still, paralyzed by fear, as his father raised his hand. For a brief moment, the dim light caught the glint of something sharp and metal. The dull thud that came after that was sickeningly final. It was the sound of life ending, a sound that echoed the storm outside but was much worse.

And then, the other screams began. Not the screams of his mother, for she was beyond screaming, but the terrified shrieks of his aunts, his grandmother, who had rushed in, drawn by the initial commotion. They were a chorus of pure, unadulterated panic, a flock of birds caught in a predator's snare. John watched as his father turned, his face full of rage and bloodlust, and his movements were unnervingly fast and violent. The scene dissolved into a blur of terror, a symphony of violence that played out in the confines of that opulent bedroom. He saw glimpses of flailing limbs, heard the sickening crunch of bone, smelled the ever-present, overwhelming odor of blood and the sharp, chemical scent that he would later come to associate with his father's work in the disused abattoir he frequented.

He remembered a specific detail: the way the lamplight caught the intricate silver embroidery on his grandmother's shawl as it fell, a stark contrast to the raw brutality unfolding around it. He remembered the sound of his younger cousin's whimpers, a tiny, lost sound swallowed by the cacophony of terror. And through it all, John stood in the doorway, a silent witness, his small body trembling uncontrollably, his mind struggling to process the unimaginable. He wasn't scared for himself; he was just deeply shocked. It was as if his very capacity for feeling had been amputated, leaving behind a gaping void where his innocent childhood should have been.

The things that happened after that were a blur. He remembered being pulled away, his small hands scraped raw from clinging to the doorframe. He remembered how cold and sterile the police station smelled and how strangers' voices were kind but distant. He remembered being questioned, his answers monosyllabic, his gaze vacant. His father, his monstrous father, had been apprehended, but for young John, the true perpetrator was not the man in handcuffs, but the darkness that had been unleashed that night, a darkness that had taken root within him.

He recalled the unnerving silence that had descended upon the house after the initial chaos. The smell of fear and death that lingered was a real presence, a constant reminder of what had happened. The rooms that used to feel like home now felt strange, haunted by the sounds of violence. The grand staircase, where he had often played, now seemed to stretch into an abyss. The polished floors, once a playground, now reflected distorted shadows that danced with his deepest fears.

In the aftermath, John was shuffled between relatives, a silent, withdrawn child. He rarely spoke of that night, the memories too raw, too horrific to articulate. But they ate away at him, a toxic mix of trauma, confusion, and a growing, terrifying understanding of how fragile life is and how cruel people can be. He learned to suppress his emotions, to build walls around the ravaged landscape of his inner world. His father's violence had not only extinguished the lives of his mother and female relatives; it had irrevocably extinguished the light within young John, leaving behind a darkness that would eventually mirror the very depravity he had witnessed.

He would wake up in the middle of the night with the smell of blood and brandy in his nose and the sound of his father's growl in his ears. He would see the blank, unseeing eyes of his mother, the terror etched on his grandmother's face. These weren't just memories; they were real experiences that he relived with such painful clarity that they drove him to the edge of insanity. This profound, formative trauma was the crucible in which John Vance's fractured psyche was forged. He didn't just lose his childhood innocence; it was brutally and violently killed, and in its place, he became aware of how predatory the world is and how terrifying the darkness that lay dormant inside him could be. The scent of copper, the sound of a storm, the sight of spilled blood – these were the triggers, the sensory signposts that led back to that night, the night his world ended and something far more sinister began to grow in its place. He had witnessed the ultimate act of betrayal, the violent obliteration of love and trust, and in its place, a seed of darkness had been sown, nurtured by fear and cemented by the unspeakable. He understood, on a primal level, the power of fear, the intoxicating rush of dominance, the chilling ease with which life could be snuffed out. This was not the foundation of a healthy mind, but the fertile soil for something far more monstrous.

The Birth of the Secondary Personality

The fractured shards of John Vance's childhood settled not like broken glass, but like molten lead, searing into his developing consciousness. The night his father's rage consumed the Vance estate wasn't merely an event witnessed; it was an existential cataclysm that ripped through the fabric of his being, leaving behind a void that his tender psyche, desperate for survival, began to fill with something else. This wasn't a conscious choice or a planned decision;

it was a basic, desperate act of self-preservation. The horrible truth of that night, the brutal deaths of his mother and female relatives, was too much for a seven-year-old mind to handle. To stay alive, it had to be hidden away in the deepest parts of his being and replaced with something that could protect him from the unbearable pain.

Dissociation was definitely the main psychological defense mechanism at work. When reality got too scary to handle, it was the mind's last chance to get away. John's mind, faced with the unimaginable violence, simply… detached. The sensory overload – the coppery scent of blood, the sharp tang of brandy, the guttural roars, the sickening thuds – was too much for his developing nervous system. To cope, his consciousness fractured, creating a chasm between the observer and the horrific events unfolding. He became an island, adrift from the storm, watching it rage from an impossible distance. This wasn't a conscious decision to "check out"; it was an involuntary physiological and psychological response, a desperate attempt to prevent his mind from shattering completely. The boy who was tucked into bed that night ceased to exist in the immediate aftermath. In his place was a shell, an observer who had seen something horrible happen but didn't really feel it, at least not the way a child should. The vivid sensory details that would later haunt his adult life were at first a shield, a collection of separate impressions that his young mind couldn't yet connect to the whole trauma.

Repression came along with dissociation. The memories of that night, the screams, the blood, the sheer brutality, were deemed too dangerous, too painful to surface. His young mind, which was naturally good at survival, pushed them down, burying them under layers of denial and forgetfulness. This wasn't a process of actively choosing what to forget, but rather an unconscious act of sealing away the most damaging psychological wounds. These memories that were pushed away didn't go away; they got worse. They caused pressure, like a deep infection, a quiet, internal storm that would eventually need to be let out. The emotional energy tied to this trauma, the terror, the grief, the confusion, couldn't simply vanish. It needed to change shape and find a new home.

And that vessel began to manifest as rage. For a child who had witnessed the ultimate act of betrayal and violence, a passive victimhood was an unacceptable fate. The helplessness he felt, the sheer powerlessness in the face of such monstrous acts, was a corrosive emotion. To counteract this debilitating sense of vulnerability, a new personality began to coalesce, one forged not from love and innocence, but from the raw, unadulterated fury that had been unleashed that night. This wasn't the controlled anger of an adult; it was a wild, primal scream that didn't have a voice of its own. This new persona was a protector, even though it was a scary one. It was designed to ensure that John Vance would never again be so vulnerable, so utterly at the mercy of others. It was a bulwark against the world that had shown him its ugliest face, a promise of retribution for the trauma inflicted.

The precise moment of psychological fragmentation was not a sudden explosion, but a subtle, insidious shift. It was the moment the internal screams of the seven-year-old boy were drowned out by a nascent, predatory urge. The boy, John, was effectively paralyzed by the horror. He could not act, could not fight, could not comprehend. But something within him, a deep-seated instinct for survival, recognized the overwhelming power of aggression. The father's violence was horrible, but it was also a cruel way to control and scare people. In witnessing this, a part of John's mind latched onto the power inherent in that savagery, detaching it from the moral implications.

This was where the secondary personality, the predator, began to take shape. It didn't become a whole thing overnight. It was a seed that grew in the fertile ground of John's trauma. This emergent persona was a reaction to the overwhelming helplessness. If John was the victim, then this other self would be the aggressor. It was a twisted form of empowerment. The fear of seeing his mother's blood, his grandmother's shawl stained red, and his aunts' screams all came together to make a strong, if scary, plan. The sheer primal nature of the violence, stripped of any humanistic context, offered a stark, albeit perverted, solution to the unbearable pain.

The dissociative state let this new person grow without "John's" conscious mind knowing it was happening. It was as if John's awareness of himself had splintered, with one part remaining in the frozen state of trauma and another beginning to awaken, fueled by the residual energy of that night's violence. This new entity didn't have to process the grief or the horror. Its goal was simpler: to rule, to control, and to hurt others before they could hurt it. This was the birth of the echo, the dark reflection that would shadow John for the rest of his life.

The anger wasn't just a way to deal with things; it was a trigger. It provided the energy, the driving force, for the repression and dissociation to solidify into distinct psychological structures. The memories and feelings that John had buried deep inside him didn't come out in tears or screams of pain. Instead, they came out in a cold, simmering rage that was always there, just below the surface of his mind. This fury was the foundation upon which the secondary personality was built. It was a primal, animalistic rage that had no morals or empathy and came from a complete lack of safety and love.

This emergent predator personality didn't have John's childhood memories; it had only the imprint of the violence. It understood aggression, dominance, and the silencing of opposition. It was a distilled essence of John's father's rage, stripped of its human context and amplified by the pure terror of the victim. The blood, the screams, the fear – these became not sources of pain, but of power for this new entity. It learned to connect the smell of blood with getting rid of weakness and the sound of screams with winning control. It was a horrible copy of life that came from death, a perversion of nature.

The splitting up wasn't just a mental break; it was a spiritual one too. The boy John Vance, with his capacity for innocence and joy, was irrevocably wounded, perhaps even effectively extinguished on that night. In his place, a fractured being emerged, a composite of trauma and survival. The secondary personality was not an alien invader; it was a part of John that was so horrible that it was a sign of how hard his mind was trying to protect itself from an unbearable reality. The trauma had made the monster, which was a creature made to live in a world that had shown itself to be cruel and unforgiving.

A clinical study of this phenomenon shows that the mind is under attack. Dissociation is the most extreme way to protect oneself from a threat that is too strong to handle. Repression acts as the vault, sealing away the most damaging memories to prevent their conscious re-traumatization. And rage, the untamed offspring of helplessness, becomes the architect of a new identity, one built on the ashes of the old, a terrifying testament to the mind's capacity to fracture and reform in the face of unimaginable horror. The secondary personality, in essence, was a survival mechanism taken to its most extreme, a terrifyingly effective way for John Vance's mind to endure the unbearable by creating a self that could not be broken in the same way. It was the birth of a monster from the ashes of a shattered innocence, a primal scream given form.

Recurring Nightmares and Visions

The phantom of that night clung to John Vance like a second skin, a chilling dampness that no amount of waking hours could fully evaporate. Sleep didn't help; it just gave him a different, more dangerous battlefield. His nights were a relentless carousel of fractured images and raw, primal fear, a visceral replay of the horrors he'd tried so desperately to outrun. These weren't the nebulous anxieties of a troubled mind; they were sharp, vivid, and terrifyingly real. The nightmares weren't just watching; they were fully immersing him, each one taking him deeper into the darkness of his past. He would be back in the Vance estate's suffocating luxury, where the air was thick with the sickening smell of spilled brandy and something much more metallic and scary. The opulent décor, once a symbol of his family's prominence, now warped into a grotesque backdrop for unspeakable acts. The mahogany dining table, which was usually full of the leftovers from a fancy meal, would be turned over, and the polished surface would reflect the flickering, hellish light of the lamps that had been turned over. The Persian rugs, once a testament to refined taste, would be soaked in a deep, viscous crimson, the intricate patterns lost to the spreading stain.

The sounds were the worst part of these nighttime trips. His father's guttural roars, which had once meant power and authority, now sounded like a monster with no human qualities. It was a sound that had no reason, no fatherhood, and was a pure expression of pure brutality. Intertwined with this were the choked screams, the desperate pleas that tore through the night, each one a shard of glass embedding itself deeper into his psyche. He could still hear his aunts' high-pitched screams and his mother's scared whimper. These were sounds that his waking mind had carefully buried, but his cruelly all-knowing subconscious brought them back to life with painful clarity. The thudding sounds, sickening and final, would resonate in his bones, a percussive beat accompanying the symphony of terror. His own small form, a phantom observer, would often be cowering behind a velvet curtain, or beneath a heavy oak sideboard, a silent witness to the unfolding pandemonium. He could feel the rough weave of the fabric against his cheek, the cold seep of the polished floorboards beneath his trembling hands. The air felt heavy and suffocating, and there was an electric fear in the air that made his heart pound against his ribs like a bird in a cage.

Sometimes, the nightmares would shift focus, zeroing in on specific, horrifying details. He would see his mother's silk dressing gown, the one she wore for quiet evenings, now torn and stained, clinging to her limp form. The delicate floral embroidery seemed to mock the violence it had witnessed. He would see that her usually bright eyes had lost their spark, and the warmth and love they always had had turned into a terrifying stillness. Then he saw his aunts' faces, which had once been beautiful, twisted in fear as they tried to protect themselves from the attack. He'd see the glint of metal, the arc of a brutal swing, and the inevitable, devastating impact. These weren't abstract images; they were hyper-realistic replays, each detail etched with an agonizing precision that defied his attempts to rationalize them away. The smell of blood, which was sharp and coppery, would fill his nose so strongly that he would wake up gasping for air, sure that the smell was still on his skin.

These nighttime visits weren't just bad dreams; they were a psychological siege. They broke down the weak walls that his conscious mind had built, leaving him open to the pure, unfiltered horror that lay beneath. The dissociation that had served him so well during the day, creating a safe distance, became a liability in the unguarded territory of sleep. His defenses broke down, and the memories he had been trying to forget came rushing back, wild and free. The psychological compartmentalization, the careful partitioning of his mind, began to break down. The molten lead of his trauma, so effectively contained, would begin to seep out, burning through the carefully constructed barriers. He would wake up in a cold sweat, with his body drenched, his heart racing, and the screams still ringing in his ears. The sheets would be tangled around him as if he had been physically fighting off an attacker, his muscles still tensed from the phantom struggle.

The line between what is real and what is a dream started to blur more and more often. During the day, pieces of these nightmares would come to mind without warning, like pieces of glass from a broken mirror. A loud noise, like a door slamming or a car backfiring, would send a rush of adrenaline through him, making him feel scared, smell blood, or see his father's angry face for a split second. Even a faint smell of alcohol from a stranger could take him back to that night, when the air was thick with the metallic taste of his father's breath. The soft texture of velvet, a material he might encounter in a hotel lobby or a theatre, could evoke the feel of the curtains behind which he'd hidden, and with it, the terrifying tableau that had unfolded. These intrusive visions were shocking, confusing, and very disturbing. They reminded him that the past wasn't just a bunch of memories; it was a living, breathing thing that had dug its claws into him.

These episodes left him perpetually on edge, his nerves frayed to the breaking point. The constant stream of nightmares and intrusive thoughts made him feel like danger was always just below the surface. This heightened state of anxiety made him hyper-vigilant, his senses constantly on alert for any perceived threat. He would flinch at sudden movements, his gaze darting around, searching for an escape route, his mind already anticipating the worst. This long-term stress showed up in his body too. He had chronic headaches and his jaw hurt a lot because it was always clenched. His sleep, when it came, was shallow and restless, a pale imitation of true rest. The exhaustion was profound, a bone-deep weariness that no amount of sleep could alleviate.

The worst thing about these recurring nightmares and visions was that they made his already volatile rage even worse. The raw, unadulterated fury that had been a nascent shield in his childhood now found fertile ground in the fertile soil of his unresolved trauma. He felt helpless in his dreams, and the pain of not being able to do anything about it or get away made him very angry. The violence he saw over and over again at night made his story even stronger: the world was a harsh, dangerous place, and the only way to stay alive was to be stronger and more ruthless than the people who wanted to hurt him. The anger wasn't just an emotion; it was a reaction, a physical response to the constant pain his own mind was causing him.

When the nightmares were particularly vivid, or the intrusive visions more potent, John would find himself teetering on the brink. The carefully constructed facade of control he presented to the world would begin to crack. A perceived slight, a moment of frustration, or even a seemingly innocuous comment could be enough to ignite the dormant inferno. The anger would grow quickly, like a tidal wave of rage that could swallow him whole. His vision would narrow, his breathing would become shallow and ragged, and his hands would clench into fists. At these times, he was no longer John Vance, the supposedly successful businessman. He was a vessel for the primal rage that had come from that terrible night. The violence his father had done to him made him feel like he was going down the same destructive path.

These outbursts could be terrifying, both for those around him and for John himself. A raised voice, a slammed fist on a table, a sudden, aggressive stance – these were the outward manifestations of the internal storm. He might lash out verbally, his words laced with venom and accusation, or he might resort to physical intimidation, his sheer presence becoming a threat. Sometimes his rage would get so bad that he would hit people, which was a scary show of raw power that always left him shaken and horrified, but also, strangely, empowered. Even though the act of aggression was harmful, it gave the person a brief sense of control and a break from the feeling of being helpless. It was a sickening confirmation of the predator persona, a dark sign that it was necessary for survival.

The cycle was cruel. The nightmares made him angry, which led to outbursts. The guilt and shame that followed the outbursts only made the trauma worse, making him more likely to have nightmares in the future. It was a self-perpetuating loop of suffering, a testament to the inescapable nature of his past. He was in a war with himself, fighting an enemy that lived in his own mind and was made up of the things he wanted to forget so badly. The violence he had seen had not only hurt his mind; it had become a part of him, controlling how he felt, how he interacted with the world, and a rage that was threatening to destroy him from the inside out. The echo of the past was not a whisper; it was a roar, and it was growing louder with each passing night. The visions weren't just memories; they were warnings of a darkness he was always in danger of falling into.

The Role of Guilt and Repression

The rage, a tempest that clawed at the edges of John Vance's sanity, was only one facet of the multifaceted psychological landscape carved by his past. Beneath the veneer of aggression, a more insidious current flowed: guilt. It wasn't the sharp, accusatory guilt of a specific wrongdoing; it was a deep, almost existential guilt that came from seeing horrible things happen and feeling powerless to stop them. He hadn't actively participated, but his survival, his continued existence while others perished, gnawed at him with an unrelenting ferocity. This feeling got worse because he felt ashamed of not doing anything, and it was hard for him to be a child who couldn't help, protect, or even cry out without getting into more trouble. This shame, in turn, morphed into a deep-seated conviction of his own inadequacy, a belief that he was somehow complicit in the tragedy simply by virtue of his inability to prevent it.

This guilt was not a constant, overt companion. Instead, it lurked in the shadowed corners of his mind, surfacing at unexpected moments, often triggered by seemingly innocuous events. The sight of a child's scraped knee, a fleeting glimpse of parental concern on a stranger's face, or even the quiet solitude of an empty room could dredge up the submerged shame. He would find himself caught in a sudden, suffocating wave of remorse, a phantom ache in his chest that felt akin to physical pain. It was the guilt of a survivor, a feeling that made you ask, "Why you?" Why did you get to live when they didn't? What is it about you that makes you worthy of this break? These questions, unanswerable and tormenting, would leave him adrift in a sea of self-recrimination, his carefully constructed defenses momentarily crumbling.

He tried to bury these feelings and push them back into the dark corners of his mind, but they were just as strong as the nightmares. In John's case, repression wasn't just forgetting; it was a conscious, active effort to get rid of these bad feelings from his mind. He would engage in a rigorous mental discipline, diverting his attention, focusing on logic, on tasks, on anything that demanded his absolute mental engagement. This was the foundation of his predatory personality: the ability to separate his mind into different areas, one for his wild, raw feelings and another for the calm, logical pragmatism he showed to the world. However, the energy expended in maintaining these boundaries was colossal, leaving him perpetually drained, his mental reserves constantly depleted.

This internal tug-of-war between guilt and repression created a psychological environment that was exceptionally volatile. He always felt like he was in control during times when he thought he was lucid. The predatory instinct, honed by years of perceived threats and the necessity of self-preservation, would surge forward, an armored knight defending the castle of his mind. This person was effective, made quick decisions, and didn't feel guilty at all, which made them emotionally strong. It helped him deal with the difficult parts of running a business, make tough choices, and give off an air of unbreakable strength. Even at these times of peak performance, though, the ghost of guilt would flicker at the edges, a small tremor that threatened to break up the carefully planned facade.

Not only did he try to forget about his trauma, but he also avoided anything that might remind him of it in a deep, almost pathological way. He carefully arranged his surroundings, subconsciously getting rid of things that could set him off. He rarely visited places that evoked memories of his childhood, and he actively shunned individuals who might, through a careless word or gesture, unlock the Pandora's Box of his past. He often had shallow relationships because he wanted to keep emotional closeness from happening, which could have led to a deeper exploration of his mind. He was afraid that any real connection would cause his carefully built self to fall apart. This isolation, while ostensibly a protective measure, also served to reinforce the guilt, as it prevented him from seeking solace or understanding from others. He was a prisoner in a cell made of fear and denial, which he had put himself in.

The conflict between the aggressive, outward-facing persona and the deeply buried guilt was a constant source of internal friction. When the guilt threatened to surface, the predatory instinct would immediately reassert itself, not just as a defense against the guilt itself, but as a means of silencing the internal accuser. The act of asserting dominance, of demonstrating power, became a perverse form of penance. He would work with an almost crazy intensity, getting more done and pushing himself harder, as if the things he did outside of work could make up for the things he did wrong inside. He desperately needed outside approval to prove his worth and show himself and the world that he was more than just the helpless child who had seen such terrible things.

There were times, in the dead of night, when the repression would break down and the raw fear of the past would come through the cracks. It wasn't always the vivid, visceral nightmares he experienced. Sometimes, it was a more subtle and sneaky way of getting into his mind. He would wake up with a profound sense of unease, a gnawing apprehension that had no logical root. His mind would feel foggy, a disorienting haze that obscured clear thought. During these times, the guilt would be so strong that it felt like a heavy blanket pressing down on him, making him feel heavy and unable to move. He would lie in bed, paralyzed by an unnamed dread, the silence of the room amplifying the internal cacophony of his unresolved trauma.

The act of forgetting, the ultimate goal of repression, was a constant, exhausting pursuit. He would do mental gymnastics, changing the way he remembered things and making up new stories that made the horror less scary. His father, a figure of monstrous brutality in his nightmares, might be re-cast in his conscious mind as a man struggling with inner demons, his actions born of a twisted love or a tragic flaw. It could be said that his mother's screams were cries of pain from an accident and that her blank eyes were a sign of shock, not violence. These mental revisions were not deliberate lies but rather desperate attempts to construct a more palatable reality, a reality where he wasn't the sole survivor of an atrocity. This self-deception was a double-edged sword; it provided temporary relief but also further cemented the divide within his psyche, pushing the true horror deeper into the subconscious, where it festered and grew.

Because of this internal conflict, John often had to carefully plan how he acted in public. He could be charming and engaging one moment, then abruptly distant and cold the next. These changes weren't random; they were often a direct result of the changing internal struggle. When the guilt was suppressed and the predatory persona was dominant, he was confident, almost arrogant. When the repression started to break down and the fear and shame started to take over, he would retreat, his defenses getting stronger and his interactions becoming more guarded and shallow. People often thought that this inconsistency was a sign of being fickle or emotionally unstable, which made him feel even more alone and made him believe that he was fundamentally flawed.

The repression also affected his perception of others. He thought that showing vulnerability was a sign of weakness, so he didn't trust it. When he encountered people who were open about their struggles, he felt a mixture of pity and revulsion. He couldn't understand why they would be willing to show their pain and seem to have no control. In his mind, they were inviting disaster, making themselves easy prey. He was judgmental because he was fighting against his own vulnerability, which he saw in others. He thought their openness was a dangerous mistake and a sign that they didn't have the strong willpower he thought was necessary to stay alive.

The guilt, when it managed to breach the fortress of repression, was a debilitating force. He felt a deep sense of lethargy and hopelessness that made him not want to do anything. During these times, the anger would go away, and he would feel empty and hollow. The predatory instinct, stripped of its fuel, became dormant, and he would find himself adrift, unable to engage with the world. These were the times when he was most open to intrusive thoughts and the return of broken images and sounds from that night. He didn't actively fight them, but he did passively endure them. He would sit for hours, staring blankly at a wall, lost in the echoes of a past he couldn't escape, a past that whispered to him how worthless he was.

It was tiring to always try to keep these two parts of his mind that were at war with each other apart. It meant that John was perpetually on guard, his internal landscape a battlefield where fragile truces were constantly threatened. The calmness he showed on the outside was a dangerous illusion, like a thin layer of ice over a deep, chaotic sea. Any external disturbance, any unexpected pressure, could shatter that illusion, plunging him back into the terrifying reality of his repressed trauma. He was a man living in a state of perpetual vigilance, not against external threats, but against the devastating resurgence of his own internal demons. Ironically, the very act of trying to forget was keeping the past alive, a constant, simmering presence that defined every waking moment and haunted every dream.

Foreshadowing Future Torment

The gnawing guilt, the shame of his childhood helplessness, wasn't merely a passive specter; it was the dark architect of 'Monster John.' It provided the blueprint, the twisted motivation for the violence that would soon erupt with terrifying clarity. John, stuck in a never-ending cycle of repression, had unknowingly made it easy for this horrible persona to grow. The trauma, which couldn't be accessed consciously, grew worse and became a force that needed to be released. When the carefully built walls of his mind finally started to break down because of the huge stress of his internal conflict, it wasn't John Vance who came out. It was a creature made of his deepest fears and biggest flaws.

His victims became unwitting vessels for his unresolved past. In their terror, their pleas for mercy, he saw distorted reflections of his own past helplessness. The child who had cowered in the shadows, unable to speak, unable to act, found a perverse echo in the eyes of those he would soon terrorize. The raw, primal fear he saw on their faces was something he had felt before. It was such a strong memory that it felt more like a present reality than a memory. He wasn't just hurting her; he was acting out a scene that he had been forced to live through and had tried to forget about. This reenactment wasn't a conscious choice; it was more like an almost involuntary urge brought on by the raw, unaddressed pain that had been carefully stored away. The instinct to attack, which had been sharpened by years of perceived threats and the need to protect oneself, turned into a weapon of revenge, not against a real enemy, but against the ghosts of his past tormentors.

The cyclical nature of his torment was, therefore, an inevitability. Every act of violence and every moment of terror he caused were desperate, though horrible, attempts to face and defeat the ghosts that haunted him. He was trapped in a loop, replaying the tragedy with himself as both the victim and, in a twisted sense, the perpetrator. The helplessness he had felt as a child was being projected outwards, onto those who could not defend themselves, thus momentarily alleviating the suffocating burden of his own inadequacy. He would find a fleeting sense of control, a perverse empowerment, in the fear he instilled, a stark contrast to the abject powerlessness that had defined his formative years. But this short break always led to a deeper descent into the storm of guilt, as the truth of his actions would start to come out once the adrenaline wore off, only to be met with more repression and another inevitable eruption of "Monster John."

This cycle of trauma, repression, and violent re-enactment would always lead to more terrible things in the future. The wounds underneath stayed open and got worse over time. John's mental defenses were weak and likely to fall apart at any moment. Every breakdown and every time he let out his pent-up anger only made the gap inside him bigger, making real healing less likely. The "Monster John" persona, which had once been a desperate way to protect himself, was changing and becoming more independent and entrenched. It was a shadow self that was starting to control his life, and it was never satisfied with being free. The world, unaware of the psychological war raging within him, would soon bear witness to the devastating consequences of a past that refused to stay buried. The echo of his childhood pain was not fading; it was getting louder, gaining strength, and ready to unleash a flood of pain on the innocent. The careful control he had over his life was a weak front, and the cracks were starting to show, letting the horrible thing that was hiding inside him out and ready to eat everything in its path. The violence wasn't an anomaly; it was the inevitable consequence of a mind trapped in the relentless echo of its own past suffering, a past that was dictating the terrifying trajectory of his future. His victims were not random; they were chosen, consciously or unconsciously, as proxies for the deep-seated pain he could no longer contain, a pain that was now manifesting as pure, unadulterated terror. The carefully orchestrated compartmentalization was failing, and the unleashed trauma was finding its horrifying expression in the dark landscape of his predatory actions, foreshadowing a future steeped in the same unspeakable horrors he had once endured.

Chapter 7: Whispers from the Abyss

The Unseen Observer

The chilling certainty of John Vance's death, which was backed up by eyewitness accounts and the grim finality of the ravine, started to fade. It was a subtle unraveling, almost imperceptible at first, like a loose thread on a meticulously woven tapestry. The town, which needed closure and the comfort of knowing that evil had been defeated, held on to the story of John's death. But the human mind is very good at justifying things, and it could also be very open to the constant whisper of doubt, especially when it was in the shadow of something amazing. The official story said that the ravine, a huge hole in the ground, had eaten him whole. Yet, its sheer immensity, its labyrinthine depths, its treacherous terrain – these were factors that defied simple pronouncements. It was a wild place where secrets could grow, and things that weren't supposed to happen often did.

The first signs weren't real proof, not by any means. They were bits and pieces, fleeting impressions that most rational people would write off as the result of an overactive imagination, anxiety from grief, or just the effects of long-term stress. A rustle in the undergrowth where no animal should have been. A shadow that looked like it was coming out of the thick leaves on the edge of my vision. The smell of woodsmoke, which was weak and out of place, came from a place that was supposed to be empty and had been searched by search parties. These were the seeds of unease, planted in the fertile ground of a community still reeling from the horrors John Vance had inflicted. They were the unseen ripples on the surface of a pond, hinting at something disturbed beneath.

Mrs. Gable, whose porch had a wide but far-off view of the edge of the ravine, was one of the first to tell people about these strange things. Even though her eyesight was getting worse in the dim light of dusk, it had always been sharp, and her memory for details was still very good. She said she had seen a figure, blurry and hidden in the twilight, near the dangerous northern slope not just once, but several times over the course of a week. "Just a flicker," she'd insisted to her neighbor, Martha, her voice hushed with an almost reverent trepidation. "Like a deer, but… wrong. Too tall, too still. Then gone." Martha, a pragmatist by nature, had attributed it to Mrs. Gable's macular degeneration, or perhaps a particularly vivid dream. But the doubt had already been planted.

Then there was Timmy Peterson, a young boy known for making things up. He swore he heard a low, guttural humming coming from deep in the ravine late one night when there was no moon. He described it as a sound that "made your teeth ache," a melody devoid of any human warmth, a resonant vibration that seemed to seep from the very rock and earth. His father, a man weary from the long, arduous investigation and the subsequent mourning, had gently chided him, explaining it was likely just the wind whistling through the crevices, or perhaps the distant rumble of a freight train. But Timmy, for all his youthful exuberance, was not prone to fabrication when it came to fear. He had been genuinely terrified, his small face pale and drawn in the dim light of his bedroom. He couldn't shake the feeling that whatever made that noise was still down there, watching.

The local sheriff, a gruff but decent man named Brody, found himself fielding increasingly peculiar calls. Hikers, drawn by the morbid curiosity that often followed such notorious events, reported strange cairns of stones, meticulously arranged in patterns that seemed too deliberate to be natural. Others spoke of discarded items – a single, mud-caked glove, a length of coarse rope that looked unnervingly similar to the kind Vance had been known to favor, a tattered piece of plaid fabric snagged on a thorn bush far from any established trail. Each report, when considered in isolation, was easily explained away. The glove could have been lost by a careless camper. The rope is a remnant of a logging operation that has long since been forgotten. The fabric is a piece of clothing that a hunter lost. But the sheer accumulation of these anomalies, the subtle discord they introduced into the accepted narrative, began to gnaw at Brody. He was a man who believed in facts and proof. Yet, he couldn't entirely dismiss the prickling sensation on the back of his neck, the vague unease that settled over him whenever he drove past the imposing silhouette of the ravine.

These whispers, these sightings that weren't confirmed, and these pieces of strangeness were the observer who wasn't seen. They were the slight change in air pressure that happens before a storm and the almost unnoticeable tremor that suggests something is more unstable below the surface. They were the town's subconscious wrestling with the unsettling possibility that their nightmare might not have ended with the fall. The ravine, with its natural mystery and huge size and depth, was the perfect place for these worries to show themselves. It was a place that naturally made people feel like they didn't know what was going on. It was like a void that took away all certainty and left only questions.

The search parties, initially so thorough, so exhaustive, had focused on the immediate vicinity of Vance's supposed final moments. They had searched the ledges that were easy to get to, rappelled down into the shallower crevices, and dragged the dark pools at the bottom of the ravine. But the ravine was far from fully explored. There were parts that were still full of thick, wild wilderness that only the most experienced climbers or those who didn't care about their own safety could get to. It was within these uncharted territories, these overlooked pockets of wilderness, that the subtle signs began to emerge.

Man Hemlock, a hermit who lived on the fringes of the town, a man whose reputation for eccentricity preceded him, became an unlikely source of corroboration. He rarely interacted with the townsfolk, preferring the solitude of his ramshackle cabin, surrounded by the whispering pines and the watchful gaze of the mountain. But on one of his rare trips to town for supplies, he had Sheriff Brody cornered. His voice was a rough rasp. "I saw smoke," he said, staring at Brody with eyes like chips of flint. "Up near the old hermit's cave. Thought it was a campfire, but… it was different. Flickered in the wrong way. And the smell. Not like pine. Like… like wet dirt and something that smells bad. He was talking about a part of the ravine that was known for being slippery and always wet, a place that even the most experienced hunters stayed away from. Hemlock knew the woods' secrets and hidden dangers because he knew them so well. His description, though vague, resonated with the other scattered reports, creating a disquieting tapestry of the uncanny.

The people in the town also started to speak in low voices, and their conversations became more anxious and speculative. The initial relief at Vance's apparent end had given way to a creeping dread. Children said they had nightmares that were very vivid and scary, with figures hiding in dark, shadowy places. Parents who were once eager to tell their kids that the monster was gone now had trouble keeping that belief. The very landscape seemed to conspire against them. The wind whistling through the trees took on a mournful, accusatory tone. The sound of leaves moving made me think of quiet footsteps. The shadows lengthened, and in their depths, people began to see things that weren't there, or perhaps, were.

A group of teenagers, on a dare to explore the perimeter of the ravine one crisp autumn evening, claimed to have seen a flickering light deep within its shadowed recesses. They described it as a solitary glow, not the steady beam of a flashlight, but a more erratic, almost organic luminescence. They'd dismissed it as a reflection from a distant car or a trick of the moonlight, but the memory lingered, a discordant note in their youthful bravado. One of them, a boy named Kevin, later confessed to his mother that the light had seemed to move, not with the predictable arc of a car's headlights, but with a strange, loping gait, as if something was crawling or stumbling through the undergrowth. He'd been too afraid to call out, too frozen by a primal fear to do anything but watch, his heart hammering against his ribs.

The feeling that they were being watched was pervasive. It was a quiet, sneaky feeling that hung over the town like a shroud. People started locking their doors more carefully, looking nervously into darkened windows, and walking faster when they were alone at night. The ravine, which used to be a clear sign of justice served, had become a place of lingering fear, a place that held the unspoken promise of more terror. The sheer scale of the place was its greatest ally, offering an infinite capacity for concealment, for survival, for the impossible.

Even Sheriff Brody, a man who prided himself on his stoicism, found himself wrestling with the implications. He replayed the details of Vance's apprehension, the desperate struggle, the precarious balance on the ravine's edge. He was sure that the reports were true and that the witnesses were honest. But the nagging thought wouldn't go away: what if the fall wasn't the end? What if the ravines' harsh embrace had been a harsh, primal form of shelter instead? The idea was as scary as it was unlikely, a seed of doubt that, once planted, would not go away. It was the unseen observer, not a real thing, but a feeling that was everywhere, a general unease that whispered through the town, a scary feeling that the darkness hadn't really gone away, just gone deeper into the ground, waiting.

The subtle signs were a testament to the enduring power of fear, and the unsettling resilience of the human – or perhaps, inhuman – spirit. They were the stories told in hushed tones over picket fences, the anxious glances exchanged in the local diner, the fleeting images caught in the corner of one's eye. They were the growing conviction that the seemingly closed case of John Vance was far from over. The ravine, a place of unforgiving beauty and brutal depths, had become a repository of their deepest anxieties, a silent testament to the fact that some monsters, once unleashed, do not simply disappear. They adapt. They last. And sometimes, they find a way to watch from the shadows, their presence felt long after they have seemingly vanished from sight. The collective consciousness of the town was shifting, a slow, almost imperceptible migration away from certainty and towards a disquieting, persistent unease, an unease born from the unnerving possibility that the unseen observer might still be very much alive, and very much aware. The sheer vastness of the ravine meant that any conclusive proof of Vance's death, or indeed his survival, was virtually impossible to obtain, leaving the town suspended in a state of perpetual, unnerving ambiguity. It was a psychological landscape as treacherous as the ravine itself, where the specter of the past continued to cast a long, menacing shadow over the present.

Anomalies in the Investigation

Detective Miller found himself adrift in a sea of paperwork, each document a testament to a case that had been declared closed, a chapter definitively shut. Yet, for him, it was a narrative riddled with unresolved punctuation, a story that stubbornly refused to end. The reports made it clear that John Vance had died in a tragic fall into the unforgiving Blackwood Ravine. But the lingering whispers, the disquieting murmurs that had threaded their way through the town's collective consciousness, had lodged themselves in Miller's mind like shards of glass. He'd been the lead detective, the one tasked with bringing closure, and the weight of that responsibility, coupled with the unsettling anomalies, had become an unbearable burden. At the time, he had dismissed many of them as coincidences: the strange sounds, the misplaced artifacts, and the rumors of strange sounds. He thought they were all due to the town's shared trauma, a desperate attempt to make sense of the things that didn't make sense. Now, in the sterile quiet of his makeshift office, a small, cluttered room in the back of the precinct, those dismissals felt hollow, their justifications flimsy against the persistent tide of doubt.

He pulled out the evidence logs, the photographs, the sworn statements, the sheer volume of which was a monument to their initial exhaustive efforts. He'd been meticulous, he reminded himself, painstakingly thorough. They had searched the ravine, sent out search parties, and talked to everyone who had even a small connection to Vance or the crimes he had committed. It was clear what needed to be done: find Vance, stop the terror, and bring some peace back to Havenwood. And they had found him, or at least, what was presumed to be him, a grim tableau at the bottom of the chasm, reduced by gravity and time into an unrecognizable ruin. The forensics had been conclusive, or so they had believed. The clothing fragments, the bone structure – it all pointed to Vance. But "all pointed to Vance" was a far cry from irrefutable proof, especially when a man like Vance, a man who had demonstrated an almost supernatural ability to elude capture and inflict misery, was involved.

Miller's gaze drifted to a faded photograph, its edges dog-eared from repeated handling. It was a picture taken from a drone that looked at a part of the ravine's western face that was too dangerous for a ground search. This was where the bulk of the search efforts had been concentrated, near the point of Vance's final known location. But this particular section, highlighted by a red marker on the print, was further down, a narrow, almost inaccessible ledge shrouded in thick foliage. During the initial sweep, a glint of something metallic had been spotted, a fleeting anomaly. A quick look around had found a tin can that had been thrown away, was rusty, and was half-buried in the mud. It had been logged as general refuse, the detritus of some careless hiker, and largely ignored. Now, however, the memory of Mrs. Gable's hesitant report about a cloaked figure near the northern slope, and Timmy Peterson's unnerving description of a resonant hum, began to coalesce around this overlooked detail. What if it wasn't just refuse? What if that glint was something more?

He flipped through the witness statements, running his finger over the signatures of people whose words hadn't seemed very important at the time. Old Man Hemlock, the secretive woodsman, had talked about smoke that smelled strange and not like pine. Hemlock was known for his eccentricities, his solitary existence lending itself to tall tales. But Miller recalled the old man's eyes, as sharp and clear as the mountain air, devoid of any embellishment. He had talked about a light that "flickered wrong" and a smell of "wet earth and something rotten." The place Hemlock had mentioned, even though it was only vaguely described, was not far from the ledge that the drone had taken a picture of. Could Hemlock have seen a fire, a signal, a clandestine operation? The thought sent a tremor of unease through him.

Then there were the teenagers, their story of a flickering, moving light dismissed as youthful fancy. Kevin, the one who'd spoken of a "loping gait," had been particularly distraught. Miller had talked to him and seen the real fear on the boy's face. At the time, he'd attributed it to the residual terror Vance had instilled in the town, a collective hallucination born of fear. But what if the light wasn't a hallucination? What if it was a lantern or torch that someone was carrying while walking in a strange way through the dangerous terrain? The ravine was a vast and complex ecosystem, its hidden crevices and shadowed ravines capable of harboring secrets for years.

He took out the forensic reports again and looked over the detailed descriptions of the remains that had been found. The pathology department had done a good job, and their conclusions were based on well-known scientific facts. But there was a footnote, a small detail that didn't seem important at the time but now, with all of these strange things happening, felt like a possible crack in their certainty. The report mentioned the presence of unusual sediment in the nasal passages and lungs of the remains. The study found that it was consistent with being outside for a long time and being buried in wet ground. But the sediment's exact makeup was… strange. It contained traces of a rare, phosphorescent fungus indigenous to the deepest, most inaccessible parts of the ravine, a fungus that typically thrived in anaerobic conditions, far from the sunlight that penetrated even the thickest canopy.

This detail gnawed at him. Yes, Vance had fallen, but did he fall all the way to the bottom of the ravine, or did he somehow survive the first impact, maybe by hiding in a crevice or a secret cave? The sediment suggested that the area had been around for a long time, even though it wasn't clear right away at the site of the discovery. It implied a journey, or a period of confinement, within a part of the ravine that was rarely, if ever, visited.

Miller's gaze fell upon a stack of reports detailing the recovered items from the ravine, items that had been cataloged and stored as peripheral evidence. One of them was a single glove covered in mud that was said to be made of thick, worn leather. The report noted its similarity to gloves Vance had been known to wear, but the similarity was deemed insufficient to definitively link it to him, especially given the circumstances. Alongside it, a length of coarse rope, its fibers frayed and discolored, and a tattered piece of plaid fabric, snagged on a thorn bush. At the time, these had been just more pieces of the grim puzzle, contributing to the narrative of Vance's final moments. But what if they weren't just things that were lost? What if they were placed there, or dropped by someone who had recently traversed those same dangerous paths? The rope, in particular, seemed a critical detail. Vance was known for his agility, his ability to scale seemingly impossible surfaces. Had he used such a rope to navigate a difficult descent, or perhaps, to ascend?

He reached for his car keys, which felt familiar and gave him some comfort. He needed to go back. Not to the ravine itself, not yet. That was a job for a more specialized team, one that was ready for the depths he thought might hold more than just a dead body. He needed to revisit the precinct's archives, to meticulously re-examine the crime scene photographs, the initial search grids, and any other documentation that might have been relegated to the 'unremarkable' pile. He was trying to find a needle in a haystack, a single thread that could pull apart the whole carefully planned story of Vance's death. He was looking for the detail that had been missed, the odd thing that had been ignored, the whisper that had been drowned out by the roar of the end.

The precinct's basement archives were a labyrinth of dusty shelves, filled with the forgotten detritus of countless investigations. The air was thick with the scent of aging paper and stale coffee. Miller navigated the narrow aisles, his flashlight beam cutting through the gloom, his mind replaying the events of Vance's capture and the subsequent search. He remembered the pressure from the town, the desperate need for resolution. The case had left a mark on Havenwood, and Vance's death, no matter how horrible, was seen as the end of that mark. He realized that they had been hurt by their haste. In their eagerness to provide closure, they had perhaps been too quick to accept the simplest explanation, too eager to believe that the darkness had been contained.

He found the box that said "Vance, John—Final Investigation." Inside, there was a messy pile of files, pictures, and other evidence. He started with the crime scene photos, images that still held the power to churn his stomach.

He focused on the little things, the small mistakes that he had missed in his first look. There was a photograph of the area where Vance's body had been found, a steep embankment leading down to a muddy pool. They had figured out the angle of the fall by looking at the path of the debris and the location of the remains. But Miller noticed something in the background, partially obscured by a cluster of dense ferns. It looked like a simple shelter, like a lean-to made of branches and what looked like an old tarp. It was hard to see and easy to miss in the chaos of the scene, and it wasn't mentioned in the first reports. Had Vance, in his final moments, sought refuge rather than succumbing immediately?

He checked this against the drone footage of the ledge that couldn't be reached. The coordinates were close to being right. He felt a shiver go down his spine. This wasn't just about finding a body; it was about understanding the circumstances that led to it. If Vance had survived the first fall and found shelter in the ravine, he might have been able to move around. In that case, the story of a simple, tragic accident would have turned into something much more complicated and much more evil.

Miller remembered a particular witness, a local hunter named Silas Croft, who had reported seeing peculiar markings on the trees near the ravine's edge, not long after Vance's capture. Croft said they were rough symbols that had been scratched into the bark with a sharp object. People at the time thought Croft's story was just the ramblings of a man who had spent too much time alone in the woods. But what if those symbols were Vance's? What if they were a form of communication, a territorial marking, or even a desperate attempt to leave a trail? Miller dug through Silas Croft's statement, his heart pounding. The symbols were not very clear, but the place Croft said they were located was in line with the area around the inaccessible ledge and the place where the lean-to was seen in the picture.

He also looked over the evidence log again for things that had been found in the area around Vance's death, not just the area right next to it. A small, waterproof pouch was found a few hundred yards downstream from the main entrance to the ravine. Inside, a collection of items: a half-eaten energy bar, a small, worn compass, and a tightly folded piece of paper. The paper, the report stated, contained what appeared to be a rudimentary map, but its markings were illegible, smudged beyond recognition. It was thought to belong to a hiker, maybe one who was lost or hurt, and their things had been strewn about. But Miller had a different view now. This wasn't just random litter; it was evidence of survival, of a plan, of a deliberate navigation of the ravine. The map, smudged or not, suggested intent. Vance wasn't just a victim of circumstance; he was a survivor, a planner, and maybe even still alive and working in the hidden depths of Blackwood Ravine. The investigation, he realized, had been concluded with tunnel vision, its focus so narrow that it had missed the broader, more terrifying picture. The anomalies weren't just whispers; they were shouting, and it was time for Detective Miller to finally listen.

Johns Isolation and Survival

John Vance's world didn't end with a bang; it ended with a confusing drop. Blackwood Ravine's jagged embrace was meant to be his grave, a quick and brutal end to a life lived on the edge. But gravity, that uncaring architect of destruction, had been... oddly kind. He hadn't plummeted to his immediate death, a macabre tableau for the inevitable search party. Instead, he had been caught by the gnarled fingers of old trees, and a cruel, jolting embrace had stopped him from falling. He was broken, but still alive.

He woke up to a symphony of pain. His left leg was a useless, throbbing appendage, twisted at an unnatural angle. He thought that the ribs had given up their strength with sickening cracks. Blood, warm and sticky, matted his hair and trickled into his eyes, blurring the already disorienting kaleidoscope of green and brown that surrounded him. Panic, a cold, sharp thing, clawed at his throat. He was trapped, injured, and utterly alone. The instinct to stay alive, a deep, primal current running beneath the surface of his fake personality, surged. He had to move. He had to survive.

The first few hours were a blur of pain and frantic, broken movement. He used the branches of the trees that had fallen as crutches, and his good leg took the brunt of the pain as he moved forward. Every time he moved his weight, white-hot flares shot through his broken limb. The thick brush on the floor of the ravine ripped at his clothes and skin, leaving small, unimportant wounds that were nothing compared to the huge damage he had already done. He was a broken thing, a piece of junk left behind in the wild that didn't care.

Thirst was a constant, nagging friend. His mouth was dry, and his tongue was thick and heavy. He remembered stories, fragments of survival lore gleaned from pulp novels and whispered conversations in the dark. Water. Look for water. He strained his ears, trying to distinguish the murmur of a hidden stream from the rustling of leaves and the distant, mocking cry of unseen birds. Finally, a soft, musical trickle came to him. It was a maddeningly slow crawl, and his body protested every inch he gained. He came to a small spring covered in moss. The water was so cold that it burned his dry throat. He drank greedily, not caring about the possible contaminants. His body's desperate need for water made him ignore any rational caution.

John's mind started to break down as the first rush of adrenaline wore off and he became very tired. The instinct to survive fought with the deeper, more corrosive darkness that had always been inside him. He wasn't a victim; he was a survivor. And those who lived changed. They didn't think about the pain; they used it. His broken mind, laid bare by the ordeal, gave him no comfort or peace. Instead, it amplified his isolation, twisting it into a perverse form of freedom.

He found a shallow overhang, a small cave formed by an ancient rockfall, that offered a meager shelter from the elements. He dragged himself into its damp, earthy interior, the scent of decay and mineral filling his nostrils. This would be both his home and his prison. The days bled into one another, marked only by the shifting patterns of light that filtered through the dense canopy above. He learned how to make the most of the little food he had left over from his body: a half-eaten energy bar and a crumpled pack of stale mints. When those ran out, hunger turned into a dull ache that never went away, with sharp pains that threatened to take over his body.

He became a kind of hunter, but his prey was small and his methods were rough. Grubs and insects, unearthed from rotting logs, became a staple. He chewed on roots, spitting out the bitter ones. His tongue got used to the earthy, often bad tastes. He learned to distinguish the edible from the poisonous through a terrifying process of trial and error, his body a living, breathing laboratory. One wrong move could lead to a painful death, but the depths of his own mind offered a quicker, and maybe better, way to die.

His hurt leg was always hurting. The initial shock had worn off, leaving a deep, throbbing ache that never truly subsided. He tried to splint it, using branches and strips of his own torn clothing, but his injured hand, clumsy and unresponsive, made the task agonizingly difficult. The wound festered, a raw, angry red blooming around the edges. He knew for sure that infection was a real and present danger. But the thought of seeking help, of surrendering himself to the world he had so meticulously escaped, was abhorrent. He made this isolation and this raw, brutal fight happen. It was a sign of how strong he was, a twisted kind of pride.

His mental health got worse along with his physical health. The solitude, which he had once craved as an escape, began to press in on him, a suffocating blanket. He talked to himself, and his voice was a hoarse whisper in the heavy silence. He argued with imaginary figures, replaying past confrontations, relishing the venom he had once spat and now relived with chilling clarity. The lines between what is real and what is not became less clear. He could see shapes in the dark and hear whispers in the wind. These were the voices of the people he had hurt and killed. They were not specters of guilt, but rather companions, distorted echoes of his own fractured consciousness.

He began to explore his immediate surroundings, hobbling on his makeshift crutches. The ravine was like a maze, with beautiful but dangerous places that were hard to find. He discovered small pockets of the ravine that offered more sustenance – patches of wild berries, fungi that, with careful preparation, proved edible. He learned how the sun moved and how the temperature changed slightly to signal the passing of time. He got to know the smells of the forest very well: the damp earth after rain, the sharp smell of pine needles, and the musky smell of animals that he couldn't see.

His thoughts, once sharp and calculating, became more primal, focused on the immediate needs of survival. He had trouble sleeping because of nightmares and the pain from his injuries. He would wake with a start, his heart pounding, convinced that he was being pursued, not by the authorities he had evaded, but by something far more ancient and terrifying. The abyss, as he called it, wasn't just the hole he had fallen into; it was also the emptiness inside of him, a darkness that was growing and taking over all light.

He found a narrow, almost hidden game trail that led deeper into the ravine. It was a path that fewer people used and that was less obvious. It went through thick bushes and over dangerous scree slopes, a path that would have stopped anyone less desperate. He saw it as a way to escape his immediate pain, a secret way to get away, and a way to disappear even more. Every step was a fight, proof of his strong will. He had become an animal, with his complex criminal mind reduced to the basic, desperate need to live. The isolation was like a furnace that changed him into something new, something stronger, and something more dangerous. He was no longer John Vance, the man who had terrorized Havenwood. He was a ghost, a shadow, a whisper in the dark, and proof of the brutal, unyielding power of survival.

The Predator Adapts

The first few weeks in the ravine were a harsh lesson that took away the civilized facade that had once defined John Vance. He had fallen not only physically, but also into a state where instinct was more important than reason. The only things that mattered to him were the gnawing pains of hunger and the constant throbbing of his broken leg. But even in this basic fight for survival, the predator's core was still there, not gone, but changed. For many people, being alone would have driven them crazy, but for him, it was like a crucible that burned away unnecessary thoughts and made his natural ruthlessness sharper. He had always been a planner, a careful architect of chaos, but now that the outside world was reduced to its most basic parts—food, shelter, and the constant threat of death—his predatory mind started to change in scary ways.

His experience of almost dying had, in a strange way, given him a lot of clarity. The huge, uncaring wilderness didn't judge you or have any consequences other than the ones you could see right away. Without outside checks and balances, a chilling self-awareness could grow. He started to see his hurt leg not just as a problem, but as a challenge to be overcome, a problem to be solved with the same cold logic he used to get around the police or trick victims. He learned to use the uneven terrain to his advantage, his gait, though awkward and painful, becoming more deliberate, more efficient. He discovered how to gauge distances with a newfound precision, how to navigate the dense undergrowth with minimal disturbance, becoming a phantom in his own makeshift domain. The ravine was no longer just a place to keep him locked up; it was his training ground.

He learned to speak by noticing small changes in the world around him. He learned to read the forest's quiet signs, like the slight tremor of a leaf that had been disturbed, the fleeting scent that was carried on the wind, and the almost imperceptible snap of a twig under the weight of an unseen creature. Because he was always afraid of dying, his senses became very attuned to these small differences. He would lie for hours, motionless, his broken body a testament to his resilience, his mind a silent observer, cataloging every sound, every movement, every scent. This wasn't just watching a stranded victim; it was a hunter actively scouting its territory, looking for patterns, and figuring out where the prey might be weak. He started to learn how the ecosystem in the ravine worked, how its animals came and went, what they did, and what their weaknesses were. This knowledge, once applied to the exploitation of human beings, was now being redirected towards his own survival, a chilling testament to his adaptability.

His way of doing things, which had scared Havenwood with his evil deeds, didn't go away; they just got better. He had to stop using all the planned theatrics he used to use because of how bad his situation was. There were no big speeches or long-lasting insults, just the pure, unfiltered desire to live and maybe even win. He found himself recalling his past actions, not with remorse or regret, but with a detached, analytical fascination. He looked at his old methods and figured out which psychological buttons he had pushed and which weaknesses he had taken advantage of. The isolation offered him an unprecedented opportunity for introspection, a dark mirror reflecting his own depravity without the distorting lens of societal expectations or legal repercussions. He was rethinking his tools, methods, and understanding of the human mind, all while stuck in his tree prison.

The hunger, once a purely biological imperative, began to take on a different quality. It wasn't just about filling an empty stomach; it was about learning how to get food and outsmarting nature itself. He became almost superhuman at finding edible plants, spotting the tiny signs of insect colonies, and following small game with a level of patience that was almost obsessive. He would watch birds as they looked for food, writing down which berries they liked best and which grubs they found. He learned to mimic their movements, to exploit their own instinctual behaviors. This wasn't just gathering food; it was a way for him to show his intellectual superiority over the natural world, just like he had done with his human prey.

His injured leg, far from being a constant reminder of his weakness, became a peculiar kind of advantage. It made him move and think about how to move in a different way. He learned to utilize leverage and momentum in ways he never had before. He discovered how to scramble over obstacles that would have been insurmountable with two good legs, how to use the dense foliage as a form of camouflage, obscuring his limping gait. He began to practice this altered movement, not just for survival, but for the sheer mastery of it. It was a physical sign of how he was changing, a constant, painful reminder that he was becoming something new, something made from the ashes of his own near-death.

The silence of the ravine, once deafening, began to hum with a different kind of energy. He started to perceive patterns in the seemingly random sounds of the wilderness. The distant hoot of an owl became a marker of time, the rustling of leaves a potential alarm, the chirping of crickets a rhythmic lullaby that masked his own stealthy movements. He realized that the lack of human noise had made his hearing sharper, letting him hear a wider range of sounds. This made him more aware, which made him less likely to be surprised and more likely to notice when something that might be a threat, whether an animal or, hypothetically, a person, was coming. He was a creature of the shadows, and the ravine was teaching him to listen to the whispers of those shadows.

He started to test himself, not out of malice, but out of a detached interest in how far he could push his body and mind. He would push himself to the brink of exhaustion, testing his pain tolerance, his ability to remain focused under duress. He wasn't hurting himself by putting himself through these tests; he was just testing his own abilities in a systematic way. He was setting a new standard for himself, a higher level of what he could handle and what he could do. The man who used to depend on complicated plans and outside help was now finding a source of strength inside himself, a raw, untamed power that had been dormant for years.

The psychological aspect of his adaptation was perhaps the most insidious. The solitude had not broken him; it had purified him. The anxieties, the social pressures, the need for validation that had once plagued him were gone. He was left with his core identity, stripped bare and unvarnished. He no longer had to play a role. He could finally be the monster he had always been, without pretending. He thought about his past victims again, not out of fear of doing it again, but out of a cold, almost scientific interest in how they reacted and what made them weak. He took their fear apart, made a list of it, studied it, and got to know it better. This self-analysis was not about guilt; it was about refining his craft, about understanding the art of fear from a new, profound perspective.

He started to see the ravine not as a place of imprisonment, but as a sanctuary. He was really free there, and the rules of the outside world didn't matter. He was no longer the fugitive John Vance. He was something else, something primal, something that belonged to the shadows and the wild. This sense of belonging, however twisted, was a powerful motivator. It made him more determined to live, not just to get away, but to do well in his new solitude. He started to picture coming back, not as a hurt and broken man, but as a creature reborn, a predator made in the abyss. His near-death experience had not been an end, but a rebirth, a terrifying metamorphosis that had honed his predatory instincts to a razor's edge, preparing him for a future he himself could only begin to imagine. He was not just surviving; he was evolving. He was becoming more than he had ever been.

Seeds of Return

The silence of the ravine had become a strangely comforting cacophony. John Vance was slowly and surely learning how to speak that language. But beneath the acquired tranquility, a different kind of noise was beginning to stir. It wasn't the rustling of leaves or the distant cry of a hawk; it was an internal dissonance, a tremor deep within the bedrock of his being. The prolonged isolation, intended by fate, or perhaps by circumstance, to be his undoing, was instead acting as a fertile ground for something far more insidious to take root. His physical survival, which showed how strong and determined he was, was a win, but wins often came with a cost, and John was starting to feel the weight of it on his soul.

The clarity he had found in the wilderness, the stripping away of societal pretense, had been a powerful, almost intoxicating experience. He had been reborn into a state of pure instinct, like a predator with no guilt or fear of what would happen. Yet, with this newfound self-awareness came a subtle, almost imperceptible shift. At first, his only goal was to survive, but that drive began to mix with something older and more deeply ingrained. It was the return of the architect, the careful planner who loved to be in charge and play with people's fears. The ravine had taught him to hunt, but it was also, inadvertently, teaching him to remember.

He would often find himself staring into the flickering flames of his meager fire, the shadows dancing on the rough-hewn walls of his makeshift shelter, and his mind would drift. It would drift back to the empty luxury of his old life, to the quiet whispers of scared victims, and to the heady rush of having all the power. These were not memories that brought him pain or regret. Instead, they were like old blueprints, carefully preserved, waiting for the right moment to be unfurled. He started to break down those past successes, not like a scientist looking at a specimen, but like an artist remembering their greatest work. He replayed the moments, the subtle inflections of voice, the involuntary flinches, the precise choreography of dread he had so expertly orchestrated. The ravine, in its infinite, indifferent expanse, had become his rehearsal space.

The physical limitations imposed by his shattered leg, once a constant source of frustration, now served a different purpose. They made him think outside the box and come up with new ways to move and approach things. But as his physical strength slowly came back, though in a different way, his mind began to change as well. The ingenuity he applied to navigating treacherous terrain started to bleed into his thoughts about the world beyond the ravine. He began to envision not just his escape, but his return. And with that return came the inevitable question: what would he do with the sharpened instincts, the honed senses, the unblunted ruthlessness he had cultivated in the darkness?

He first noticed it during the quiet times, when he didn't have to worry about staying alive. A stray thought, a fleeting image, a visceral urge that felt both alien and intimately familiar. He would be tracking a rabbit, his movements slow and deliberate, when a memory of a particular victim's scream would flash through his mind, not with a sense of horror, but with a curious, almost nostalgic recognition of the sound. It was as if his past actions were not just echoes, but seeds lying dormant in the fertile soil of his loneliness, waiting for the right time to grow again.

The fear he had once caused in others was a strong drug that he had gotten used to giving out. Not having it in his life now left a hole, a quiet, nagging emptiness that just living couldn't fill. He had conquered his immediate surroundings and tamed the wild to some extent, but the deep desire to impose his will on the chaos of the world and impose his dark order on it remained. The ravine had been a crucible, refining him, hardening him, but it had also, paradoxically, intensified the very urges it had seemingly suppressed. He wasn't broken; he was being remade.

There were times, usually in the dead of night, when the wind howled through the canyon, that he would feel a phantom echo of the terror he had once so expertly manufactured. It felt strange, like hearing a familiar song from a dream you had long ago. He would close his eyes, and the images would flood back – not of his victims' suffering, but of his own calculated machinations. The careful planning, the psychological chess game, and the long, painful wait all came back to him with an almost intoxicating clarity. He realized, with a chilling certainty, that the isolation had not purged him of his desires; it had merely postponed their fulfillment.

The absence of human interaction was a double-edged sword. On the one hand, it had freed him from the constant vigilance needed to avoid being caught and the mental energy needed to keep up the act. On the other hand, it had removed the primary outlet for his deepest, darkest inclinations. He had sharpened his hunting skills to an almost superhuman level, learning to read the small differences in the wild and predict the movements of prey with amazing accuracy. But the wild offered a different kind of challenge, a different kind of reward, than the raw, human fear he had come to crave.

He started to question the narrative of his own survival. Was he merely a fugitive clinging to life, or was he a warrior in strategic retreat, gathering strength for a triumphant return? The latter felt more potent, more aligned with the man he had become. The ravine was not a prison, but a sanctuary, a place where he could shed the constraints of his former identity and embrace the primal force that lay within. He was no longer John Vance, the hunted criminal. He was something more elemental, something that belonged to the shadows, something that understood the language of fear better than anyone.

When he dreamed, it wasn't about his death, but about his rise. He saw himself not as a broken man crawling from the wilderness, but as a force of nature, a storm that had gathered strength in the quiet depths, ready to unleash its fury upon an unsuspecting world. These were not nightmares; they were visions, premonitions of a future he was actively, if unconsciously, building. Instead of breaking him, the trauma of his own downfall gave him a deep understanding of how weak he and others are. And with that understanding came a renewed, terrifying appreciation for the power he wielded.

He began to catalog his every thought, his every instinct, with a renewed intensity. The silence of the ravine was no longer just a space for survival; it was a canvas for his psychological re-evaluation. He wasn't just running away from his past; he was picking it apart, figuring out how it worked, what made it so appealing, and how strong it still is. The predatory urges that had been pushed down by the strong urge to protect oneself were now coming back, not as intrusive thoughts but as a deep, resonant call. He was like a coiled spring, his energy accumulating in the quiet darkness, preparing for the moment of release.

The world outside, he imagined, would have moved on, would have forgotten the monster that had once stalked its streets. But John Vance was not someone who forgot things. He was a creature of meticulous planning and enduring obsession. His absence was not an end; it was merely an intermission. The seeds of his return, nurtured in the dark, fertile soil of the abyss, were beginning to germinate. He was not just surviving the wilderness; he was preparing to reclaim his dominion, to remind the world of the terror it had tried to bury. The silence of the ravine was a deception; it was the deep, ominous hush before a storm.

Chapter 8: The Ripple Effect

Oakhaven's Lingering Unease

By all outward appearances, Oakhaven had tried to hide the ashes of John Vance's reign of terror by making things seem normal. Months had bled into each other, and the town's wounds were only slightly healed by the never-ending cycle of seasons. Spring had melted the frozen ground and coaxed buds out of bare branches. Summer had brought a false warmth, a brief feeling of peace. Before, the sound of children's laughter was muffled by a general sense of fear. Now, it echoed in the parks as they tentatively came back to life. Conversations could be heard through open windows in the evening. But under this facade of recovery, there was a disturbing undercurrent, a tension that was almost tangible and wouldn't go away. The shadow of "Monster John" wasn't a ghost that had been laid to rest; it was a constant, nagging feeling of unease, like a phantom limb that still hurt from being cut off.

The memory of Vance's careful cruelty had become a part of Oakhaven itself. Every flicker of a streetlamp, every creak of an old house, and every rustle of leaves in the wind now had a dark meaning. The ordinary had become extraordinary, not because it was amazing, but because it could be dangerous. When a car backfired in the distance, it would send a wave of fear through a quiet street. People would look up and scan the darkness for a threat that wasn't there but was always in their minds. Neighbors who used to smile and say hi to each other easily now looked at each other with more awareness, and their conversations were filled with a hesitant suspicion. Did they really see that figure hiding in the background? Was that shadow moving too purposefully? Fear had not gone away because Vance was gone; it had changed, becoming sharper and more dangerous.

The police, who seemed to be restoring order, were actually dealing with the same widespread fear that the townspeople were. Every little thing that went wrong, every small crime, was looked at with a level of scrutiny that came from past trauma. A broken window at the bakery and a prowler near the old mill were no longer just normal calls. They were faint but terrifying echoes of how John Vance used to plan things out carefully and kill people without feeling anything. Detective Miller, who had seen a lot of bad things in his life, was haunted by the thought of Vance's intelligence and how he could blend in and operate in plain sight before disappearing back into the shadows. They didn't have any solid leads, and Vance's disappearance was so outrageous that it left a huge hole in their understanding. This showed how much power he still had over their minds.

The local news outlets, which were used to getting sensational headlines from Vance's capture, found themselves subtly increasing the town's worries. Articles, which often used careful language, would talk about "unexplained occurrences" or "heightened police presence," which kept the fear alive, though less obviously. These reports, no matter how well-meaning, reminded Oakhaven that it was weak and that the monster had not really been caught, just… gone. Local officials used the word "rehabilitation" to talk about Oakhaven, but it felt empty, like a shallow attempt to cover up the deep psychological scars.

For those who had been directly affected by Vance's terror, time did not bring them much comfort. The families of the victims were always on high alert, and their lives would never be the same. A knock on the door or a phone call out of the blue still made her heart race. It was a natural instinct to protect herself that had become second nature. The routines of daily life that used to be comforting were now full of triggers that brought back memories of what had been lost. Vance's eerie calm and his ability to control fear with such precision stayed with them all the time, like a dark passenger in their waking hours and a frequent visitor in their nightmares.

Vance's evil seemed to have left its mark on the very landscape of Oakhaven. The huge, boarded-up, and falling-down shape of his old house was a stark reminder of the terrible things that had happened there. People walking by would instinctively speed up, their eyes darting to the dark windows as if they were expecting to see a ghostly figure watching them. People used to see the woods around them as a fun place to hang out, but now they were more cautious about them. The sound of leaves rustling and twigs snapping were now seen through the eyes of Vance's hunting skills. The wilderness that had become his home had also become a symbol of his wild darkness, a place where the impossible had come true.

The town's efforts to rebuild its sense of community also seemed forced. Public events that used to be lively were now quiet. People stood together in groups they knew, talking quietly and smiling a little too hard. Yes, the shared experience of fear had brought them together, but it was a bond made in fear, and that fear could make people feel alone even in a crowd. The unspoken question hung heavy in the air: had Vance really disappeared, or was he just waiting and watching, like a spider in its web, for the right time to attack again? This all-encompassing question, which was never answered and may never be, was the real ghost that haunted Oakhaven. It was a feeling of unease that kept true healing from happening and kept the embers of fear burning. The lack of concrete proof of Vance's return did nothing to calm the growing paranoia; in fact, it seemed to make it worse, letting people's imaginations run wild with the scary possibilities. The town, which was desperate for closure, was instead stuck in a cycle of anxiety, which shows how deeply and lasting John Vance's reign of terror affected them. The silence that followed his supposed death wasn't a peaceful one; it was a pregnant hush, a breath held in anticipation of a threat that might never fully materialize but had become a permanent resident of Oakhaven.

The Detectives Obsession

The flashing neon sign for "Rosie's Diner" lit up the rain-soaked asphalt in a bright way, making it a beacon in the dark, oppressive Oakhaven night. Detective Miles Corbin held a lukewarm cup of coffee in his hand. The bitter taste was something he was used to. The town slept outside, or at least pretended to. The people inside were lulled by the fake calm that had settled over the town like a shroud since John Vance's reign of terror had suddenly ended. But Corbin couldn't afford to sleep; it was a fragile peace that he fought against. His nights were a never-ending digging, a trip back into the void that Vance had so skillfully created.

The case files, which were stacked precariously on the worn vinyl seat of the diner booth, were always with him. They were more than just paper and ink; they were pieces of a puzzle that wouldn't fit together and pieces of a nightmare that wouldn't go away. Vance. The name itself was a poisonous whisper in Corbin's head, like a ghost limb that kept twitching. Officially, Vance was dead, a victim of his own carefully planned death, lost in the harsh wilderness around Oakhaven. The official report, written by men who had never really dealt with Vance's terrifying intelligence, was a neat ending, a neat bow on a very disturbing package. But Corbin couldn't agree. He wouldn't.

His coworkers, who hadn't been forced to retire early or move to a different, less stressful jurisdiction, had tried. Captain Davies, a man whose gut was as thick as his sense of practicality, had given soft warnings at first, then stronger orders. "Vance is dead," he said, his voice full of tiredness that matched Corbin's own. The town is getting better. You should do it too. Davies, on the other hand, didn't get it. He hadn't spent weeks going over Vance's carefully kept journals, following the twisted paths of his logic, or feeling the cold tendrils of his intelligence wrap around his own thoughts. He hadn't seen the small inconsistencies and almost invisible cracks in the story that everyone else had easily accepted.

Corbin's obsession didn't come from a desire for fame or a need to prove himself. It was a deep, primal feeling that something was very wrong, a discordant note in the symphony of Oakhaven's supposed recovery. Vance was a master of trickery, a puppeteer who loved to pull strings from behind the scenes. It felt like his last act, his final, grand illusion, when he disappeared so cleanly and completely. Corbin didn't see it as an end; he saw it as a brilliant act of misdirection.

He had looked at every piece of evidence, every photo, and every witness statement a thousand times. He had gone back to the empty woods where Vance's supposed remains had been found, the burned-out remains of a campsite that seemed too staged and too convenient. He'd spent hours looking at the grainy security footage from the night of Vance's last known movements, looking for a hint of doubt or a moment when the cold calm that had become his trademark slipped. He even talked to forensic anthropologists and told them to look at the little biological evidence again to see if there were any signs that the identification might have been wrong. Their polite, professional refusals only made him more determined.

Vance's reign of terror was marked by the careful way he committed his crimes. He didn't just pick his victims at random; he picked them with terrifying accuracy, dissecting and understanding their lives before killing them. Vance had looked into their lives, learned their routines, their weaknesses, and their biggest fears. He had moved among them like a wolf in sheep's clothing, and no one noticed him until he decided to show himself. Then he was gone. There was no trace, no whisper, and no loose end that the story of his death couldn't easily explain away. That part bothered Corbin the most. Vance was too smart and too careful to do something so final without a reason.

He thought back to the days right after Vance's supposed death, when everyone in Oakhaven felt a huge sense of relief. The town let out a collective breath, and the fear that had been suffocating them for a moment lifted. But for Corbin, the quiet that came after the screams was scarier than the screams themselves. It was the quiet of a predator waiting for its prey, the quiet of a carefully set trap. He could see it in the townspeople's eyes, the quick glances, the nervous tremors, and the way they still jumped at loud noises. They wanted to believe Vance was gone, but the part of them that had been hurt beyond repair knew better.

Corbin's personal life had suffered because of his pursuit. His marriage fell apart because of the stress. His wife, Sarah, couldn't stand the constant shadow that Vance cast over their lives. "You're not here, Miles," she begged, her voice raw with a pain he couldn't ease. "You're lost even when you're at home." You're looking for ghosts. He had tried to explain how Vance's influence was sneaky and how certain it was that he was still out there, a ghost in the background. But the words didn't seem enough, and the explanations didn't make sense. Sarah finally left, taking with her the last bits of the life Corbin had known. All he had left were the case files and the nagging obsession.

His bosses thought his dedication was a dangerous obsession. Detective Harding, a young officer who wanted to make a name for himself, had once openly made fun of Corbin's constant questions. "Still chasing boogeymen, Detective?" he sneered, his voice full of youthful arrogance. Corbin just looked back at him, his own eyes hard and steady. "Some monsters don't stay buried, Harding. Especially the ones who know how to hide in plain sight. Captain Davies had given him a formal reprimand for the comment, along with a stern lecture about how things are done in the department and how important it is to move on. But Corbin couldn't let it go. He wouldn't stop until he had answers, until he could be sure that Vance was either really gone or still a threat.

The obsession had turned into a lonely trip. He felt more and more alone, and his coworkers looked at him with a mix of pity and fear. He was the detective who couldn't let go. He saw Vance's shadow in every strange thing that happened, and he haunted the empty office late at night, bathed in the pale glow of his computer screen. His apartment had turned into an extension of his office, with maps of Oakhaven and the wilderness around it covering the walls, marked with pins and strange notes. There were notes about Vance's friends, his money problems, and his mental state. It was all there, a jumbled picture of a mind focused on one thing.

He had begun to see patterns and small connections that other people had missed. There had been a lot of small acts of vandalism in the town in the months after Vance went missing. For example, a window was broken at the library, graffiti was painted on the town hall, and there were a lot of other small acts of destruction that seemed random. Each one by itself was not important and could easily be explained away as the actions of bored teens. Corbin, on the other hand, saw a disturbing echo of Vance's methods: his ability to make people feel uneasy and chip away at the town's fragile sense of security. Were these just random events, or were they planned to see how the town and he would react?

He had even started to think that there might be a link to a string of unexplained disappearances in nearby towns, cases that had been quickly closed because there wasn't enough evidence. If Vance were still alive, could he be working farther away, using the hunting skills he learned in Oakhaven to hunt in new places? The thought made him shiver, and a cold fear gripped his chest. It was no longer just about Oakhaven; it was also about stopping a monster who had shown he could avoid capture and stop more tragedies from happening.

It was becoming clear that his obsession was taking a toll on his body. Dark circles had settled under his eyes for good, and his once sharp features were now lined with tiredness and a grim determination. He lived on old donuts and lukewarm coffee, and his body was just a way for his mind to keep going. He slept in fits and starts, and Vance's creepy smile and disembodied laughter haunted his dreams.

Corbin was looking at a picture of Vance one very late night when the rain was pounding on the diner window. The picture was from a better time, a community picnic from years before the terror started. Vance, who was younger then, smiled widely, and his eyes were bright and full of warmth that seemed completely strange now. Corbin ran a rough finger along the edge of his face. Vance was very careful and paid close attention to every little thing, even when he wasn't committing crimes. It was in the way he looked, talked, and moved. And it was how he vanished.

He remembered a small detail from the first investigation that had seemed unimportant at the time. Vance was a creature of habit and didn't like to leave any of his things behind. But at the place where he was thought to have died, some things were found that looked like they had been put there. A silver Zippo lighter, a leather-bound notebook that had seen better days, and a single, tarnished silver cufflink. Were these the unintentional remains of a man in need, or were they planned breadcrumbs left for a certain group of people? Corbin felt a rush of adrenaline and a new sense of purpose. Vance was too smart to be careless. If these things really belonged to Vance, they felt like a message. A tease.

He took out a new notebook and started to write quickly with his pen. He started to draw, to make diagrams, and to connect the threads that seemed to be unrelated. The cufflink. He had seen a similar design in a fashion magazine that Vance used to read. The lighter—Vance had been a smoker, but he always liked disposable Bic lighters better than fancy silver Zippos. The notebook was also strange. Vance wrote a lot, but his journals were always in plain black covers, not the old, embossed leather that was found. These things didn't belong to Vance, or if they did, they were carefully chosen and arranged to create a certain effect.

This was it. This was the crack in the armor, the small difference that screamed of lies. Vance was still alive in that empty clearing. He had planned his own death and carefully set up his own disappearance. But why? And where had he gone? The questions were like fire in Corbin's mind, feeding his obsession. He was sure, deep down in his bones, that Vance was still out there. He knew that this lonely, all-consuming quest was the only thing that stood between Oakhaven and the monster that had, for the time being, gone back into the shadows. He had made a promise to himself and the town that had been through so much to find out the truth, no matter what it cost. The hunt had just started, and the night was still young.

New Patterns New Fears

The first wave of relief that swept over Oakhaven after John Vance's supposed death had long since faded, leaving behind a constant, low-level hum of worry. Detective Miles Corbin, on the other hand, thought that "unease" was an understatement. He thought it was a carefully planned change, a small adjustment to the fear level that would keep the town on edge without causing the full-blown panic that had characterized Vance's rule. The open, brutal acts of violence were gone. Instead, there was a more subtle kind of terror that played on people's perceptions and made them doubt. It was Vance's signature, which showed how good he was at psychology. He hadn't just stopped existing; he had changed and adjusted his strategies to fit this quieter phase of his game.

Corbin first noticed the small changes not in quiet whispers or scared looks, but in the boring reports that came across his desk. A series of small acts of vandalism, which at first were thought to be the work of bored teens, started to show a disturbing pattern. It wasn't just random damage; the defacement had a planned, almost artistic quality to it. Someone had painted a single, bright red symbol on the town's beloved war memorial, a bronze soldier standing guard in the middle of the square. Corbin knew it right away from Vance's journals: a stylized raven, a common symbol that Vance used to show off his intelligence and ability to observe and attack from above. This wasn't just a random act; it was a statement, a scary message to anyone who was paying attention.

Then there was the event at the Oakhaven Public Library, which is a place where people go to think quietly. Over the course of one night, the books on the shelves had been carefully moved around so that they were in a specific, thematic order that made Corbin shiver. There were books about local history next to books about folklore and mythology, and there were also books about how to manipulate people's minds and how to hide. It was a carefully chosen collection of information, a subtle, intellectual tease, as if Vance were saying,

"I am still here, and I still have the knowledge that once fascinated you." The librarians were confused and thought it was just a prank by people who were really into certain genres, but Corbin saw the careful planning and the true purpose behind it. It was too exact and too much like Vance's known interests to be a mistake.

There was no denying the ripple effect. The community tried to keep up appearances of normalcy, but the small acts of intimidation slowly eroded their sense of safety. The red raven symbol, which first appeared on a lamppost near the school and then on the back door of the town's only grocery store, became a sign of trouble. It wasn't a violent threat, but it was a constant reminder that the darkness was still there. People in Oakhaven began to watch their kids more closely, conversations in the town square became quieter, and the town's once-busy atmosphere seemed to be stuck in a permanent twilight. Corbin could feel the change, the fear that was getting stronger, and the quiet paranoia that Vance had so skillfully built up.

He was drawn to the edges of Oakhaven, to the places that Vance might have thought were his own. The old mill on the edge of town, which had been left to rot as a reminder of Oakhaven's industrial past, became a popular place to hang out. Corbin would spend hours there, and the only sounds were the creaking of old wood and the scurrying of things he couldn't see. He was looking for a sign, a clue, anything that would prove his gut feeling that Vance was still around. He would run his fingers over the graffiti, feeling a strange connection to the familiar raven symbol carved into the crumbling plaster. He understood the mind that had planned these subtle provocations in a sick way.

The local newspaper was excited to report on the town's recovery at first, but then it started getting letters from people who didn't want to be known. They weren't threatening or demanding; instead, they were philosophical, asking rhetorical questions about fear, the illusion of safety, and the lasting power of the human mind. Eleanor Vance, the editor, called them the ramblings of a disturbed person, but Corbin saw the sophisticated vocabulary, the carefully thought-out arguments, and the nihilistic worldview that was similar to Vance's own. He thought that Vance might be using these letters to see how people were reacting, to see if his message was getting through and if the seeds of doubt he was planting were taking root. This was a very advanced type of psychological warfare that was done in secret.

Corbin's investigation into the town's seemingly random events started to show a bigger, scarier picture. He noticed that there were a lot more stray animals than usual in the weeks after Vance went missing. Corbin thought of Vance's interest in animal behavior, his ideas about pack dynamics, and the basic instincts that kept animals alive, even though they didn't seem to have anything to do with each other. He remembered certain parts of Vance's journals that talked about how he had watched and changed the behavior of the animals in the area. Now, packs of wild dogs roamed the edges of town, which was a small disturbance to the peaceful scene. People said they were seeing more foxes in neighborhoods, and there were even rumors of a big, very aggressive coyote near the edge of the woods. Was this just a coincidence, or was Vance, in his own sick way, causing a small ecological disturbance that mirrored the social unrest he was creating? It was a long shot, but Corbin knew that Vance would think about every little thing.

The vandalism also started to mean something more specific and symbolic. The red raven showed up not only on public buildings, but also on the homes of well-known people who had spoken out against Oakhaven's return to normalcy. A tiny, almost invisible scratch on a car door or a single dead bird on a doorstep were not acts of aggression; they were planned acts of intimidation. They were meant to make people uneasy, cause trouble, and make them doubt their own safety and that of their neighbors. It was a quiet, mental siege meant to weaken the town's trust from the inside. Corbin was more and more sure that Vance was no longer working alone. The complexity and number of these events pointed to a network, maybe a group of people who had been recruited or influenced by Vance.

He went back to the case files from the first investigation and read through the details of Vance's supposed last days. He paid attention to the things that were found at the campsite, which he had previously thought were fake. The tarnished cufflink, the leather-bound notebook, and the silver Zippo lighter. He no longer thought of them as random leftovers, but as deliberate signs. He realized that the notebook didn't have Vance's own thoughts in it. Instead, it had carefully copied passages from different philosophical and psychological texts that had been subtly changed to fit Vance's twisted view of the world. There was a small, almost invisible crest on the Zippo lighter. It was a heraldic symbol that Corbin vaguely remembered from an old Oakhaven family tree. This family had fallen out of favor decades ago. After a lot of hard work, he found out that the cufflink was a specific design from a long-gone luxury brand. It was a piece that antique jewelry collectors would have loved. These things weren't just random objects; they were coded messages that someone was supposed to figure out or that a certain observant detective was supposed to find.

Corbin's growing suspicion was that Vance hadn't just vanished; he had planned a careful rebirth. His presence in Oakhaven, or at least his influence, was slowly coming back, like poison getting into the water supply. The town was getting better, but it was only on the surface, like putting a bandage over a wound that was still hurting. Vance was playing a long game, and Corbin was afraid that he was the only one who really understood how high the stakes were. The new patterns of fear were more complicated, more sneaky, and a lot more dangerous because they were harder to understand and fight. They were the whispers in the dark, the shadows at the edge of sight, and the slow, creeping fear that Vance had always been good at creating. He was testing the waters and the town's strength, and Corbin knew that this was just the start of his planned return. Once again, the raven had flown away.

The NearVictims Struggle

The quiet in Clara's small apartment was fragile and could be broken by the sound of floorboards creaking or the sound of a siren in the distance. Every sound, no matter how harmless, made her heart race, her muscles tense, and her breath catch in her throat. It had been eighteen months since she had seen the inside of John Vance's private cabin. It had been eighteen months since she had fought her way out of the suffocating darkness and into a kind of freedom. But the freedom felt like a coat that someone else had borrowed, didn't fit right, and was likely to slip off at the first hint of wind.

Her days were carefully planned to keep the monsters away. She woke up before dawn and walked quickly through the streets of a town that still felt strange to her. Then she went straight to the bakery where she worked. The rhythmic kneading of the dough, the comforting smell of yeast and sugar, and the mindless chatter of early morning customers were all things that kept her grounded. She found comfort in the things that were certain, like the flour on her hands and the warm glow of the ovens. It was very different from the scary, unpredictable things that had always been a part of her life.

But even the most ordinary things were dangerous. A careless word, a quick movement, or a shadow that fell too long could all bring back memories of her time in captivity. She would stare blankly at a customer's face, lost in the echoing emptiness of Vance's cellar. The smell of burnt toast could take her back to the cabin, where the smoke smelled bad and she was scared of the fire he had promised to start. She would have to go to the back room, where her hands would shake and she would focus on her breathing and the solid feel of the stainless steel counter under her fingers until the shaking stopped.

Dr. Ramirez, Clara's therapist, had been very helpful in guiding her through the dangerous terrain of her trauma. They met once a week, and their sessions were a safe place for Clara to talk about the heavy burden of her past. Dr. Ramirez was patient, and her voice was like a soothing balm as she helped

Clara untangle the roots of her fear. She taught Clara how to ground herself, how to deal with things, and how to slowly and painfully rebuild trust in herself, in others, and in the world outside.

Dr. Ramirez would often say to her, "He's gone, Clara," and she would look at him with steady, reassuring eyes. "John Vance is gone." "You are safe."

Clara held on to those words and said them over and over again. But the echo of Vance's scary words and the fact that he always seemed to show up when she least expected it made her resolve weaker. She remembered how casually cruel he was, how smart he was, and how he could turn her own thoughts against her. He wasn't just a killer; he was also a master of psychological warfare and a manipulator. And the fear that he could just show up again, that the peace they had worked so hard to build could be broken in an instant, was always there.

She stayed away from the news, especially the ones about Oakhaven. The town used to be a lively community, but now it meant something dark to her. She didn't want to go back to its shadows, hear its quiet whispers, or feel its very real unease. She had run away in a panic and had no plans to look back. But it seemed that Oakhaven had a way of getting in the way of her carefully planned life.

A few weeks ago, a small, local newspaper that she didn't ask for showed up in her mailbox. It was a flyer from a regional distributor. She was about to throw it away, but the headline "Oakhaven Residents Report Strange Incidents" caught her eye. Her heart was in her throat. She quickly read the article, her eyes moving over the strange acts of vandalism and scary events. The symbol of the red raven. It was there, and the way it was described was very cold. She felt cold blood. It was Vance. He was back. The certainty, quick and harsh, hit her like a cold wave.

She had been very anxious for the next few days. Every shadow seemed to grow longer, and every car she didn't know parked on her street made her spine tingle with fear. She looked closely at people's faces, looking for a sign of recognition or a flash of the predatory glint she remembered seeing in Vance's eyes. She was sure, and it scared her, that if Vance was really back in action, she would be one of the first to know. Her heightened sensitivity to his presence, which was a result of her extreme trauma, had become both a curse and a possible warning system for her.

One night, as she was walking home from work, she saw a man standing across the street from her apartment building. He was plain and unremarkable, with a dark jacket and a baseball cap pulled low over his eyes. But the way he stood still and seemed to be watching her building made her teeth hurt. Her heart raced as she sped up. She didn't look back, but the feeling of being watched stayed with her, and a cold fear crept up her spine.

After she got inside her apartment, she locked the door and checked the deadbolt twice. She looked through the peephole, but there was no one on the street. But the unease stayed. There was a small change in the air, but Clara could feel it. It was the same feeling she had in the days before Vance was caught, a low hum of evil that seemed to come from the air itself.

She tried to ignore it, saying it was just paranoia from her past trauma. But the memory of the article in the newspaper, which talked about the raven symbol, kept coming back to her. Vance was good at playing psychological games and making people feel scared by bringing up their deepest fears. He was gone, but his twisted legacy and influence seemed to be coming back to life.

Clara picked up her phone and held her fingers over Dr. Ramirez's number. She thought about it. What could she say? "I think someone is watching me"? "I saw a man who made me feel uneasy"? It sounded like the ramblings of someone who was losing their mind. She didn't want to be afraid and be a victim again. She had worked so hard to take back her life and be more than just the girl who got away from John Vance.

But as she looked out her window at the street below, which was only dimly lit, a new kind of fear began to grow. It wasn't the fear that kept her from moving; it was a deeper fear, a premonition. She remembered the little things that Vance had been obsessed with and the subtle ways he had used to control his victims. He was a creature of routine and pattern. And if he really did come back, it wouldn't be a sudden explosion of violence; it would be a slow, creeping rise.

Clara knew for sure that she was at the front lines of whatever Vance was planning. She was still alive, which made her a living proof of his cruelty and, she thought with a shiver, maybe his biggest failure. But now it looked like she might also be an unintentional sign of his return. The shadow that had fallen over Oakhaven, which she had tried so hard to get away from, was getting longer, and she had a terrible feeling that it was already reaching for her. Finally, she called Dr. Ramirez's number. When she spoke, her voice was barely a whisper. "Dr. Ramirez," she said, her voice shaking. "I think he might be back."

A Pattern of Psychological Warfare

The strange things that were happening in Oakhaven were more than just vandalism or a few people feeling uneasy. Clara, even from the distance she had put between herself and others, felt the sneaky tendrils of a familiar pattern. It wasn't the violent outburst she had seen with her own eyes; it was something much more planned, a slow burn meant to destroy the town's peace. If "Monster John" was still alive, this was a new phase for him. Psychological attrition, a more advanced and terrifying type of warfare, had taken the place of the open violence and raw, primal fear that had characterized his last reign of madness.

She was becoming more and more afraid that John Vance had always had a strange kind of intelligence. It was a smart person who loved to play with fear and the beautiful pain of waiting. His past actions, the careful choice of victims, and the carefully staged scenes all showed that he knew how to use suggestion and how doubt could damage a person's mind. It looked like he had improved his skills now. The red raven, which he had once used as a simple signature with a rough, almost artistic touch, was no longer just a signature. It was a whisper in the dark, a promise of threats that were not seen. Each time it showed up, whether it was written on a fence post or spray-painted on a store window, it was a planned act of psychological warfare meant to cause fear and disagreement.

The people of the town, who had no idea how deep the darkness had once wrapped around them, were now feeling it come back in a more sneaky way. It wasn't the sudden, sharp shock of a violent attack; it was the slow, gnawing worry of not knowing. The broken windows, the statues that had been vandalized, and the strange phone calls that came in late at night and were eerily quiet were not just random acts of vandalism. They were carefully planned disruptions, each one a small crack in the foundation of Oakhaven's collective mind. It seemed that Vance was no longer just trying to hurt them; he wanted to take away their sense of safety and turn their own minds into tools of their torture.

Clara remembered how Vance had messed with her mind and made her doubt her own senses and sanity. He had enjoyed how confused she was and how far apart what she knew to be true and what he made her believe were. This new campaign was just another part of that same sneaky plan, a bigger use of his sick art. He was no longer going after just one person; he was going after the whole community, using their shared weakness as his battlefield. The strange things that were happening here and there, even if they seemed small to someone who wasn't there, were the first signs of this psychological war. Vance was seeing how the town would react and getting ready for something much worse.

The change from open violence to mental manipulation was a chilling sign of Vance's ability to change and his unwavering dedication to his sick goals. It indicated a more profound, strategic perspective, acknowledging the enduring effects of fear even after the physical threat had diminished. He was moving past the immediate thrill of fear and into the long-lasting power of dread. At first, Clara's fear was her own, but now it was a shared, widespread thing that hung over Oakhaven like a shroud. He was taking back control not by using physical force, but by changing how people saw things, making everyone feel like they could be a target, and breaking down the trust that holds a community together.

The red raven symbol itself was a brilliant piece of psychological warfare. It was a ghost from his past crimes that had come back to haunt him in the present. It wasn't just a sign that it had come back; it was a psychological weapon meant to bring back memories of his reign of terror, remind the town of how weak they were, and fan the flames of their deepest fears. For those who remembered how brutal it was, it was a scary sign of things to come. It was an unsettling sign for those who had only heard the quiet stories. Vance knew how powerful symbols could be because they could tap into deep-seated fears and shared memories. He was using the raven to tell a story about his return, to make it seem like it was going to happen no matter what, and to convince Oakhaven that he was an unstoppable force.

The article Clara found in the newspaper, which reported on "strange incidents" in a detached way, was exactly the kind of subtle way Vance would have spread the word. It wasn't an open statement of his presence, but a carefully controlled leak of information meant to make people uneasy without showing his hand. He did well when things were unclear and in the dark. He could make the town's fear worse without getting involved by letting rumors and suspicions grow. The local authorities, who probably thought the problems were too small to matter, wouldn't be able to see the bigger picture of the planned psychological torture. They would be chasing shadows, treating symptoms while the real problem—Vance's sneaky plan—kept happening without them seeing it.

This change in Vance's way of doing things scared Clara the most. It was a real prison that she had to get out of. But this new kind of terror was an attack on the mind, a distortion of reality itself. It was a kind of control that was much harder to get away from, a darkness that could get into even the safest places. The man who had once locked her in a cellar was now trying to lock up an entire town in a state of constant fear, making them prisoners of their own fears. He was showing that his ability to be cruel wasn't limited by physical boundaries; it was an expanding force that could reach out and touch everyone.

It was scary how smart this campaign was. It talked about a mind that hadn't been broken by its past run-ins with the law or by being held captive, if he had been held captive. Instead, it looked like it had been sharpened and honed by what it had been through. Vance wasn't just a killer who acted on impulse; he was a strategist and a tactician of terror. He knew that the best way to break someone's spirit wasn't to destroy it right away, but to slowly take away their hope and make them feel scared all the time. He was creating an environment where people would start to doubt each other, suspect their neighbors, and isolate themselves—exactly the conditions that would make them most vulnerable.

Clara knew how the ripple effect worked. Her own survival and escape from Vance's grip had thrown his carefully planned world off balance. He had been caught, and his methods were made clear. But if he was really in charge of these new events, it meant he had learned from his mistakes. He knew that confronting someone directly was dangerous and that going back to his old ways would probably get him caught quickly. Instead, he was playing a longer, more subtle game that would let him get back some control and power without drawing too much attention right away. He was weaving a web, and every little thing that happened was another strand, carefully placed to trap the town in a suffocating fear.

The red raven wasn't just graffiti; it was a psychological trigger that reminded them of the predator that was hiding just out of sight. It was a promise that the darkness hadn't really gone away; it was just waiting, changing, and getting ready to attack again. Vance was no longer just a person; he was a legend, a monster. By bringing back his symbol, he was bringing that legend back to life, making it real again, and bringing back the fear he had once caused. This wasn't just random acts of violence; it was a planned and systematic effort to spread fear, a brilliant act of psychological warfare meant to break the town's spirit and regain his power through widespread fear. He was showing a scary level of intelligence behind the craziness, a planned accuracy that made him even more dangerous than before. Clara felt sick when she realized that his main goal was not just to scare people, but to paralyze an entire community, make them relive their worst nightmares, and finally break them, one psychological blow at a time.

Chapter 9: The Predator's Return

The First Signs of Revival

For weeks, there had been a low hum of unease in Oakhaven, but it suddenly turned into a deafening scream. It started with a call from Mrs. Gable, the owner of the old bookstore on Elm Street. She was frantic and choked up. When Sheriff Brody finally understood her, her voice, which was usually as steady and calming as the smell of old paper, was a shaky tremor. She was cleaning out the back room, which doesn't get much use, when her broom got stuck on something under a pile of old newspapers. She thought at first that it was a tear in the floorboards, but it was something more planned and evil.

His stomach turned when Brody got there. The air in the bookstore was thick with the sickly sweet smell of decay, which always seemed to cling to the edges of Oakhaven's beautiful facade. Mrs. Gable stood near the counter, her face pale and her hands wringing, her eyes wide with fear that matched the growing fear in Brody's own chest. He had been sheriff long enough to know the signs of real fear. The back room was dark, and the light that came through the dirty window made dust motes dance. And there, under the yellowed pages of old local histories, was where the bad smell came from.

It was a small, poorly made wooden figure, no bigger than a child's doll, but the details were very accurate. Its arms and legs were bent at strange angles, and its head hung to one side in a strange way. But it was the face, or rather, the attempt at a face, that made Brody feel sick again. Two sharp pieces of dark glass were pushed into the wood where eyes should be, and they shone in the dim light. And then he saw it, written in what was clearly dried, dark blood on the effigy's chest: a single, bright red raven. The symbol, which used to be a scary footnote in Oakhaven's darkest chapter, was now a loud declaration.

This was not a random act of vandalism. This was a sign. And Brody knew for sure that the messenger was John Vance. This knowledge made his stomach feel like a block of ice. The statue was too planned out and too symbolic. It was a twisted version of the victims Vance had so cruelly tormented, a reminder of the evil that had once held Oakhaven captive. The care that went into building it, the gruesome details, and most importantly, the unmistakable mark of the red raven all pointed to the predator's return. People in the town had talked about weird things happening, like unsettling graffiti and a growing sense of unease. But it was easy to write them off as the work of bored teens or the lingering worries of a community trying to move on from the past. But now there was no doubt.

The news spread quickly through Oakhaven, fanned by the cold wind of fear that had come back. People who were whispering turned into people who were screaming in fear. The red raven, which had once only been a nightmare for a few people, was now a part of the town's collective mind. It wasn't just a mark; it was a return. The shock was so strong that it knocked the breath out of Oakhaven. People who had tried to convince themselves that the past was really over and that Vance was either dead or locked up forever had to face the scary truth that he was still alive and, worse, that he was back.

Sheriff Brody was on the phone with Clara, and his voice was tight with a grim sense of urgency that matched the fear that was now coming from every part of Oakhaven. "It's him, Clara," he said, his voice heavy with a burden he had hoped to never have to carry again. "The statue in Mrs. Gable's bookstore had the raven. And the… how it was made. You can't be wrong about it. It's the same careful horror. He went into great detail about the scene, and with each word, his voice got quieter. He painted a picture of the gruesome discovery that was slowly but surely tearing down any peace Oakhaven had managed to build.

Clara listened, her heart like a heavy stone in her chest. She had felt it, right? The small change in the air, the darkness that had been slowly creeping into their lives. She had pushed it aside as her own lingering fear, a ghost of something bad that had happened to her in the past. But Brody's confirmation was a brutal fall back into the abyss. "The effigy…" she whispered, her voice barely audible. "He used to make those, didn't he?" Little, twisted things. To make fun of them."

"Yes," Brody said, and the word was full of tired fear. "He did." And this one… It has the same horrible art style. The eyes made of glass and the twisted limbs. And the black bird. Clara, written in blood. Not this time paint. "Real blood." He stopped, and the silence on the other end of the line was full of fear that wasn't spoken. "This isn't just vandalism anymore. This is a sentence. He's back again. And not only is he leaving his mark, but he's also making sure everyone knows it.

The suggestion hung in the air like a heavy blanket. Not only was John Vance, the man behind their worst fears, still alive, but he was also working to bring back his reign of terror. The carefully crafted illusion of normalcy that Oakhaven had held on to was shattered when they found that small, blood-stained statue. The random events of the past few weeks, which had been written off as isolated acts of mischief, were now seen in a terrifying new light: the planned, deliberate beginning of a full-blown resurgence. Vance wasn't just coming back; he was making a terrifying, visceral announcement of his presence.

The town reacted right away and in a big way. The quiet worries of the past few weeks turned into a full-blown panic. Doors that had been left open were now locked. The kids stayed inside, and instead of laughing, they whispered in fear. People on the street who used to be friendly now all had the same unspoken fear. The air in Oakhaven felt thicker, as if it was full of the memories of what John Vance could do. The red raven, which had once been a sign of a terrible event in the past, was now a sign of a terrible event in the present, a clear and undeniable sign that the monster had come back.

Brody told more, but his voice was strained. Clara, they found it stuffed inside an old display case. Put away like it was a hidden treasure, a horrible prize. Mrs. Gable found it while cleaning out the back to give away some old books. When I got there, she was screaming. A sound that was raw and pure, and it still rings in my head. He took a deep, shaky breath. "The town is in a panic. People are scared. They're talking about leaving and blocking themselves in their homes. Clara, they remember. They can't stop thinking about what he did, and the thought of him coming back is breaking them.

He talked about what was going on at the bookstore, how quiet and respectful the few people who dared to look were, and how efficiently his deputies secured the area. The blood, which was dark and thick, had dried into a dark stain on the rough wood, showing how serious the killer was. The effigy itself was a disturbing work of macabre art. Its shape suggested great pain, and its glass eyes showed a chilling emptiness. Brody talked about how they were carefully writing down every detail and putting the effigy in a bag as proof, but he knew, with a certainty that ate at him, that this was more than just proof. It was a call to arms.

"We've sent out a warning to everyone in town," Brody said in a low voice. "More patrols and more people watching the streets." But what can we do, Clara? He doesn't just break windows and spray paint anymore. He has gotten worse. This is a direct message. He says he's here, he's watching, and he's ready to play his games again. His voice was full of weariness, and the weight of the town's fear was heavy on his shoulders. He may have thought too much that they had buried the darkness with Vance's supposed death or capture. Now, he had to admit that the darkness had only been sleeping, waiting for the right time to wake up.

The effigy wasn't just a sign; it was a personal insult. Vance knew how important it was and how scared it would make not only the general public but also Clara. He was reaching out to her, his arms twisted around her in a way that made her feel safe. His methods, which used to be obvious and violent, had changed into something much more sneaky. This wasn't the mindless rage of a crazy person; it was the planned cruelty of a predator who knew how to use psychological warfare. He used the town's deepest fears as weapons, and the red raven was his flag.

"I saw the article in the paper you talked about," Clara said, her voice getting sharper. "The one that talks about the "strange events." It was so... out of touch. Almost like they didn't care. He would want it reported this way. Enough to make people uneasy, but not enough to make them really worried. Brody, he was just seeing how things were going. Seeing if anyone could figure it out. And now, with this…

"He doesn't have to be subtle anymore," Brody said with a grim look on his face. "This statue… There is no room for doubt. The whispers are done. The guessing is over. Oakhaven knows. And they are scared. They see their neighbors and their own homes in a new way. Clara, he's already winning. "He's splitting us up with fear." He talked about how paranoia was growing, how people's interactions with each other were changing in small ways, and how people were becoming more withdrawn and suspicious of their neighbors. "It's exactly what he wanted." To tear us apart, piece by piece, before he even shows up. He's not just going after our property anymore; he's going after our minds, our sense of safety, and even our will to believe in a peaceful future.

It was scary to learn that John Vance had not only survived, but had also carefully planned his return, improving his methods and making them even more terrifying. Clara remembered how smart he was and how he could break down fear and take advantage of every flaw. His previous reign of terror was marked by brutal violence and a deep, immediate fear that left his victims broken. But this new stage, which included psychological warfare with symbols and the intentional spread of fear, was much more advanced and sneaky. He wasn't just a killer anymore; he was a master of fear, and Oakhaven was now his canvas. The red raven, covered in blood on a rough statue, was a clear sign that he had come back to life. It was a scary promise that the darkness had come back, stronger and more terrifying than ever. The only sound after Brody's words were the distant wail of a siren, which was a sad counterpoint to the town's waking nightmare.

Johns Renewed Purpose

The wind whipped John's torn coat around him like a shroud as he stood on the edge of the old quarry. The scarred ground below yawned, a sign of a past that Oakhaven had tried and failed to bury. He took a deep breath and smelled the damp earth and pine needles, which were very different from the sterile air of his prison. Years had gone by, not because the seasons changed, but because his own thoughts moved slowly and painfully. His body showed signs of survival, like the way his cheeks were hollow and his shoulders were hunched, but inside him, something much stronger had been made. The raw desperation of those lonely years had stripped away the last traces of the man he used to be, leaving behind a core of pure, unadulterated determination.

Even from this far away, the whispers of Oakhaven seemed to reach him. He thought about how fear would grow in their hearts, like a sweet, intoxicating scent that made the fire inside him burn even more. They thought he was gone, a ghost that had been sent to haunt their dreams. They were wrong. He hadn't been kicked out; he had just been getting ready. He wasn't broken by being alone; it had made him stronger. It had helped him sort through the pieces of his broken mind, find the true essence of who he was, and accept it with a passion that was almost religious. He was more than just a survivor; he was a master of terror, and his best work was still not finished.

He didn't just come back on a whim; he had carefully planned it out. In his mind, it was a symphony of revenge playing out in a silent theater. The red raven, which had once been just a symbol, was now his flag, a sign that he would never leave. It was more than just a mark; it was a promise he had made to himself in the dark corners of his loneliness. He remembered how beautiful and scary those early works were, like the twisted figures that had been his dark proclamations. Making them had been a ritual, a way to bring order to the chaos that was going on inside him and give physical form to the pain he was causing. Now, those rituals would come back to life with a new purpose and a sharper cruelty.

Being alone had let him break down fear into its most basic parts. He had looked at its tendrils and how it could sneak into even the strongest minds. He knew that real fear didn't come from sudden violence, but from the slow loss of hope, the creeping dread, and the gnawing uncertainty. His past crimes, though violent, had been… simple. A raw outpouring of anger. Now, his plan was much more complicated. It was like a psychological chess game where the pieces weren't pawns, but the souls of the people who lived in Oakhaven. He was the grandmaster, and every move he made was meant to cause the most trouble and despair.

There is no doubt that revenge was a strong motivator. The humiliation of being caught and the suffocating embrace of being locked up were two things that hurt him deeply. But it wasn't just revenge. It was a completion. He thought of himself as a tool, a force of nature set free to fix an imbalance and get rid of the town's complacency and self-deception. They had tried to forget and cover up their sins with a fake sense of peace. He was here to remind them of the darkness that lay beneath the surface, the darkness that resided within them as much as it resided within him. They wouldn't look in the mirror that was him.

The pain inside him and the broken pieces of his mind had always been his crucible. But the pain had changed in his solitude. It was no longer a burden to carry; it was a huge source of strength. His craziness wasn't a flaw; it was his strength. It let him see the world in a way that other people couldn't, and it helped him understand the basic instincts that even the most civilized men have. He saw the fear in their eyes, the brief flashes of panic that showed how fake their carefully built facades were, and he knew it was his own reflection, but bigger and more distorted.

He walked down from the quarry, each step carefully planned and a reminder of why he was there. The path, which had once been overgrown and dangerous, now felt familiar, like it was in his muscle memory. He wasn't a man going back to a place; he was a force going back to where it belonged.

The comforting lies that Oakhaven told themselves were about to be broken. The red raven didn't just mean he was back; it also meant they would have to face the truth. He was the personification of their hidden guilt, the voice of their unspoken sins, and he had come to get them.

He stopped at the edge of the woods, where the smell of pine and wet earth was familiar but now had a new meaning. He had learned to read the small signs of the wild, live off of what little it had to offer, and become one with its quiet rhythm. This basic way of life had stripped away the artifice of civilization, showing the raw, wild core of his being. He was a predator, and he had to be one. His senses were so sharp that they were almost unbearable. The sound of leaves rustling, twigs snapping, and birds calling from far away were all signs that he understood with an instinctual clarity that no amount of training could match.

He had been able to put his philosophy into words after years of thinking about it. It was a twisted tapestry made up of trauma and a deep understanding of how weak people are. He thought Oakhaven was a town full of hypocrites, where people kept secrets and didn't talk about their problems. They had celebrated how strong and united they were, but he knew the truth: they were weak and broken. His presence was just the thing that would bring these cracks to light and make them into big wounds. He wasn't destroying Oakhaven; he was showing what it really was, something that had always been there but hidden.

He thought about the effigy, the small, rough doll he had given to Mrs. Gable. It was a perfect example of how he was going to do things differently. Not the obvious violence of his past, but a planned, mental attack. The details were very important: the glass eyes, which looked like shards of frozen despair; the twisted limbs, which looked like the souls of his victims; and the blood, which was a visceral reminder of how easily he could end a life. The red raven, written in that thick, dark liquid, was his signature, the clear sign that he had come back. It was a message that wasn't spoken, but felt like a deep, primal fear.

He smiled, which was a rare, scary look that didn't reach his eyes. Making that effigy was more than just an act of defiance; it was also an act of freedom. It was like getting rid of a skin, getting rid of the doubts and fears that had been bothering him even when things were at their worst. He had shown himself that he could still make people afraid, that he could still bring out the primal fear that was his birthright. The years had not dulled his edge; they had made it sharper.

He remembered the exact details of the effigy and how carefully he had built it. Every bend in the wood and every piece of glass was put there on purpose. It was a piece of art, even if it was ugly, that was meant to touch the deepest fears of anyone who found it. He had thought about how they would react, how they would gasp in horror, and how the town would be filled with cold fear. He had loved the idea of how scared and helpless they were. It showed that he was still a force to be reckoned with and that he was still alive.

His goal was not just to hurt people, but to tell the truth. He thought of himself as a surgeon, cutting away the rot that was hiding under Oakhaven's calm surface. They had let themselves get too comfortable and thought that the darkness was gone. He was here to show them that the darkness was a natural part of being human and that he was its most devoted follower. It wasn't an accident that he ruled with fear; it was a cleansing.

He kept going, and the landscape opened up in front of him like a map he knew well. He knew every secret path, every dark corner, and every place where a man could go and come back at will. His time in the wild had taught him how to hide, how to be patient like a hunter, and how nature itself is harsh and efficient. He moved with a quiet grace, like a ghost in the dark, and his presence hardly changed the natural order.

He stopped to look at the lights of Oakhaven twinkling in the distance. Each light represented a life, a family, or a story. And each one was a possible victim, a blank canvas on which he would paint his dark masterpiece. He didn't see them as people, but as parts of a bigger organism that was sick and needed drastic treatment. He thought that his actions, no matter how cruel, were acts of mercy. He was giving them a chance to face their biggest fears, let go of the false sense of safety, and accept the basic truth of their lives.

The internal monologue was always there, a low hum of self-affirmation and fear of what was to come. He thought about the things he had done wrong in the past, but not with regret. Instead, he looked at them with a detached, analytical eye. He looked at each act and each victim, looking for lessons learned and ways to improve. He had studied his own darkness, and his lessons got scarier and scarier. The last chapter of his life was just a prologue, a prelude to the big opera of his return.

He thought about Brody, the Sheriff. He may have had good intentions, but in the end, he was limited by his strict adherence to rules and systems that couldn't understand the true nature of the evil he was. Brody was the order that John wanted to tear down, the weak structure of politeness that John hated so much. They had been like a predator and prey in the past, playing a game of cat and mouse. But the roles had changed. John was no longer the mouse; he was the hawk, circling, waiting, and completely without remorse.

Clara. The name kept ringing in his head, a dissonance that wouldn't go away. She was the key, the one who knew, maybe more than anyone else, how bad he was. In his twisted mind, she had been a witness, a victim, and a fellow traveler on the dark path. His return was more than just a message to the town; it was a cruel invitation to her to relive the nightmare they had both been through. He knew that the red raven effigy would deeply affect her and bring to life the fears he had worked so hard to keep hidden.

He wasn't a man who was only motivated by one thing. His reasons for doing things were complicated. They included a deep sense of injustice, a deep sense of being cut off from other people, and a strong desire to force his will on a world he saw as weak and unworthy. He thought of himself as an artist, and the minds of the people of Oakhaven were his canvas. Fear, despair, and the shock of the unexpected were his tools, not brushes and paints. The red raven was his mark of ownership on their fear.

The time alone had not been a punishment, but a test. It had helped him let go of the last bits of who he used to be and accept the horrible truth of who he was. He was no longer John Vance, the troubled person who was fighting his demons. He was the embodiment of those demons, a force let loose on a world that had long since forgotten what real terror was. His new goal was not only to get back what he had lost, but also to change it, to make his craft into an art form that would leave a lasting mark on the soul of Oakhaven. The predator had not only come back; he had changed.

The Detectives Race Against Time

Detective Miles Brody's office, which was usually a place of controlled chaos, was now filled with a frantic energy that matched the knot in his stomach. The walls, which used to be covered in case files and crime scene photos, now felt like they were closing in on him, each one a silent accusation. The monster they had locked up, John Vance, was back. The effigy on Mrs. Gable's porch was proof beyond a doubt. It was a stark red raven drawn in Vance's unmistakable blood-red ink. Brody's victory was bitter and tasted like ashes in his mouth because he had always said Vance could get away. A huge wave of fear washed over the relief of being right. The fear that had haunted his sleep for years, the phantom whispers of Vance's return, had materialized into a terrifying reality.

He ran a hand over his tired face, and the stubble on his chin showed that he had already been awake for several nights. The department's initial excitement, which was followed by quiet whispers of "We knew it," quickly faded, leaving behind a grim understanding of the huge job ahead. Vance wasn't just back; he was back with a scary message. The effigy was a statement because it was so carefully made and placed. This wasn't the crazy violence of their past fights; this was something planned and practiced. It was a mental weapon meant to destroy the town's weak sense of safety before any real harm was done.

Detective Sarah Jenkins said, "He's changed, Miles," her voice tight with fear and grim determination. She was stretched too thin, and her usual sharp focus was now showing signs of stress. The files that were strewn across Brody's desk were proof of their quick, strong reaction. They were going over every piece of information and detail from Vance's previous reign of terror, looking for a new angle or a new way to understand things. "The violence was always there, but this… this is a different kind of monster." He's not just killing people anymore; he's playing games. And he's the one making the rules.

Brody nodded and stared at the blurry picture of the effigy. The glass eyes, which looked disturbingly real, seemed to stare back at me, accusingly. The twisted limbs and rough but powerful image of pain were a message straight from the depths of Vance's mind. "Sarah, he's been alone for five years." Five years for a man like him to think and improve his methods. We always paid attention to how strong and angry he was physically. We didn't realize how much those years hurt his mind, or maybe how much they made it sharper.

The pressure was heavy in the room. For Vance, every second that passed felt like a win. The public, who had been lulled into a false sense of security, was now on the verge of panic. The whispers that had always followed Vance, the scary name "Monster John," were no longer just whispers. They got louder and echoed through the town, fueled by the terrifying fact that he was back. The media, alerted by the clear proof of a repeat offender, were already circling like vultures, ready to feast on the town's fear. Brody knew he had to get ahead of it, control the story, or at least show that they were doing more than just reacting.

Brody said in a strong voice that cut through the nervous tension, "We have to change our strategy." "We can't treat this like we're dealing with the same person. The original profile is no longer useful. We need to look into this new threat, this… change. We need to think like him and be ready for him. What does he want? What is the main goal of this psychological warfare besides getting back at someone?

Jenkins leaned forward and tapped a part of a crime scene report from Vance's last spree that was highlighted. "The pattern before was random, like a storm. There was a build-up, but the targets didn't seem to make much sense. It feels personal now that Mrs. Gable is here. A planned insult. Was she a target for a reason? Or is this a sign of something else to come? She is weak and old. It's a clear message to everyone else: "I can get to anyone, anywhere."

Brody thought to himself, "He's not interested in a quick kill this time, that's for sure," as he looked closely at the effigy's construction. The twine, the pieces of fabric, and the hair that looked too real were all made by a very careful craftsman, even if his medium was fear. "He wants to make people scared. To make us unable to move. To make us feel as powerless as he did when he was in jail. And he's showing that he can do it. People in town are already on edge. "One more red raven, one more incident, and we'll be in full-blown panic."

The internal resources were stretched too thin. All of the available officers were on high alert, with their usual patrols increased and their investigation units working double shifts. But Brody knew that manpower alone wouldn't be enough. They were outsmarted and outmaneuvered. Vance had the upper hand because he was unexpected. He had five years to his advantage.

"We need to look over all of his psychiatric evaluations from when he was in prison," Brody said, his mind racing with ideas. "I want to know if any psychologists saw this coming, if anyone noticed a change in his thinking or a new way of doing things. We need to know why this is getting worse. Was it the isolation itself? Or was there something outside that had an effect?

Jenkins nodded and started to pull up files on her tablet. "Dr. Aris was the main psychiatrist. He would be the first person to talk to. He always said that Vance was a one-of-a-kind case: very smart and very troubled. He thought Vance saw his crimes as a way to show how unhappy he was with society. He believed that Vance could change how he did things.

"Art, huh?" Brody laughed, and the word tasted like vomit. "He's making nightmares, not great works of art." But if he thinks of it as art, we need to know how he makes art. What is the main idea of this new show? What does he want to say with this return? He stopped for a second, a scary thought coming to him. "Clara. What does she have to do with this? She was the only one who seemed to know what he was thinking and feeling. Did he get in touch with her? "Or is she just another piece on his messed-up chessboard?"

The name Clara Thorne hung in the air like a ghost from their past. In Vance's twisted mind, she was more than just a survivor and a witness. Her testimony was very important in getting him convicted, but it was clear that the whole thing had an effect on her as well. Brody had been keeping an eye on her to make sure she was safe, but he had never thought that Vance might use her or her connection to him as a weapon.

Brody said in a low, urgent voice, "We need to talk to Clara." "Right away." If Vance is going after someone or using someone as a pawn, she is the most likely link. She might have ideas that we really need right now. She might be able to tell us what he wants to do and what he is thinking.

Jenkins' forehead wrinkled. Do you think he's trying to talk to her? Or using her to send us a message?

"Both." Or not at all. Brody said, "That's the problem," and he was very angry. "We're just guessing, Sarah." We're responding. Vance is setting the pace. He is the conductor, and we are trying to keep up with his terrifying symphony. He got up from his chair and walked around the small office. The burden of responsibility was almost too much to bear. For years, he had tried to show that Vance was still a threat, and now that threat was real and scary. He was in charge of the Oakhaven PD's reputation and, more importantly, the safety of its people.

"We need to put together a team just to study Vance's mind," Brody said, his mind racing. "Forget about the steps for a minute. I want them to look into every interview, every piece of his manifesto, and everything else he ever wrote or said. I want them to build a profile of the evolved John Vance. What sets him off now? What are the new things that he's obsessed with? What are the small changes in his beliefs?

"And in the meantime?" Jenkins asked, and her eyes stayed on him.

"While we wait, we send troops to the ground. More patrols and a more visible presence. We need to calm the public down and show them that we're fighting back, even if we can't see what we're doing. We need to search the area around Mrs. Gable's for any evidence that may have been missed. We should also get ready for the worst. If Vance is stepping up his psychological warfare, the next step could be anything. He might be trying to trick us. He might be planning something much bigger than just another effigy.

He stopped by the window and looked out at the town, which was quiet and unaware. The long shadows cast by the afternoon sun made the streets look strange and scary. Oakhaven had tried to hide its demons and act like the nightmare was over. John Vance had found them, cleaned them up, and was now ready to let them go again. The race against time wasn't just about finding Vance; it was about understanding him, about outthinking him, before he could plunge Oakhaven back into the abyss.

Vance's return was so bold, and the way he planned his first move said a lot.

He was not just a prisoner who had escaped; he was a strategist who had come back to the battlefield. The last chapter of his terror, which he thought was the end, was now just the beginning. Brody felt a cold fear settle in his stomach. They had caught him before, but that was because of how he had acted in the past. At this point, he was a mystery, a ghostly force working on a new, more dangerous level.

Brody said, "We need to widen our search parameters," and turned back to Jenkins. "He's shown that he can get away from being watched, so just keeping him in one place isn't enough. He could be hiding in plain sight or in a place that no one would expect. Are there any empty buildings or old factories on the edge of town that could be used as a temporary base? He needs to plan and get what he needs. He'll pick a place that matches how he feels right now—something out of the way, something that isn't noticed, something that looks like his own exile.

Jenkins was already writing down notes, and her fingers were moving quickly across the digital notepad. "There's the old Miller cannery, which has been empty for years. It's deep in the woods, so it's not easy to get to. And the old train station is a maze of empty cars and tunnels that haven't been used in years. Both could be places to hide. "We'll send units to sweep those areas very well."

"And the timing," Brody said, his mind still racing. "At night, the effigy was put up. He is a being of the dark. He does well in the dark. We need to be able to predict what he's going to do, not just react to it. If he wants to scare people, he'll probably attack when it will have the biggest effect. At dawn, dusk, or when people are worried. He doesn't use brute force; he uses psychological impact. That effigy wasn't just a warning; it was a way for him to show off his skills and make fun of them.

He took a new notepad and drew a simple picture of Vance's face. Then he drew a second, darker figure next to it. It was a more abstract, more threatening figure, a chaotic mix of sharp edges and shadows. "This is what we have to deal with now. Not the same man we caught five years ago, but something else. We can project our worst fears onto him because he is a blank slate, and he knows how to use that to his advantage. He is a mirror that shows the darkness that Oakhaven has tried to ignore.

The fear was always there, eating away at him, but Brody pushed it down. He had to be the rock, the steady hand. It was important for the lives of the people in Oakhaven. "I want a complete lockdown on anyone he used to know. Anyone who might have helped him or cared about his cause. We need to keep an eye on their movements and communications. He might not be working alone, or he could be using old contacts to get information or resources.

Jenkins looked up, her face serious. "We've already begun that." But Miles, it's a huge network. And a lot of them have either spread out or gone into hiding. "It's like chasing ghosts."

"Then we become ghost hunters," Brody said, his voice getting harder. "It's not just about catching a criminal anymore. It's about keeping a town from falling apart. Vance wants to tear down Oakhaven, piece by piece, and he's starting with their sense of safety. The effigy was the first shot. We have to think that his next move will be even worse and more personal.

He hit the desk with his hand, which made Jenkins jump. "We don't have much time left, Sarah." He is out there and playing. And if we don't figure out his game quickly, he's going to win. The words hung in the air, a scary and real truth. The predator had come back, not only from prison but also from the depths of his own twisted mind. He was now a much more dangerous and unpredictable enemy than ever before. Brody knew for sure that this would be a race to the very end, and it made him feel sick to his stomach.

Exploiting the Towns Fear

The digital clock on Detective Brody's desk said 3:17 AM, a silent reminder of the hours that had passed without giving him a break. The effigy, which was now in a bag and tagged, sat on a different table. Its glass eyes stared blankly, accusingly, at Brody, who looked tired. He had looked at the crime scene photos a dozen times, and each time he saw something new that made him uneasy: the way the twine was knotted just right, the edges of the cut fabric that were unnaturally clean, and the faint, almost invisible smudge of what could be dirt or something much worse near the base. It was a show, and Vance was the star. Oakhaven was the unwilling audience.

Brody knew that the town was vulnerable after years of relative peace. People told scary stories about Vance's reign of terror to kids, and the memory of it had faded into a grim legend. But the effigy had broken through that comfortable forgetting, shattering the false sense of safety. The whispers were getting louder now, not just in the quiet aisles of the grocery store, but also in calls to the police station that were full of fear and in the air of Oakhaven, which was now full of tension. Vance was a master manipulator, and he was expertly fanning the embers of their long-dormant fear into a raging inferno.

Detective Sarah Jenkins said, "He's not just teasing us, Miles," her voice hoarse from not getting enough sleep and drinking too much coffee. She was bent over a map of Oakhaven, tracing a path with her finger from Mrs. Gable's quiet suburban street to the town square. "He is in charge of it. He wants us to know he's there and feel him. Her finger landed on a small park, a patch of green that is usually full of families but is probably empty after dark. "Think about it. Early in the morning, the effigy was found. Who found it? Someone was out for an early walk, and someone else was already scared. The newspapers also ran with it. "Instant spread of the terror throughout the town."

Brody rubbed his temples, and the pain behind his eyes got worse. "He's using the town's own infrastructure against us." The media, people's natural curiosity, and their fear. "He's using their reactions as weapons." He looked at the map, and his stomach tightened. Vance wasn't just hiding; he was making sure people knew he was there on purpose. Oakhaven was the prize in a psychological war.

"And it's working," Jenkins said, her voice barely above a whisper. "My sister called me last night. Her kids don't want to go to the park. People are locking their doors earlier and checking them again. The mailman on Elm Street said he saw someone hiding in the shadows, but it was just a shadow. "He's making a ghost, and now everyone can see ghosts."

Vance's return wasn't a chaotic explosion; it was a carefully planned campaign of fear. The effigy was just the first act, a way to show what they wanted to do. Brody thought of Vance hiding somewhere and watching Oakhaven through a warped lens, his mind a complex algorithm for making people feel scared. He wasn't just looking for physical weaknesses; he was also looking for the town's collective mind, looking for the cracks, the fears, and the old worries that lay hidden beneath the surface of everyday life.

"We need to guess what he's going to do next, Sarah." How can you make people more afraid in a town like this? Brody thought out loud as he walked around his office. "He knows we're searching for him. He knows we're getting things ready. So, he won't face them directly next. It will be something that shakes people's faith in themselves and makes them doubt their own safety and senses.

Jenkins pointed to a small clock tower on the edge of town that wasn't being used anymore. "How about something you can see? Something that makes everyone look up to see how he affects them?

Brody's eyes followed her finger. The tower with the clock. It had been broken for years, standing watch over the town without making a sound.

It was the perfect blank slate for Vance's sick art. "A public taunt, though. Something that says, "I'm here, and you can't ignore me." For example, if he were to change the clock face. With something that stands for something. Something that talks about time running out or maybe time being messed up.

"Or something more personal," Jenkins said, her eyes hardening. "He's always been interested in symbols." Do you remember the pictures of the raven? What if he used the clock tower to show someone something special? "Everyone can see a message that is meant for you or the department."

The thought made Brody feel uneasy again. There was no doubt about Vance's intelligence, and he was even better at being cruel in a psychological way. He wouldn't just leave a dummy on a porch; he'd make the whole town his own creepy theater. He would make Oakhaven a part of its own terror.

Brody leaned over the map again and said, "We also need to think about the environmental factors." "He needs to move, get supplies, and set up his next… display." He'll use the dark places and the spaces that aren't used anymore. The old industrial area on the south side, the abandoned quarry, and the thick woods on the north side. These are places where he can work without being seen and change the world around him to have the biggest effect.

"The quarry," Jenkins said, her forehead furrowed. "It's a maze of dangerous drops and paths that have grown too big. People stay away from it. Things can go missing there. The quarry would be perfect for a dramatic scene that plays on the idea of falling or being lost.

Brody nodded, and a dark picture came to mind. Vance, who was standing on a ledge, was setting up a scene that could be seen for miles. He was a shadow against the setting sun, a creepy puppet master playing with the lives of the townspeople. He wouldn't just be there; he would be a constant threat, a figure carved into the landscape of their fear.

Brody said in a low, measured voice, "He wants us to chase shadows and wear ourselves out." "He's making traps." Every empty building, every dark alley, and every sound in the leaves could be a deliberate attempt to waste our time and money. He is using Oakhaven itself against us. Fear is what he uses to hurt people.

Brody hated the idea that Vance was in charge of the story and setting the pace of their investigation. He was the one who hunted, not the one who was hunted. But Vance had changed the rules of the game. This was no longer a simple manhunt; it was a battle of wits and a deep dive into the broken maze of a troubled mind. Vance was a predator who knew that real power came not only from being physically strong, but also from changing how people saw things.

Jenkins looked at the map and said, "He could be leaving subtle clues, breadcrumbs that are meant to send us on wild goose chases." "Or, he could be using the town's well-known landmarks in scary new ways." Maybe the old theater? What if he put something on the screen when there was no movie playing? A scary message for everyone in town. Or even the town hall itself. "A symbol of authority that has been weakened."

Brody imagined it: the dark theater, the audience waiting in silence, only to see not a movie but Vance's warped vision. Or the bare front of the town hall, which is usually a sign of order and government, now covered up or damaged by his symbol. It would be an attack on their sense of safety and a planned breach of the places they thought were safe and well-known. He was going after Oakhaven's sense of who it was and what was normal.

Brody's voice got stronger as he said, "He's not just trying to scare us; he's trying to break us." "He wants us to feel like we can't do anything and are useless. He wants to show that he can always stay one step ahead, no matter how many resources we throw at him. He is using the town's fear as both a shield and a weapon.

It was especially scary to think about Vance using the natural world to his advantage. He had always been able to find new ways to do things. The woods that surrounded Oakhaven, which were usually a place to have fun, could turn into a suffocating maze. Picture him leaving markers that aren't meant for us to follow but to confuse us. Or making every shadow seem scary by using natural sounds like the hoot of an owl or the snap of a twig to keep people on edge all the time.

"He could also be using the radio waves," Jenkins said, as a sudden thought hit her. "Sending out distorted messages or static at certain times. Enough to make people uneasy and raise their paranoia. He is a threat not just to their bodies, but to their whole lives.

Brody's mind raced as he thought about all the things that could happen. Vance was a scary artist, and Oakhaven was his canvas. He was a conductor, and the town's fear was his band. The effigy was the first note of the symphony of dread, which was just beginning. He had to find the score and figure out what the composer meant before the final, terrible crescendo.

Brody thought, "He might even be changing the town itself in small ways." The words hung in the air. "Leaving graffiti that looks random but isn't." Putting things in different places in public. Small changes that are hard to notice but add up to make you feel uneasy, like something is wrong. He wants us to question what we see and think about what is real.

Jenkins was already looking at satellite pictures of Oakhaven and zooming in on places that fit their wild ideas. "The old amusement park, which has been closed for years. Even in the middle of the day, it's a scary place. Think of Vance using the broken down Ferris wheel and other rides as a backdrop for his fear. A monument to happiness that has now become a symbol of sadness.

A chill ran down Brody's spine. Vance had a twisted sense of art, and the old, forgotten places in Oakhaven were perfect extensions of his own broken mind. He wasn't just going back to Oakhaven; he was taking it back, one act of terror at a time. He was making the town a part of his twisted redemption.

Brody stressed, with a strained voice, "The key is that he's not doing this for himself." "He's doing it for us." He wants to see how we respond. He wants to see us fall, to feel as scared and alone as he did. "The more scared we are, the stronger he gets."

The fear that Oakhaven felt was heavy on her body. Brody felt it pushing down on him, always reminding him of how important the situation was. For five long years, Vance had been carefully planning his return, his escape, and the terror campaign that would follow. He had been watching, learning, and changing. And now he was using that knowledge to take advantage of the town's very structure, turning their natural fears into his most powerful weapon. It was a war, but not with guns; it was psychological warfare. Vance was determined to win by making sure that everyone in Oakhaven was always scared.

The Trap is Set

He watched from his vantage point, a spectral observer cloaked in the anonymity that Oakhaven's sprawling periphery offered. The town, which used to be his personal playground, now felt like a carefully planned chessboard, with its unsuspecting residents as pawns in a game he had been perfecting for years. Detective Brody and his eager assistant, Jenkins, were good, he would say. They were smart, diligent, and their recent nocturnal deliberations within the confines of their sterile precinct hadn't escaped his notice. Their talks were like the frantic running of mice; they were easy to understand for someone who had learned to read the small signs of fear and excitement long ago. Of course, they were looking for him. They were carefully picking apart every strange sound and unsettling detail, looking for a pattern or logic that would lead them to his carefully built lair. But they were looking for a hunter, when in fact, a shepherd was about to catch them.

His trap wasn't meant for brute force or even a direct, head-on fight. That would be rude and not very effective. No, his trap was a beautiful, sneaky thing made from the threads of their own investigation and spun from their own need. He had observed their routines, their predictable routes, the very rhythm of their pursuit. They thought they were getting closer, that the net was getting tighter. In a way, it was. But it was a net he had thrown, a carefully placed trap that would lead them exactly where he wanted them to go. He had thought of every possible explanation and every possible conclusion they could come to. The effigy, which was a flashy introduction, had done its job perfectly by distracting them and pulling them into a story of rising fear. They were interested in the obvious signs of his presence, like the symbolic gestures and the easy-to-understand displays. They were searching for the monster in the shadows, when the monster was already holding the spotlight, directing their gaze to whatever illusion he chose.

He was especially happy with what they had to say about the clock tower. It was a sweetly romantic idea to turn a broken monument into a public display of fear. They thought he would send out images and leave mysterious messages for everyone. They were so close, but they couldn't see anything. The clock tower was just a trick, a distraction. His real theater of operations was somewhere else, in a place that was much more powerful and personal. He had purposely let rumors about his old haunts, like the abandoned quarry and the thick woods, come out, knowing that they would cling to these familiar ghosts. They thought of them as possible hiding spots that made sense based on what he had done before. In a way, they were walking right into the arms of his carefully planned illusion.

He knew that the key was to not only predict what they would do, but also why they would do it. Brody and Jenkins were motivated by a need for closure, for the terror to come to an end once and for all. They wanted an end, a sense of closure. And in his own sick way, he wanted it too. But his conclusion would be on his own terms, a grand finale, a work of art in psychological theater. He wasn't just hiding; he was putting together a symphony of fear, and the climax was coming up fast. He had to make sure the audience was there, the stage was ready, and the last act would leave a lasting impression.

Like a fisherman skillfully playing a line, he had been subtly directing their attention for the past few days. The note that was thrown away near the old mill and the anonymous tip about a shady person near the old train tracks were not just coincidences. They were planned breadcrumbs that were placed in such a way that they would lead them on a wild goose chase, using up their resources, energy, and patience. The false trails were stones carefully placed in a path that would not let them escape, but would lead them to a meeting point. He knew they would see these as signs of his growing boldness and carelessness. They would think he was a killer who was getting careless, like a predator who was playing his hand too well. They would never guess that what they thought was his carelessness was actually his way of being in charge.

He remembered a specific conversation that he had heard through the high-tech surveillance equipment he had carefully set up weeks before. Brody's voice was full of frustration as he fought against the growing sense of unease that was spreading through the town. He talked about how Vance could use their fear as a weapon and make Oakhaven itself a tool of terror. He loved it. They were starting to see how powerful he was and how much he could change things. But knowing was a long way from getting over it. He was more than just a killer; he was a sculptor of fear and an artist of the mind. And Oakhaven was the best thing he was working on.

They thought it was the quarry. A place where things could go missing. Yes, a place where things could go missing. But it was also a place where things could be found if you knew where to look. He had spent days carefully getting the place ready, not to escape, but to show something. He had made some paths clear, lit up some features, and most importantly, made sure that the story he wanted to tell would be impossible to ignore. He had even made small changes to the landscape that made things feel a little off, a sense of unease that would grow as they looked into things more. The trash that looked like it was just thrown around was actually very carefully placed. Each piece was a planned object, a prop in the play he was about to direct.

He had even thought about how the weather might affect his mind. A sudden storm or a thick fog coming in from the river could make people feel even more alone and vulnerable. He had thoroughly scouted the quarry, making maps not only of the physical terrain but also of the subtle changes in the atmosphere. He knew exactly when the sun would cast long, spooky shadows and when the wind would howl through the cracks, making a sound that was hard to understand. He wasn't just setting a trap; he was planning an experience that would break them, shatter their composure, and leave them completely exposed.

They had also talked about radio frequencies. He admitted that the idea of sending out distorted messages was a bit over the top. But it also worked to plant seeds of doubt and make people feel scared for a long time after the broadcast ended. He had, in fact, tried short bursts of static that were just enough to be creepy and make the townspeople wonder why it was so quiet. It was a low-level hum of worry, a constant reminder that he was there, even if he wasn't seen. And now that hum would grow into a deafening roar.

He watched the patrol cars, whose headlights cut through the darkening sky like nervous fireflies. They were looking around the edges, in the usual places, and in the obvious ones. They were easy to guess. They were following the rules of a normal investigation. But he had thrown those rules away a long time ago. He was playing a different game, a game of psychological warfare, in which the battlefield was the mind and the goal was to completely control it.

He then turned his attention to a specific part of the quarry that he had carefully chosen. It was an overhang, like a natural amphitheater that looked out over a steep drop. From this point of view, you could see for miles, and more importantly, you could be seen. He made sure that the way to this area looked deceptively easy, even welcoming. It felt like a natural path, a continuation of their search that took them deeper into the heart of his design. There were small signs, of course, for those who knew what to look for, like faint scuff marks on the rocks or a piece of vegetation that had been moved. But to Brody and Jenkins, who were so focused on their goal, these would seem like nothing more than random disturbances, the result of nature, not a predator's planned staging.

He laughed, a low, guttural sound that got lost in the sound of the leaves moving. They wanted to find him so badly that they were willing to do anything to end this. They thought they were closing the net and making him act. They couldn't believe that they were actually walking into it on purpose. He had taken advantage of their preconceived ideas about how criminals act. They thought he would be trapped and in a lot of trouble. They didn't think he would be in charge of the whole thing, like the conductor of their impending fall. He wasn't running; he was taking them to their own stage.

The excitement and fear that came with the anticipation throbbed inside him. This wasn't just about getting even, getting justice, or even ending his rule. This was about leaving a mark. This was about making a mark so deep and scary that Oakhaven would always be remembered in the history of his dark art. He had read about the great plays and the carefully thought-out psychological warfare campaigns. He had learned from the best manipulators, people who knew that true power didn't come from brute force but from carefully and devastatingly manipulating the human mind. And he was about to give his best work. Not with tripwires and nets, but with carefully cultivated fear, strategically placed illusions, and the promise of a conclusion that would be anything but a simple arrest, the trap was set. It would be a show, and Oakhaven and its dedicated detectives would be the only ones who could see it

Chapter 10: The Reckoning

The Final Confrontation

The quarry floor was a rough, broken stone and shadowy area that had been shaped by neglect and the constant erosion of time. A light, steady rain that had started an hour earlier made the dangerous ground even more slippery, turning loose scree into a possible deathtrap. There was a strong smell of wet dirt and something else in the air, something metal and slightly sour. It smelled like something was about to happen, or maybe it was the smell of blood. Detective Brody's breath rose in the cold, and all of his senses were on high alert, with every nerve screaming a silent warning. Jenkins, who was younger and less experienced than him, held his sidearm with a white-knuckled grip and looked into the dark that surrounded them on all sides. They had followed the breadcrumbs, the twisted path of carefully placed clues and carefully planned misdirections that had brought them to this empty mouth, this natural amphitheater of their worst fears.

Brody looked at the sheer rock faces, the rusty remains of machinery that had been left behind, and the open mouth of the abandoned mine shaft that dropped into a black hole. At that moment, he felt a primal prickling on the back of his neck and the cold, hard truth that he was being watched and hunted. Just as he had thought and planned, they had walked right into it. The quarry, a place of long-gone industry and whispered local legends, was the perfect setting for the last act. He knew that Vance, this "Monster John," would pick a place that was like his own broken mind: beautiful and dangerous, with hidden depths and steep drops. They had hunted a ghost, a ghost made up of fear and rumors, but now, right here, the ghost was very real and very dangerous.

A sound came from above, first soft and then louder. It was a rhythmic scraping, like claws on stone. It wasn't the breeze. It wasn't the rain. It was on purpose. Brody raised his hand to tell Jenkins to stop. His heart was pounding against his ribs in a frantic rhythm. His mind raced as he tried to put together the pieces of Vance's complicated game. The effigy, the strange notes, the fake sightings—all of these were meant to draw them in, separate them, and get them to this exact point where they would be at his mercy. And now, from the shadows of the overhang he had expected, a person came out. It wasn't a monster in the usual sense; it was a man, thin and wiry, standing out against the bruised sky at dusk. He was so still that it was scary, like a predator, and it made Brody feel even worse.

"Vance!" Even though Brody's voice was steady, it sounded strained. He kept his gun aimed, with his finger close to the trigger. "It's done. Come out into the open. "You are surrounded." The words sounded empty, like a desperate plea against the quarry's complete lack of interest. He knew with a chilling certainty that Vance had long since made the word "surrounded" useless.

The figure stayed still for a moment, and then a low, humorless chuckle came down. There was a sound that seemed to come from the stone itself. It was a dry, rough sound that promised no surrender, only a strange kind of victory. "Surrounded, Detective?" You don't understand. "I have surrounded you." The voice, which was louder because of the quarry's acoustics, was eerily close, as if Vance were speaking directly into Brody's ear.

A bright beam of light suddenly shot down from the overhang, pinning Brody and Jenkins in its harsh glare. It was a strong industrial spotlight that could turn night into a strange, bright day. Then another one appeared, and then another, until the quarry floor was covered in beams that lit up every move they made, making them look like easy prey. Jenkins flinched and squinted his eyes against the sudden brightness. "He… he's got spotlights," he said, his voice full of disbelief.

Brody said, "He's ready for this, Jenkins," looking up at the shadow above. He could see Vance better now. He wore dark, useful clothes that made him blend in with the shadows, but his face was brightly lit, with a scary mix of triumph and something like sadness. This face had seen and done too much; it had become a mask for the abyss.

"Vance, do you think this is a game?" Brody pushed harder, his voice getting harder. "Do you think this is a play or something?"

"Isn't it?" There was a mocking sweetness in Vance's voice. "The last act. Detective, this is the end of all your hard work. You've worked so hard and been so determined. You did exactly what I told you to do. And now, you're exactly where I want you to be. He slowly and carefully waved his arm around, pointing to the whole quarry. "Look around you. This is my theater. And you, gentlemen, are my stars, even though you don't want to be.

There was a small but steady tremor in the ground. Then, a low grinding noise started coming from deep inside the mine shaft. It got louder and more insistent, like a machine groaning that talked about great weight and great power. Brody's blood turned cold. He had thought about using explosives, traps, and a secret stash of weapons. He hadn't thought about this. "What is that?" Jenkins whispered, his eyes wide with fear.

"It's a counterweight system," Vance said, his voice becoming more like a teacher's. "Smart, isn't it? Used mining tools that have been repurposed. It is meant to… change the path of the rockfall. From right above the main door. He stopped for a moment to let the meaning sink in. "Or maybe from a different, more beautiful place."

Brody got it right away. The carefully planned route they had taken and the seemingly easy way down into the quarry were all lies. They weren't just stuck; they were put there. Vance had definitely set up a section of the quarry wall that was very dangerous and right below it.

"You've been looking for me in the obvious places for so long, Detective," Vance said, his voice getting more and more smug. "The old railway bridge, the woods, and the mill that is no longer in use. You searched for the hunter. But I've always been the shepherd, leading my flock to the slaughter.

A loud roar filled the air before Brody could do anything. It was the sound of metal grinding, earth collapsing, and tons of rock giving way. The ground shook violently under their feet. A stream of rocks, dust, and other debris began to fall from the quarry wall. It didn't fall straight down, but at an angle, just as Vance had said, toward the exact spot where they were standing. It was a scary, unnatural rain of death.

"Get out of the way!" Brody yelled and pushed Jenkins hard. They rushed to hide behind the rusted hulks of broken machinery, but the quarry floor didn't offer much protection. The ground shook, and rocks the size of cars bounced and rolled, making the earth shake. Dust filled the air, making it hard to see more than a few feet. A smaller rock hit Brody's shoulder and spun him around, causing him to feel a sharp pain. He fell hard and lost his breath.

He coughed and spat dirt out of his mouth, and it was hard for him to get up. The sound was amazing, like a symphony of destruction that was too loud to hear. He could hear Jenkins yelling, but the noise made it hard to hear. He looked around at the messy scene, his eyes stinging from the dust. And then he saw him. Vance was not running or hiding; he was standing still in front of the bright lights. He was looking. He looked calm, almost detached, as he looked at the mess he had made.

"You didn't give me enough credit, Detective," Vance's voice was clear enough to cut through the noise of the roar. "You thought you could outsmart me. You thought you could trap me. But you were just doing what I wanted you to do.

Brody pushed himself up to his feet, even though his shoulder hurt a lot. He could see Jenkins struggling to get out from under a pile of fallen debris, with his leg pinned under a jagged slab of rock. Brody's calmness as a professional was broken by panic, which was cold and sharp. He yelled, "Jenkins!" and started to walk toward him.

Vance looked on, his face unreadable. "Such loyalty," he said softly, almost to himself. "Good in its own way." It's too bad it will be so… unrewarding.

A new sound came out of the noise as Brody stumbled toward his partner: a high-pitched, metallic scream followed by a loud bang. The ground in front of Vance's quarry shot up. A piece of reinforced concrete that had been buried under years of dust and debris had been violently thrown out. And from it, like a ghost rising from the ground, came Vance's carefully made weapon.

It was a modified hydraulic press, a huge machine made of steel and pistons that was much bigger and stronger than anything Brody could have thought of. Under the spotlights, its shiny metal surfaces, which had somehow escaped the rockfall, glinted in a bad way. And at the top, a huge, sharp blade that could easily cut through rock or flesh.

Vance said, "My last flourish," and his voice was full of a creepy pride. "The ultimate tool for… reclamation." He pointed to the press. Detective, this quarry has kept secrets for decades. It's time for it to eat more.

Brody stood still, horrified by what he had just realized. Vance wasn't just trying to kill them. He was planning a carefully planned demolition, and the rockfall was a cover for the use of his final, terrible tool. And the controls… Vance had the controls.

"Do you want to be the monster, Vance?" Brody growled, his voice hoarse from anger and fear. "Do you want to be God? Now let's see how you like the taste of what you made. He pulled out his gun, and the cold steel felt good in his shaking hand. He didn't pay attention to the pain, the dust, or the rocks that were about to fall. His focus became sharper, zeroing in on one desperate goal.

Vance laughed again, which made Brody's nerves crawl. "Brody, you're still thinking like a detective." Still looking for the easy shot and the move that everyone else does. But this isn't about being easy. This is about what must happen. He turned a dial on the control panel of the press. The huge blade started to slowly and steadily fall, its descent marked by a low, threatening hum.

Brody shot.

The shot broke through the air like a sharp, defiant punctuation mark against the roar of the rockfall and the press's groan. The bullet hit the control panel. There were sparks, and the blade that was coming down stopped with a shuddering lurch. Vance swore, a long string of sharp, angry curses. He lunged at the panel, desperately trying to reset it.

Brody got the chance he needed. He ran toward Vance, ignoring the pain in his shoulder. His movements were jagged and frantic. When Jenkins heard the press stop humming, he worked even harder, pushing against the rock that was holding his leg down.

Vance turned around as Brody got closer, his eyes full of rage. He had not realized how strong Brody's will was. He didn't see a detective; he saw a man with a basic need to protect, a force of nature that had been set free by the threat to his partner. Vance let go of the controls and lunged at Brody with a wicked-looking hunting knife in his hand.

The two men hit each other hard. The quarry floor turned into a battlefield, with dust, falling rocks, and raw, desperate violence all around. Brody fought with a strength he didn't know he had because of the adrenaline and rage that were coursing through him. He blocked Vance's knife thrusts, and the sound of steel hitting steel echoed through the quarry, making the rockfall seem even worse. He saw his chance when Vance swung too far and left a small opening. Brody hit Vance's temple with the butt of his gun.

Vance staggered back, confused, and his grip on the knife slipped. Brody took advantage of the chance. He tackled Vance, and they both fell to the ground, which was full of dangerous debris. The knife slipped away and got lost in the mess. They rolled around, fighting, their bodies a mess of fatigue and need. Vance was still dangerous, even though he was weaker. He moved with a crazy energy. He hit Brody's jaw with a strong punch, which made stars burst behind Brody's eyes.

But Brody held on, his grip was like iron. He could hear Jenkins yelling words of encouragement and feel the pressure on his leg ease a little as his partner kept fighting. The rockfall was getting quieter, and the loud roar was slowly turning into a rumbling echo. The spotlights, on the other hand, stayed, shining their harsh, unyielding light on the scene.

Brody screamed and twisted, slamming Vance's head against a sharp piece of stone. Vance stopped moving. Brody got up quickly, breathing heavily and in a lot of pain. He looked at Vance, who was lying still on the ground, and then at the hydraulic press, which had stopped working and had a huge blade ready to kill. He looked at Jenkins, who was now able to pull his leg free. His face was twisted in pain.

"He's… he's done?" Jenkins's voice was hoarse and he wheezed.

Brody knelt down next to Vance and felt for a pulse. It was there, but it was weak and thin. They caught the hunter. The shepherd had led his flock, not to death, but to a painful, brutal end.

The silence that followed was deep, with only the sound of water dripping from the quarry walls and the two detectives' ragged breathing breaking it. The big show was over. The audience was spellbound, terrified, and finally the person who did it was brought to the stage of their own death. It wasn't the clean, victorious arrest Vance had hoped for, but it was the end. An end that was bloody, brutal, and unforgettable. Brody looked up at the sky. The rain was now a steady downpour, washing away the dust, blood, and lingering smell of fear from the cursed quarry. The time had come for Vance, Oakhaven, and the two men who had dared to chase the monster into the heart of its own making.

Johns Psychological Unraveling

The rain stuck John's thinning hair to his scalp, and each drop was a chilling reminder of the flood that had been his life. He stood in the middle of the chaos, the loud noise of the quarry wall falling down was a symphony that scared and excited him at the same time. The sound was so basic and destructive that it was like the storm that was raging inside of him. He had planned every painful detail and every careful step that had brought them, and him, to this point. Detective Brody. The man who had the guts to tear apart his carefully built world and peel back the layers of his carefully crafted persona to show the raw, festering wound underneath.

His sharp but distant gaze flickered over the scene. The spotlights, which shone like uncaring stars, lit up the carnage and turned the natural amphitheater into a grotesque stage. He saw Brody, a man of raw, desperate courage, running toward Jenkins, who was trapped under the rubble with his partner. A wave of something like pity, cold and sharp, hit him. Faithfulness. What a strange and fragile idea. He had held on to it before. Before it had been twisted, ruined, and finally broken into a million pieces that couldn't be fixed.

The hydraulic press stood in front of him, a huge sign of both his intelligence and his despair. Its blade, a sharpened maw of steel, hung in the air, a silent promise of death. He had planned it, cared for it, and brought it to life from the depths of this forgotten place. It was his best work, the last thing he did to show the world that he didn't care about them. And now it was ready to carry out its awful plan.

The machine made a low hum, like a guttural growl that shook the soles of his boots and the marrow of his bones. It was the sound of doom coming, a sign that the end was near. He felt a tremor run through him, not of fear, but of a deep, almost spiritual release. The walls that had been carefully built over the years, the lies that had been carefully planned, and the fake calm were all falling apart. The dam finally broke under the constant, soul-crushing pressure.

He saw Brody fighting his way toward Vance, his face a mask of grim determination and blood on his shoulder. The detective's eyes, full of righteous anger, met his across the rocky, dusty ground. In that brief moment, John didn't see an enemy; he saw himself. A man pushed to the edge, fighting for something or someone. It was a realization that hit him like a physical blow, a sudden burst of clarity in the chaos around him.

He had spent so much time making up his story, putting himself in the role of the wronged, the victim, and the avenger. He had convinced himself that his cause was right and that his punishment was unavoidable. But as the rain fell on him, the spotlights shone down on him, and the groaning press promised to kill him, the carefully woven tapestry of his delusion began to come apart. The edges frayed, showing the worn-out threads of his broken past.

His mind was racing, but not with plans or angry words; it was full of broken pictures. A child's small hand reaching out and then being taken away. The cold, clean white of a hospital room. The sound of quiet, pitying voices. The heavy weight of accusations that aren't spoken. The empty feeling of being left behind. These were the real people who brought him down, the evil spirits that had crept out of the dark corners of his mind.

He remembered how hurtful it was when his mother looked at him with disappointment and how cold and indifferent his father was when he didn't say anything. He remembered the teasing on the playground, the feeling of being left out, and the constant, gnawing feeling that he was fundamentally flawed and unlovable. These memories, which had been buried under layers of anger and resentment for a long time, now came rushing back, a tidal wave of pure, unfiltered pain.

He wanted to get back a sense of control and force his will on a world that had taken away even the most basic rights of living. He thought that by hurting others and having power, he could make the scars of his own pain go away. But the truth was clear and undeniable: he was only continuing the cycle and becoming what he said he hated.

The rockfall made a deafening noise, but John could hear something new: the frantic, desperate beating of his own heart. It was a scary sound, but it was also a sound of deep, terrifying freedom. The mask was coming off. The carefully built structure of "John Vance," the angry mastermind, was falling apart, showing the scared, broken child underneath.

He saw Brody lunge at him and heard a primal scream come from his throat. The detective's raw, wild rage was very different from what was going on inside John. Brody was fighting for his life, for justice, and for his partner. What was John fighting for? To get away from the heavy burden of his own life? To finally give in to the darkness that had always been with him?

Brody's eyes were fixed on John's as he got closer. A brief moment of recognition and understanding passed between them. Two men, on opposite sides of a chasm, both silently agreed that they were being pushed to the edge by things they couldn't control. For Brody, it was the never-ending search for the truth. It was the weight of his own past that he couldn't escape for John.

When Brody tackled him, he felt a shock and they both fell to the ground. The impact was violent and shook everything up, sending debris flying everywhere. He felt the rough ground against his skin and the sharp pain of gravel against his skin. He was no longer on stage, no longer the conductor of this creepy symphony. He was just a man, broken and beaten, trapped in the storm he had started.

Vance's knife, which he thought made him powerful, slipped away and got lost in the chaos. He fought with Brody, their bodies locked in a desperate, brutal dance. He could feel the detective's raw strength and the unbreakable will that drove him. And in that raw, physical fight, the last bits of the carefully crafted image he had built for himself fell apart. There was no mastermind or monster, just John, a man who was drowning in his own sadness.

He hit Brody's jaw with a desperate, flailing punch. For a brief moment, he saw the detective hesitate, with stars bursting behind his eyes. A feeling of triumph, like a dying ember of his old ambition, surged through him. But it went out just as quickly as it had started. Brody held on with a grip that felt like a vise and a will that was like a force of nature.

The sounds of the quarry slowly faded away, leaving behind the ragged gasps of effort and the desperate grunts of struggle. The rockfall was slowing down, and the noise was turning into a dull rumble. But the spotlights stayed, their harsh light holding them down like specimens in a microscope. John saw the unending beams of light and felt very ashamed. He had tried to control the story and set the rules for his last act. Instead, he had been exposed, stripped bare, and all of his deepest fears were laid out for everyone to see.

Then, another hit. Brody hit his head against a sharp rock. The world swam, a dizzying mix of pain and confusion. The fight left him limp, like a broken puppet whose strings had finally been cut. He felt his muscles relax and his body give in to what was going to happen.

He lay there, the rain soaking his clothes and the cold getting into his bones. He heard Brody's heavy breathing and the sound of his partner Jenkins trying to get free. He saw the stopped press, a silent, threatening guard. He saw

Brody get up, tired but victorious, and kneel next to him.

He felt someone touch his neck and look for a pulse. A weak, thready beat. They caught the hunter. The shepherd had led his flock not to a glorious victory, but to a brutal, shameful loss. And at that moment, when his awareness started to fade, John understood. He hadn't planned out a big scheme. He was a prisoner of the ghosts that had haunted him for a long time, and they had caused him to fall apart. The rain kept falling, a cleansing flood that washed away the dust, the blood, and the last traces of the man he had pretended to be. The time had come, but instead of the loud applause he had hoped for, there was only a deafening silence, broken only by the sad cry of his own broken soul.

Sacrifice and Survival

The cold, steady rain was starting to soak through John's clothes, which was a scary change from the fire that had been in his mind just a few moments before. The loud noise of the quarry wall falling down, which had once been a symphony of destruction that echoed his inner turmoil, had now turned into an unsettling, guttural groan. It was the sound of what happened next, of a world that would never be the same again, just like his own. The harsh and unyielding spotlights kept shining down on the once-natural amphitheater, turning it into a grotesque stage set for a tragedy he had carefully, and sadly, written. He saw Detective Brody, a man with raw courage written all over his body, scrambling toward Jenkins, his partner, who was buried under a mountain of rubble. John felt a fleeting, almost involuntary feeling, like pity, that was like a cold, sharp shard of empathy he had buried a long time ago. Faithfulness. It was an idea he had once loved, but life had changed it, bent it, and finally destroyed it.

The hydraulic press was a huge monument to his twisted genius and deep sadness that stood in front of him. Its blade, a sharp, shining mouth of tempered steel, hung in the air, a silent, powerful promise of death. He had thought it up, nurtured its scary potential, and brought it into being from the depths of this abandoned place. He had put everything he had into this work, which was his last, desperate stand against a world that had thrown him away so carelessly and cruelly. And now it was ready to carry out its horrible, horrible job. The machine made a low hum, like a deep, resonant growl that shook him to his bones and through the soles of his boots. It was the sound of doom coming, a scary prelude to the end of the show. He felt a tremor go through him, not of fear, but of a deep, almost spiritual release. The years of carefully built walls, the complicated web of planned lies, and the tiring mask of fake calm were all falling apart. The constant, soul-crushing pressure had finally broken the dam, letting the flood that had been trapped for so long out.

His sharp gaze moved across the ruined landscape, but it felt strangely far away. He saw Brody fighting his way toward Vance, his face a mask of grim determination and a dark stain of blood on his shoulder. The detective's eyes were full of righteous, unyielding rage as they met John's across the dust-covered space. In that brief, thrilling moment, John didn't see an enemy; he saw a mirror. A man pushed to the edge of the world, fighting with everything he had for something or someone. It was a realization that hit him like a physical blow, a jolt of unexpected, almost painful clarity in the middle of the chaos and madness. He had worked on his story for so long, making himself out to be the victim, the wronged party, and the righteous avenger. He had carefully convinced himself that his cause was completely just and that his punishment was completely unavoidable. But as the harsh lights shone down on him, the rain kept falling, and the press, which was groaning and threatening, promised to destroy him completely, the carefully woven tapestry of his delusion began to come apart. The edges frayed, showing the sad, broken threads of his past.

His mind was no longer full of strategic calculations or poisonous statements. Instead, it was a kaleidoscope of broken, haunting images. A small hand from a child that was outstretched and then violently taken away. The sterile, unforgiving white of a hospital room, where voices are low and despair is sterile. The sound of whispers full of pity and unspoken accusations. The heavy, all-encompassing weight of being alone. These were the real people who destroyed him: the sneaky, unending demons that had crawled out of the dark, forgotten corners of his mind. He remembered how much it hurt when his mother looked at him with disappointment. That look could freeze the soul. He remembered how cold and indifferent his father's silence had been, like a hole that had swallowed him whole. He remembered the mean things kids said to him on the playground, how they made him feel like he was unlovable and flawed. These memories, which had been buried for a long time under layers of hardened anger and festering resentment, now came rushing back, like a huge wave of raw, unfiltered pain. He had desperately tried to get back a sense of control and make the world do what he wanted, even though it had systematically taken away his most basic rights. He had tricked himself into thinking that he could somehow erase the deep, permanent scars of his own pain by using power and causing pain. But the truth, which was clear and cruel, was that he was only continuing the cycle, becoming the monster he said he hated.

The deafening roar of the rockfall that was coming to an end was a horrible noise, but in its fading echoes, John heard a new sound: the frantic, desperate beating of his own heart. It was the sound of fear, but it was also the sound of a deep, terrifying freedom. The mask was finally coming off, and there was no going back. The carefully built structure of "John Vance," the vengeful mastermind, was falling apart, showing the scared, broken child that was underneath. He heard Brody scream, a primal sound of pure, unadulterated desperation. The detective's raw, wild rage was a sharp, painful contrast to the way John was falling apart inside. Brody was fighting to stay alive, for justice, and for his partner. What was John fighting for? To get away from the heavy, suffocating weight of his own life? To finally give in to the all-consuming darkness that had been with him for so long and would never leave? As Brody got closer, he and John locked eyes. A brief moment of recognition and a terrible understanding passed between them. It was the silent, unspoken understanding between two men who were separated by an unbridgeable gap and pushed to the limit by forces they couldn't control. For Brody, it was the never-ending search for the truth. For John, it was the crushing weight of his own unyielding past that he couldn't escape.

Brody tackled him, and they both fell hard to the ground. The impact was terrible, shaking the stage for his grand, tragic opera and sending debris flying everywhere. He felt the rough, immediate embrace of the earth and the sharp pain of gravel against his skin. He was no longer on stage, and he was no longer the conductor of this horrible, creepy symphony. He was just a man, broken, completely defeated, trapped in the terrible storm he had caused. Vance's knife, which he thought was a sign of his power and authority, slipped away and was lost in the chaos. He fought with Brody, and their bodies were twisted together in a savage, primal dance. He could feel the detective's raw, unyielding strength and the sheer willpower that drove him forward. And in that raw, very physical fight, the last bits of his carefully built up persona melted away like fog in the morning sun. There was no mastermind or calculating monster; there was just John, a man who was drowning in his own despair. He was able to hit Brody in the jaw with a desperate, flailing punch. For a brief, thrilling moment, he saw the detective hesitate, with stars bursting behind his eyes. A wave of something like triumph washed over him, like a dying ember of his old anger and ambition. But it went out just as quickly as it had started. Brody held on, his grip like a vise that wouldn't let go, and his will was like a force of nature.

The sounds of the quarry, the rockfall, and the groaning machines slowly faded away. They were replaced by the ragged, desperate gasps of effort and the brutal, grunting sounds of their fight. The rockfall was slowing down, and the noise was turning into a low, scary rumble. But the spotlights stayed, their harsh, unrelenting glare pinning them down like specimens under a cold, scientific microscope. John saw the steady beams of light and felt a deep, crushing wave of shame wash over him. He had tried to control the story and set the terms for his last, dramatic act. Instead, he had been exposed, stripped bare, and his deepest, most vulnerable fears were on display for everyone to see. Then, another hit. Brody hit his head on a sharp, jagged rock. The world was a dizzying, painful kaleidoscope that made it hard to see. The fight left him limp, like a broken puppet whose strings had finally been cut. He felt himself relax as his body gave in to how unavoidable it all was. He lay there, the rain soaking through his clothes and the cold getting deeper into his bones. He could hear Brody's heavy, ragged breathing and the faint, muffled sounds of his partner Jenkins trying to get out of the rubble. He saw the stopped press, a silent, threatening guard that had not done its job. He saw Brody get up and kneel next to him, looking tired and like he had won a hard-fought battle. He felt someone touch his neck and look for a pulse. A weak, thready beat. The hunter was caught. The shepherd had led his flock not to a glorious, triumphant victory, but to a brutal, humiliating loss. And at that moment, as consciousness slowly and steadily faded, John finally got it. He wasn't the mastermind behind some big plan to get back at someone. He had been a prisoner of the ghosts that had haunted him for his whole, broken life. The rain kept falling, a never-ending, cleansing downpour that washed away the dust, blood, and last, fading traces of the man he had tried so hard, and so tragically, to be. The time for reckoning had come, but instead of the loud applause he had wanted, there was only a deep, deafening silence, broken only by the sad, lonely cry of his own broken soul.

Brody held his breath as John Vance's eyes, which had been glazed and unfocused, finally stopped moving. The noise from the quarry was slowly fading away, and the sounds of survival were taking its place. The groans of Jenkins under the rubble were a desperate contrast to the silence that had settled over Vance. He felt a deep tiredness come over him, a tiredness that went beyond the physical and into his bones. The rain, which had seemed so refreshing a few minutes ago, now felt heavy and oppressive, with each drop like a small weight on his already heavy soul. He had fought a monster, or at least what he thought was a monster. But in the end, he didn't see a monster, but a broken man whose past he couldn't escape. The win felt empty because of how much of a waste it all was.

He heard a shout, a strained, desperate sound, and turned to see Detective Miller coming out of the swirling dust and debris on the other side of the quarry. His face was covered in mud and he looked determined. He was moving toward them slowly but surely, which showed how determined he was. "Brody! Are you okay? Miller's voice was hoarse, but it was full of relief that Brody could only feel inside.

"Jenkins… he's trapped," Brody said, his voice rough from the fight and the weather. "Vance… he's gone." The last word hung in the damp air, a cold, final sound. He forced himself to get up, even though his muscles were screaming in pain, and he stumbled toward Jenkins, following the sound of his partner's muffled cries. Miller was already there, and his strong body was pushing against a fallen rock that was holding Jenkins's legs down.

Miller grunted, "He's pinned good, Brody," and his face twisted with effort. "Almost a whole section fell down."

Brody joined him, and the adrenaline that had helped him fight Vance turned into a desperate burst of energy. They pushed hard, their bodies straining, and the rough concrete and sharp stone scraped against their skin. The rain kept pouring down, making it hard to see and making the already dangerous ground even more dangerous. Every move was a fight against gravity and the weight of the earth that could crush them all.

Brody's lungs were on fire as he gasped, "We need more leverage." "Miller, see if you can find a good place to put something under it." "I'll try to get rid of some of the smaller rocks." He started to pull away loose debris, his fingers raw and bleeding, and his mind was a million miles away from the danger right in front of him. He saw the faces of the victims, the families Vance had broken, and the lives that would never be the same. He could see the deep sadness in Vance's eyes that had led him to do such terrible things. He saw Jenkins, his friend and partner, trapped under a lot of rocks and fighting for his life.

The quarry had just changed from a scary scene to a grim picture of sacrifice and survival. The costs were very clear in the rescue efforts. Every brave act and every moment of selflessness happened against a background of deep loss and trauma that wouldn't go away. Vance's reign of terror was over, but the scars it left behind would never go away.

Miller let out a triumphant yell, a loud, throaty sound of effort and relief. "Got it!" A rebar! Please give me some space! He moved a piece of twisted metal under the edge of the slab. Brody got into position and took a deep breath. Then, with a coordinated heave that felt like it would tear them apart, they were able to move the huge weight. Jenkins cried out in pain, but it was quickly followed by a lot of relieved breaths.

"My legs… I think they're crushed," Jenkins said, his voice weak.

Brody knelt next to him, his heart breaking. He saw the broken arms and legs, as well as the bare bone. He would have nightmares about it for weeks, if not months, to come. He carefully looked over Jenkins, trying to keep his hands steady even though they were shaking. "Wait a second, Jenkins." We're going to get you out.

At first, the sound of sirens getting closer was a welcome relief for their frayed nerves. Then it got louder and louder. There was help on the way. But even as the first emergency vehicles arrived, their flashing lights cutting through the darkness, Brody knew that the real trouble was just beginning. The physical wounds would heal, with time and skilled medical attention. But the emotional and psychological toll, the sacrifices made not just in the heat of the confrontation, but in the aftermath, would linger.

He looked back at Vance's body, which was lying still among the rubble. There was no triumph in his gaze, only a profound sense of sorrow. Vance had sought to rewrite his narrative, to impose his will through violence and destruction. He had ended up a victim of his own creation, consumed by the darkness he had so desperately tried to weaponize. The final confrontation had demanded immense courage, from Brody, from Jenkins, from Miller, and even, in his own twisted way, from Vance. They had all, in their own ways, made sacrifices. Vance had sacrificed his humanity. Jenkins had sacrificed his physical well-being. Brody, he knew, had sacrificed a piece of his own innocence, a sliver of the man he once was, in the brutal dance to stop the madness.

As the paramedics swarmed the scene, their efficiency a stark contrast to the chaos that had just unfolded, Brody felt a profound sense of gratitude for the lives that had been spared, for the swiftness with which Jenkins was being attended to. But he also felt the weight of what had been lost. The lives Vance had extinguished, the futures he had stolen, the profound, immeasurable grief he had inflicted upon so many. The resolution had come, but at a cost so steep, so devastating, that it would echo in the lives of everyone involved for a long time to come. The darkness had been confronted, but the shadows it cast were long and deep, and Brody knew, with a chilling certainty, that they would continue to linger long after the rain had finally stopped. He would carry the weight of this night, of Vance's brokenness and Jenkins's suffering, for the rest of his days. Survival, he understood with a heavy heart, was not always a clean victory. It was often a messy, painful, and deeply scarring testament to the resilience of the human spirit, and the devastating cost of confronting true darkness.

The Aftermath in Oakhaven

The rain, which had been a constant source of pain all night, finally let up. The downpour turned into a steady drizzle as dawn painted the bruised sky in shades of gray and muted violet. The quarry, a huge hole in the ground, was now a place of controlled chaos. The flashing blue and red lights of emergency vehicles tried to break through the darkness. Their synchronized pulses were a jarring contrast to the quiet, almost reverent whispers of the first responders. The air was thick with the smell of wet earth, ozone, and blood, and it smelled like the end. Finally, the reign of terror by John Vance, which had smothered Oakhaven for weeks, was over. But the relief was short-lived and fragile, mixed with the deep sadness of what had been lost.

Detective Brody, whose uniform was torn and stained, moved like a tired man who had looked into the abyss and made it submit. His eyes, which were usually sharp and clear, now looked tired and haunted. He had seen the dark side of life, not just in Vance's eyes, but also in the broken bodies, the ruined landscape of the quarry, and the echoing silence left by the people Vance had taken. Every rock that fell and every piece of equipment that was left behind seemed to show how much this night's reckoning would cost. He nodded curtly and professionally to the officers who were coming in, silently acknowledging the shared burden and trauma they were now responsible for dealing with. The immediate threat was over, but the effects of Vance's insanity were just starting to spread, touching every part of their quiet town.

Detective Miller, whose face was lined with fatigue, was in charge of the difficult job of securing the scene. His voice was a low rumble that cut through the constant rain. He talked to the paramedics who were taking care of Jenkins, his partner, whose groans of pain were a constant, painful reminder of what they had won. The officers were told the sad news that Vance had died. It was a stark, bare truth that hung over them like a shroud. There were no cheers or shouts of victory, just a group sigh that seemed to let out all the stress that had built up over weeks of fear and doubt. The monster was dead, but the scars it left behind were deep and always reminded them of how fragile their peace was.

The town of Oakhaven began to wake up as the first rays of sunlight slowly broke through the clouds, casting long, distorted shadows on the quarry floor. They didn't know that something big had happened in the heart of the town. The familiar sounds of everyday life, like getting ready for breakfast and going to work in the morning, would soon be broken by the news that had spread like wildfire. At first, they would feel shocked, but then they would feel a flood of emotions, including relief, grief, confusion, and a deep-seated fear that had been so brutally awakened. The carefully built illusion of safety in their private part of the world had been broken forever.

The news spread through Oakhaven like a huge wave, and each family got it with a mix of disbelief and deep, gut-wrenching relief. The quiet whispers of the past few days, full of fear and speculation, were replaced by loud crying and hesitant hugs. The coffee shops, which were usually full of people talking in the morning, were now places where people came together to mourn. Neighbors found comfort in sharing their fears and the realization that the nightmare was finally over. Mrs. Gable, whose son was one of Vance's first victims, sat by her window with the morning paper in her shaking hands and her eyes fixed on a blurry picture of John Vance, a man who had been their worst nightmare. A single tear ran down her weathered cheek, not out of sadness, but out of a deep, painful emptiness. The anger that had fueled her days and haunted her nights had finally found a way out, leaving behind an empty space where it used to be.

A small group of people started to come together in the town square without saying a word. They were all drawn together by a need for support. They stood in the cold, damp air, a sea of faces showing the pain of living in the dark. Old Man Hemlock, who had always been a calm presence in Oakhaven, put his hand on the shoulder of young Sarah Peterson. Her father had been one of Vance's last victims. His face was a map of a life lived outside. His rough, calloused hand sent a strong, silent message of comfort that showed how strong the community was. The empty spaces where laughter and conversation should have been, as well as the lack of certain faces, hung heavy in the air, reminding everyone of Vance's terrible legacy.

Sheriff Brody stood on the steps of the town hall, his face tired but determined, and spoke to the growing crowd. Even though he was tired, his voice had the authority and truth of what had happened that night. He talked about how scared Vance was, how quickly and decisively his deputies acted, and most importantly, how the terror was over. He talked about how brave his officers were and how dedicated they were to keeping the people of Oakhaven safe. He also didn't shy away from talking about the terrible loss of life that Vance's actions had caused. He talked about Jenkins, his partner, how he was still recovering, and how grateful the whole town was to him.

"This has been a dark time for Oakhaven," Brody said, his voice echoing as he looked around at his neighbors, friends, and other townspeople. "We faced a threat that put our courage, strength, and sense of safety to the test." We faced that darkness tonight, and we came out of it not unscathed, but not broken. He stopped for a moment, his voice breaking a little as he said, "We remember those we have lost." We won't forget about their lives, even though they ended too soon. They are carved into the very fabric of Oakhaven, a solemn reminder of how valuable life is and how important it is to enjoy every moment.

Then he talked about how to move forward, how to heal and rebuild. "The scars from this will stay with us as a reminder of what we've been through." But they don't make us who we are. We are all part of a community, and we will heal together. We will help each other, rebuild, and make sure that Oakhaven stays a safe and hopeful place for many years to come. His words, which were simple but deep, brought some light to the darkness that was still there. They all nodded in agreement, knowing that the road ahead would be hard but that they would walk it together.

The next few days were a blur of quiet activity. There was an official investigation going on at the quarry. It was a sad process of going through the rubble and putting together the last, awful moments. With a strong sense of duty, the town council started talking about ways to make Oakhaven safer so that such a tragedy would never happen again. There were talks about having more police officers on the streets, starting neighborhood watch programs, and other ways to make people feel more responsible for their community. Oakhaven had once taken for granted the innocence that had been replaced by a sober awareness of the constant threat of darkness, which could be found even in the most beautiful places.

The funerals were very sad, and each one showed how deeply the town had lost something. Families who were grieving deeply found comfort in the support they got from their neighbors. Flowers, a bright splash of color against the muted colors of mourning, filled the churchyards as a silent tribute to the lives that had been so cruelly cut short. The air was heavy with the smell of roses and lilies and the sad sounds of hymns that talked about everlasting peace. Each eulogy was a moving tribute, a way to honor lives that had been cut short, and a way to show how much love and laughter had been taken away. Sarah Peterson, who was young and had red-rimmed eyes but a surprisingly steady voice, talked about her father's infectious sense of humor, his unwavering kindness, and how he could always make her laugh, even on the darkest days. Her words, spoken with a maturity far beyond her years, touched the hearts of everyone who was there to mourn. They showed how love can last even in the face of unimaginable loss.

The families of the victims, who were all going through the same thing, came together in an unexpected way. They got together often to talk about their memories, help each other, and find strength in their shared grief. They were the living proof of Vance's destructive legacy, but they were also proof of Oakhaven's strength. They promised to honor their loved ones by living their lives to the fullest, cherishing every moment, and making sure that their stories and the lessons learned from this terrible event would never be forgotten. They had a quiet determination in their eyes, a determination to take back their lives from the fear that Vance had cast over them.

The psychological scars stayed even as Oakhaven slowly and painfully began to heal. A more subtle form of anxiety took the place of the hushed whispers of fear. It was an unease that spread throughout the town. People were constantly looking over their shoulders, and the sights and sounds of their daily lives were now tinged with a heightened sense of caution. People used to see the woods as a peaceful place to get away from it all, but now they saw them with suspicion. The sound of leaves rustling and twigs snapping made them think of hidden danger. Kids used to be able to run around and play, but now they had to stay closer to home. Their laughter was quieter, and their games were a little more aware of the darker sides of the world.

Detective Brody, even though the immediate threat was over, couldn't stop thinking about how Vance's reign of terror had affected him mentally. He often thought back to the quarry, the raw intensity of his fight with Vance, and the heartbreaking sight of Jenkins trapped under the rubble. The victims' faces and stories of lives stolen haunted him while he was awake and in his dreams. He could see the fear in the eyes of the people in the town and how slowly they were getting back to normal. He knew that his work was far from over. The fight for justice was over, but Oakhaven's emotional and mental healing was going to take a long time.

He made it a point to see Jenkins at the hospital often, and the grim look on his partner's face always gave him strength. Jenkins stayed very positive, even though he was in a lot of pain and faced a long recovery. His dry sense of humor and strong will showed how strong he was. "Just you wait, Brody," he would croak, a weak smile on his lips. "I'll be back on the beat before you know it." Someone has to watch over you; you don't want to get into too much trouble when you're out there alone. Their friendship, which was built on shared trauma, was a strong force and a light of hope in the dark times that followed.

The huge hydraulic press, a horrible sign of Vance's twisted genius, stayed at the quarry as a grim reminder of the destruction it had almost caused. Eventually, it was taken apart, and its parts were cataloged and stored as evidence. However, the memory of how scary it was stayed with people, a clear reminder of how close Oakhaven came to total destruction. The quarry, which had once been a place of work and then of fear, was now a quiet place for people in the town to remember, mourn, and start the process of taking back the land from the darkness that had taken it.

The Oakhaven Summer Festival, a beloved yearly event that usually brought the town together in a festive mood, had a different feel that year. Even though the celebrations were smaller, the feeling was one of deep gratitude. The fireworks, which are usually a beautiful show of light and color, seemed to burn a little brighter and longer, as if they were fighting against the shadows that were trying to cover them. The laughter of kids playing in the park was a sweet song, a promise of a future where happiness could grow again, even though they were still aware of what was going on.

Sheriff Brody stood on the edge of the celebrations, watching his town slowly regain its spirit. He felt a mix of quiet satisfaction and sadness that would last. The reign of terror was over, and the immediate danger was gone. But the experience had changed Oakhaven and him in a big way. He had seen the worst of human nature, the depths of evil that one person could do to so many. But he had also seen the amazing bravery, unbreakable strength, and deep love and community that existed in his town.

Things would never be the same at Oakhaven. The innocence was gone, and in its place was hard-earned wisdom and a sober understanding of how dark things could be. But instead, a new strength had grown, a deeper understanding of how valuable life is, and an unbreakable bond formed in the fires of shared hardship. John Vance's reign of terror would always be a part of Oakhaven's history. It was a sad time that reminded everyone how fragile peace is and how strong the human spirit is to overcome even the darkest times. The time for reckoning had come. The scars would stay, but so would the quiet, strong hope of a town that had faced its worst nightmare and come out of it, against all odds, into the dawn. The aftermath in Oakhaven was not the end; it was a deep and life-changing beginning.

Ambiguity and Lingering Shadows

After John Vance died, Oakhaven was quiet, but it wasn't a peaceful quiet. It was full of unasked questions and the echoes of fear. Detective Brody found himself walking around the precinct's hallways, which he knew well but now felt a little strange. Every creak of the floorboards and every distant siren seemed to call Vance's name, not as a defeated enemy but as a ghost. Yes, he had looked into the void, and for a moment, he thought he had won. But the polished surface of his desk showed a man who was troubled, a man who knew that defeating a monster was only the first, and maybe the easiest, step in a long, hard journey. Vance's reign of terror was over in the quarry, where he died in the mud and rain. The violence he had done to others had killed him. But Brody thought the real reckoning was just beginning, not for Vance, but for Oakhaven itself and for the people who had to put the pieces of broken lives back together.

He kept going back to the case files, which were full of carefully written accounts of Vance's fall and the coldly logical reasons he had given for his terrible actions. It wasn't just how cruel Vance was that bothered Brody; it was also how clearly he had explained his twisted view of the world. There was a scary logic to his insanity, a twisted logic that was hard to put into words. Vance wasn't a mindless brute; he was a cruel craftsman who had turned his own deep-seated trauma into a symphony of destruction. Brody read and reread the psychological profiles, the reports on Vance's childhood, and the claims of abuse, looking for a clear answer: a single event or flaw that had turned a man into such a horrible shape. But the more he read, the less sure he was. The lines between victim and perpetrator, between the wounded and the wounding, seemed to blur, creating a disquieting ethical grey that offered no easy comfort.

The town, on the other hand, was trying to put itself back together, and each person living there was unknowingly a seamstress in this group effort. The first wave of relief, which was so strong in the days after Vance's capture, had started to fade. In its place was a deeper, more introspective unease. People still got together and told stories, but the conversations had a different feel to them. They didn't just talk about Vance; they also talked about how fear is sneaky and how easy it is to peel away the facade of normalcy to show how vulnerable someone really is. The woods around Oakhaven, which used to be a peaceful place to escape, were now eerily quiet, as if the trees were watching the darkness that had taken root. The kids kept playing, but their laughter was a little more hesitant. They whispered about "the monster," a real-life bogeyman that wasn't made up.

Brody went to see Jenkins in the hospital. His partner's slow, painful recovery was proof of how bad the night had been. Jenkins's body was covered in casts and bandages, and his voice was a raspy whisper, but he still had a hint of his old sarcastic humor. "Still chasing shadows, Brody?" he rasped, a weak smile on his face. "Don't forget to keep an eye on your own back. Sometimes, the monsters you hunt are the ones that live inside you. Brody felt something when he heard the words spoken with tired wisdom. He had seen the darkness in Vance, fought it, and won, but the shadow it cast was long and seemed to stretch far beyond the quarry, reaching into the heart of Oakhaven and into the quiet corners of his own mind.

The quarry, which used to be a place of industry and later a place of terrible events, was still a scar on the landscape. Investigators carefully went through the debris, which was a sad ritual of remembering and rebuilding. Every broken tool and piece of Vance's twisted machinery was a real connection to the terror and a silent witness to the lives that had been lost there. The big hydraulic press, which was the main part of Vance's scary design, had been carefully taken apart, and its huge structure had been turned into a pile of cold, sterile evidence. But its absence seemed to leave a void, a ghostly shape etched in the minds of those who had seen its evil presence. The earth, still wet and bruised, held the secrets of that night, a silent reminder that no one was safe from the reckoning.

Brody went to the town's library not to find peace, but to learn more. He read a lot about trauma, the psychological effects of violence, and the complicated relationship between nature and nurture that could lead to such darkness. He read about serial criminals, what drove them, and how they acted. He saw a very familiar pattern in Vance's carefully documented life. Vance wasn't an exception; he was an extreme example of a deeply ingrained human ability to be cruel, which gets worse when people suffer and isn't stopped by society. The realization was not comforting; it was very disturbing. It suggested that the source of such darkness wasn't something outside of people, but something inside of them, a dormant potential waiting for the right set of circumstances to bring it out.

He would often look out of his office window and watch the people in the town go about their lives. Their faces showed a new kind of alertness. The easy friendship that used to exist in Oakhaven before Vance was gone. Instead, people were more guarded and subtly acknowledged that they were all vulnerable. People still smiled and laughed, but their happiness was deeper now. They appreciated the little moments of peace more. Oakhaven's innocence was gone for good, replaced by a hard-earned, sobering understanding of how fragile life is. The darkness had been faced, and its physical form had been defeated. However, the psychological effects, the lingering shadows of fear and trauma, were still very strong and were slowly changing the town and its people.

One night, Brody was at the edge of the woods, where Vance had first started to show himself and where the first whispers of fear had started to spread through Oakhaven. The air was cool, and the smell of pine needles and wet ground was strong in the evening. He stood there for a long time, the silence closing in on him. It wasn't an empty silence; it was full of stories that weren't being told. He didn't hate Vance; instead, he felt sorry for him and understood how broken he was and how twisted his reasoning had been. Yes, Vance was a monster, but he was also a victim, a sad result of his own pain. And in that moment of understanding, Brody didn't feel free; instead, he felt a heavy sense of duty.

He knew that the official case was over and that the person who did it had been caught and punished. The town was starting to heal, rebuild, and move on. But for Brody, the end was still a long way off. He had to deal with Vance's story, which showed how bad people can be, and the unsettling fact that once such darkness was let loose, it left permanent marks. He looked out at the trees getting darker and the shadows getting deeper, forming shapes that seemed to make fun of the fragile peace that Oakhaven had fought so hard to get back. He knew that the monster was dead and the immediate danger was over. But the question that would always haunt him, the chilling uncertainty that would stay in the quiet corners of his mind, was whether the darkness had really been defeated or just moved back, waiting for another broken soul to find its echo. The real legacy of John Vance wasn't just the lives he took, but the unsettling knowledge he gave to Oakhaven: that even in the most peaceful places, the seeds of evil could lie dormant, waiting for their chance to grow in the unsuspecting soil of everyday life. And when Brody turned his back on the quiet, watchful woods, he felt a chill that had nothing to do with the cold of the evening. It was a feeling that the shadows, no matter how faint, would always be there.

About the Author

Justin Pettyjohn is a writer who is known for writing psychological thrillers that explore the darkest parts of the human mind. Justin has a great eye for detail and a knack for building unbearable suspense. He looks at the thin lines between sanity and madness, the long-term effects of trauma, and the scary question of what really makes a monster. People have praised their previous works for having complicated plots and characters, as well as for making readers question what is good and evil long after they have finished reading. Justin Pettyjohn lives in Raleigh, North Carolina, where they probably spend their time looking for the hidden shadows in the quiet corners of everyday life.

Also by Justin Pettyjohn

Books of fiction that are guaranteed to captive your imagination:

The Fallen Immortal: Dracula's Greatest Enemy

Once the most feared general of Dracula's immortal legion, Theron Bloodbane is cast into eternal exile—betrayed, marked for death, and hunted by the very darkness he once served. Stripped of his title, pursued by unholy beasts, and bound by a cursed sigil that calls his enemies to him, Theron discovers a chilling truth: Dracula no longer seeks dominion—he seeks the extinction of mankind and the dawn of an endless night where humanity becomes nothing more than blood in chains.

Haunted by his past and tormented by the horrors he helped unleash, Theron finds an unexpected spark of salvation in a secluded village untouched by shadow—and in Lauren, a mortal woman whose quiet strength awakens something long thought dead within his immortal heart. She is light where he is darkness. Hope where he is despair. And her existence may be the key to breaking Dracula's reign forever.

As love blooms in the shadow of annihilation, Theron must choose: embrace the monster he was… or become the weapon destiny demands to destroy the darkest lord of all time.

A tale of forbidden love, ancient vengeance, and one vampire's fight to reclaim his soul—and save the world from eternal night.

www.ingramcontent.com/pod-product-compliance
Lightning Source LLC
Chambersburg PA
CBHW041732300726

48981CB00005B/321